THE LAST CLOSE CALL

LAURA GRIFFIN

BERKLEY
New York

BERKLEY
An imprint of Penguin Random House LLC
penguinrandomhouse.com

Copyright © 2023 by Laura Griffin
Excerpt from *Liar's Point* copyright © 2023 by Laura Griffin
Penguin Random House supports copyright. Copyright fuels creativity, encourages
diverse voices, promotes free speech, and creates a vibrant culture. Thank you for buying
an authorized edition of this book and for complying with copyright laws by not
reproducing, scanning, or distributing any part of it in any form without permission.
You are supporting writers and allowing Penguin Random House to continue to
publish books for every reader.

BERKLEY and the BERKLEY & B colophon are registered trademarks of
Penguin Random House LLC.

ISBN: 9780593546734

First Edition: October 2023

Printed in the United States of America
1 3 5 7 9 10 8 6 4 2

Book design by George Towne

For Doug

ONE

EVIE WAITED UNTIL the third ring to pick up.

"Are you bailing?" Hannah asked.

"Sorry."

"Evie, you *promised*."

"I'm not up for it tonight." She stripped off the sexy black tank top that she'd ridiculously put on earlier—because Drew liked it—and grabbed her terry cloth robe off the chair.

"What happened?" Hannah asked over the din of conversation, and Evie pictured her sister in the crowded sports bar where they had planned to meet.

"Nothing."

"Not *nothing*. Spill it."

Evie tied the belt and sighed. "I saw him tonight."

"Who?"

"Drew. He came by to get Bella after work."

Or at least, he'd claimed he had come from work. Given the beer on his breath, he had probably been to a happy hour with "the team" first.

"Oh, Eves. I'm sorry."

She padded barefoot across the hardwood floors that she and Drew had happily picked out together. After checking the lock on the patio door, she peered out at the dim yard. Her daughter's swing swayed in the breeze, and her Big Wheel sat abandoned on a carpet of crunchy brown leaves.

"I know that sucks," Hannah said. "Why don't you come out with us? You'll feel better."

"I'm already in bed."

"You are not. It's barely nine o'clock."

Evie returned to the bottle of merlot by the fridge and topped off her glass.

"Come on," Hannah persisted. "We're playing darts. Blake says he'll even let you win."

Evie smiled. Her sister's boyfriend was a gem, a genuine *nice guy.* But she didn't want to be a third wheel again.

"Really, I'm not up for it."

"Well." She heard the resignation in Hannah's voice. "You're still coming Thursday, right?"

"Absolutely." She took a hearty swig at the thought of her sister's Thanksgiving potluck, which was sure to be an awkward mix of friends and coworkers. Evie had offered to bring a pie, but Hannah had assigned her mashed potatoes in a transparent attempt to make sure she didn't cancel.

"What time are we eating again?" Evie asked.

"Um . . . I don't know. Four, probably?"

So eight, then. Which was fine. Evie would be there all evening, which would cut into the ice cream binge that would inevitably accompany her first holiday in six years without Drew.

And Bella's first holiday ever without her mother.

Tears burned Evie's eyes, and she took another gulp.

"So get this," she told Hannah. "He took my silver locket." Fury tightened her chest as soon as the words were out. "You know the one he gave me for Mother's Day? He stole it right out of my jewelry box."

"Oh, come on," Hannah said. "You probably misplaced it."

"No. I did not."

"Evie, the man drives a Porsche. What would he want with a silver locket?"

"He knew it would needle me." She headed down the hall and paused at Bella's room to switch off the light, ignoring the lingering scent of baby shampoo as she closed the door.

"Do you want me to come over?"

"No, I'm fine. I'm just being, I don't know, *emotional*."

"Hey, you're allowed to be emotional. Your ex is a prick. How about we walk the lake tomorrow? We can catch up."

Evie stepped into the bathroom and confronted her reflection in the mirror above the sink. Messy hair, sallow skin, dingy bathrobe. She opened the medicine cabinet and eyed the contents. The prescription sleeping pills called out to her. But she had more willpower than that. She closed the cabinet.

"What time?" she asked Hannah.

"Let's do nine. I'll meet you at the bridge."

"Are you sure? Nine sounds early."

Evie was fine with it, but Hannah's body clock didn't work that way. She hadn't had kids.

"All right, let's make it ten," Hannah said.

"Ten at the bridge."

"It's a date. Love you, Eves."

"You, too."

She set the phone down and stared at her reflection as she took another sip. A four-mile loop around the lake would do her good. Maybe she'd stop at the grocery afterward and get some fresh produce. She could make soup. Or maybe a pie for next week. She stepped into the bedroom.

A man in a ski mask stood in the doorway.

Her wineglass crashed to the floor as she registered everything at once—the wide shoulders, the black clothes, the heavy boots.

His hands were empty, but the latex gloves he wore turned her throat to dust.

"Don't scream, Evelyn."

Her heart seized. He knew her *name*.

She thought of her cell phone in the bathroom only a few feet away. She could lock herself inside and then—

He stepped into the bedroom and pulled the door shut with a terrifying *click*.

Evie's mind raced, even as time slowed to a crawl. She had to survive this. Whatever happened, she had to survive for Bella.

What did he *want*? Her heart thundered as her eyes returned to those gloved hands.

God help me.

She inched toward the bathroom, stalling for time.

"How"—she cleared her throat—"how did you get in here?"

The hole in the mask shifted—a flash of white teeth as his mouth formed a smile.

"I've been here."

TWO

Eight weeks later

THE LUCKY DUCK was half empty, which was just how Rowan liked it.

Johnny Cash drifted from the speakers. A young couple occupied a high-top table in the corner, and several regulars sat at the bar, chatting up Lila as she pulled a pint.

Rowan's favorite booth was taken, so she grabbed one near the window beneath a neon **SHINER BOCK** sign. Lila darted her a questioning glance, and Rowan gave her a nod as she slid into the torn vinyl seat.

She grabbed the plastic menu behind the condiment bottles and looked for something decadent. She was starving, she suddenly realized. For the past five days, she had subsisted on cereal and microwave popcorn.

As she skimmed the choices, Rowan tugged the scrunchie from her hair and combed her hand through it. She probably should have showered or at least put on a clean sweatshirt before coming here. Oh well. Too late now.

"You finally came up for air."

She looked up as Lila slid a Tanqueray and tonic in front of her.

"*Thank* you," Rowan said. "You read my mind."

Lila sipped a ginger ale—her hydration beverage of choice when she was working.

"Busy night?" Rowan asked.

"Not really." She shrugged. "Good tips, though."

"Has Dara been by?"

"*Yes.*" Lila's eyes sparkled, and she tossed a springy brown curl over her shoulder. "She was here earlier. With a date."

"Oh yeah?"

"They left after an hour, so you'll have to get the scoop. Are you eating?"

"Yes, but I can't decide."

"Try the nachos," Lila said. "We've got fresh guac today."

"That sounds good."

A couple walked into the bar and claimed a pair of stools on the corner. Lila eyed them as she nursed her drink. "I have to get back. I'll give Sasha your order."

"Thanks."

Lila returned to her post, and Rowan scanned the faces around the room, trying to guess people's stories. It was a game she played whenever she came here alone. All the singles tonight were regulars. Ditto the two guys shooting pool in the back. Her attention settled on the couple at the high-top. Based on their age, they might be students at the University of Texas, maybe seeking a night away from the crowds on Sixth Street. But they had a seasoned look about them. The woman's makeup was perfect. And they both exuded the stiff body language that screamed *first date*.

Rowan watched them subtly from her booth. Head tilts. Intense eye contact. The woman arched her brows as she sipped her margarita through a straw, displaying just the right amount of interest in whatever the guy was saying.

He rested a hand on his knee and looked confident—but slightly nervous—as he expounded on whichever first-date topic he'd selected for the evening.

A chime emanated from Rowan's purse. She pulled out her phone and read a text from the Austin lawyer whose client Rowan had been working for all week.

Got your email. Omg TY!!

The words were followed by three halo emojis, and Rowan felt a swell of pride.

Anytime, she texted back. So glad I could help.

This attorney had sent her three referrals over the past six months, and now there would likely be more on the way. Rowan's anemic bank account was finally getting a boost. It couldn't come soon enough. Her December credit card bill had just come in, and she hadn't even wanted to look at it.

"Rowan Healy?"

She jerked her head up as a man stepped over. Tall, broad-shouldered, dark hair. He wore a black leather jacket with droplets of rain clinging to it. Rowan darted a glance at Lila. Her friend didn't look up, but she lifted an eyebrow in a way that told Rowan she'd sent this guy over here.

"Who's asking?" Rowan responded, even though she had a sneaking suspicion she knew, based on his deep voice. Not to mention the super-direct look in his brown eyes.

"Jack Bruner, Austin PD." He smiled slightly. "Mind if I sit?"

She sighed and nodded at the empty seat across from her.

He slid into the booth and rested his elbows on the table. He looked her over, and she managed not to squirm.

"You're a hard woman to reach."

Ha. He had no idea how true that was.

"How'd you know to find me here?" she asked.

"Ric Santos told me you hang out here."

She couldn't hide her surprise at the mention of Ric. She hadn't known they were friends. But she probably should have guessed. Law enforcement was a tight-knit group.

She gave him what she hoped was a confident smile. "Look, Detective, I appreciate you coming all the way out here, but I'm afraid you've wasted your time."

"Just listen."

Two words.

A command, but not. When combined with that slight smile, it was more like a statement. Something she was *going* to do, even if she didn't realize it yet.

Rowan felt a surge of annoyance. But again, she gave him a nod.

Sasha appeared at the table and rested her cocktail tray on her hip. "Can I get you something to drink?" she asked the detective.

"A Coke, please."

She nodded. "Rowan?"

"I'm good, thanks."

She walked off, her cascade of blond hair swinging behind her.

Rowan settled her attention on the detective.

"I'm with APD's violent crimes unit, as I mentioned on the phone," he said.

With every call, he'd politely identified himself and given a callback number. Rowan had called the number once and—equally politely—left a message with her response. But he'd stubbornly ignored it.

"I'm working on a case," he said, "and I could use your help."

Rowan nodded. "Like I told you before—"

He held up his hand and gave her a sharp look. *Listen.*

"It's a serial offender," he continued. "Eight sexual assaults." His dark brows furrowed. "This guy's careful. We've only recovered one DNA profile, the second attack in the series."

"If you've only got one profile, how do you know it's the same guy?"

"Because—"

Sasha was back already with a flirty smile. She placed the detective's soft drink in front of him, and he nodded his thanks.

"Because we know," he said after she left.

Rowan looked the man over. He had an athletic build, but not the steroid-infused look she was used to seeing with young cops. Then again, he wasn't that young. The touch of gray at his temples told her he was maybe ten years older than she was, probably late thirties. Or maybe it was the wise look in his eyes that told her that.

She sipped her drink and waited for more.

"A while ago we had the sample analyzed by a genetic genealogist," he said. "Spent a lot of money and time on that. They ran into some kind of wall, and the results were inconclusive, they said."

"What's 'a while'?"

"Come again?"

"How long ago did you have it analyzed?"

He hesitated a beat.

"Four years."

Rowan's breath caught. In terms of DNA technology, four years was like four decades. A lot had changed in that time—new techniques, new tools, new profiles in the databases.

But she tried to keep her face impassive as she folded her hands in front of her.

"I appreciate your effort to track me down," she said. It told her a lot about what kind of detective he was—precisely the kind that had prompted her to shift careers. "But unfortunately, I don't do police work anymore. You could say I'm retired."

"That's not what Ric told me."

She gritted her teeth. Damn it, she'd *known* doing him a favor would come back to bite her.

"Ric said you're selective, not retired." He paused, watching her. "He told me you gave him an assist recently and that your help was invaluable."

"I know what you're doing," Rowan said. She was immune to flattery, even from smooth-talking detectives who liked to play head games. "And I can appreciate the pressure you guys must be under with a serial case. But I'm not in that line of work anymore."

He leaned forward, and she eased back slightly.

"Let me be straight, Rowan." His eyes bored into hers. "I need your help right *now*. Not next month or next year. Not whenever you get bored with what you're doing and decide to come out of retirement. I don't care if I sound desperate. I'm on a ticking clock here."

Her stomach tightened at his words. And his prediction that she would backtrack on her career change irked her.

But he held her gaze across the table, and she felt that inexorable *pull* that had turned her life upside down too many times to count.

She took in the detective's sharp eyes and the determined set to his jaw. She admired that determination—she had it, too—but she had to resist this time.

At this very moment, she had an inbox full of requests from prospective clients who were willing to pay top dollar for her work. *Positive* work. *Rewarding* work. The kind of work that made her get out of bed in the morning with a sense of purpose. She'd spent three years building her reputation as one of the best in her field, and the last thing she needed to do was put all those clients on hold and get sucked back into the vortex of police work.

A buzz emanated from beneath the table, and Jack Bruner took out his phone. His expression remained blank, but she caught the slight tensing of his shoulders.

A callout. Someone was dead or bleeding or in some emergency room somewhere.

He pulled out his wallet and tucked a twenty under his untouched Coke. Then he took out a business card and slid it across the table.

"My cell's on the back. Call me if you change your mind."

He scooted from the booth, and she felt small as he towered over her. He held out his hand.

Against her better judgment she shook it.

THE WIPER BLADES *swish-swish*ed as Jack made his way down the crowded street. Emergency vehicles lined the curbs, and even his narrow Jeep barely fit through. A cop in a yellow poncho stepped in front of him and lifted his hand. Jack held his badge up to the windshield, and the guy moved between a pair of parked cars and waved him through.

Jack scanned the street as he rolled forward. He spotted a gap between two patrol units and quickly maneuvered into the tight space. His twelve-year-old Jeep had way too many miles on it, but you couldn't beat the turning radius.

Cutting the engine, he looked around. He had never been here, but the place was familiar. One-story houses, tidy lawns, short driveways. Jack had grown up in a neighborhood much like this one, only the streets had been named after trees instead of birds. According to the map on Jack's phone, this particular subdivision was adjacent to a greenbelt. Mockingbird Lane was on the edge of the neighborhood, and all the homes to the west of him backed up to the woods.

Jack grabbed the police hangtag from the console and hooked it on his mirror before getting out. Cold rain pelted him, and he hunched into his jacket as he walked toward the barricade. Another yellow poncho moved to intercept him.

"This is a restricted area."

The kid was short and stocky, midtwenties. His cheeks were flushed, and Jack could see the collar of his uniform was soaked through, despite the poncho and hat. He gave Jack a hard stare and clenched his teeth, probably to keep them from chattering.

Jack flashed his badge and then tucked it away. "Lieutenant Hood around?"

The kid leaned closer. "Lieutenant Hood? Don't know."

"How about Detective Rollins?"

The kid's eyes remained guarded. "I saw Detective Hansen inside."

Jack nodded. "What about Rollins?"

"I don't know."

"Go find out."

The guy frowned. "You want me to—"

"See if Rollins is in there. I need a word."

The cop's expression went from guarded to flustered. Clearly, he'd been planning to man the barricade all night, not mingle with a bunch of older detectives who probably scared the shit out of him.

His Adam's apple bobbed as he looked Jack over. "And . . . your name again?"

Jack handed him a business card, then turned away as the cop walked off.

Through the pattering rain, Jack surveyed the houses. The one directly in front of him had an abandoned skateboard in the grass and a Christmas wreath still on the door. His attention settled on the neighboring home, where the front porch was cordoned off with yellow tape. A poncho-less officer was stationed at the door, and Jack watched as his messenger stopped to inquire about Detective Rollins.

Jack turned his attention to the other side of the street. Lights were on in most of the homes, and more than a few people stood outside watching the action from the shelter of their dry front porches. Others stood in their windows, observing everything through rain-slicked glass that put an imaginary layer of protection between them and whatever Bad Thing had happened to someone else.

Jack did a slow 360 and stopped facing west, the direction of the greenbelt. A dense thicket of oaks and junipers sloped down to a swollen creek, and the feeling of dread that had been eating away at him since before Thanksgiving was back again.

Crime scenes were fragile, especially ones like this. Evidence got trampled, run over, washed away. And tonight's weather wasn't helping. Any shoe impressions would be long gone, and people coming and going—even the careful ones—would track in debris, some of it microscopic. Investigators had a narrow window to gather observations and evidence, and the smallest detail could make or break a case.

Jack glanced at the greenbelt again and noticed the flicker of flashlights in the trees. At least they were looking, but Jack doubted there was anything left to find.

Although, who knew? Even the most careful criminals could make mistakes.

"Jack?"

He turned around to see Heidi Rollins stalking across the lawn in her rubber boots.

"This better be good. I'm freezing my ass off."

Heidi wore an oversize barn jacket and had her dark hair pulled back in a bun. She stepped into the street and glared up at him.

He smiled. "Long time no see."

She crossed her arms.

"Congratulations on the promotion."

She laughed. "That was three years ago."

"Still."

He took her point, though. He should have reached out to her long before now. They'd gotten their start together with Austin PD and even dated for a while. But the romance had fizzled, and a year later she moved to San Antonio, where she'd climbed swiftly up the ranks with SAPD. Heidi was ambitious and smart, and Jack hadn't been surprised when he heard she'd been promoted to homicide.

She sighed heavily, and he noticed the faint wrinkles around her eyes that hadn't been there the last time he saw her. He knew he had some, too.

"What gives, Jack?" She checked her watch. "I've got CSIs all over my crime scene, and I'd like to at least get a glimpse of what they're scooping up before it gets shipped off to the lab."

"Tell me about your victim," he said.

"Why?"

"I heard she was strangled."

Her gaze narrowed. "Where the hell did you get that?"

"Grapevine."

She muttered a curse and looked over her shoulder. Then she turned back to him. "Cause of death is *undetermined*, obviously."

"Sexual assault?"

Her lip twitched. "Undetermined."

"Was she home alone?"

She sighed again. "Cut the crap, Jack. Why did you drive all the way down here in this rain?"

He'd always liked how she didn't waste time.

"I'm investigating a string of sexual assaults," he said. "There's a choking element, and I'm wondering if it's related."

She frowned. "I hate to tell you, but we get sadistic assholes down here, same as y'all do up in Austin."

"This one's different."

"And what makes you think they're connected?"

"I'm hoping they're not."

Her attention shifted to something behind him, and her expression changed. "My lieutenant's here. I need to go." She looked at him. "Call me tomorrow. I'll share what I can."

Which might be nothing. Or she might ignore his call.
She moved to leave.

"*Wait*. Just tell me one thing."

"I need to go, Jack."

"Anything odd with the lamp?"

"The lamp?" She frowned. "What do you mean?"

"Maybe a towel or a blanket thrown over it?"

She stared at him, and the feeling of dread was back again.

"No lamp," she said. "But there's a T-shirt draped over the television."

A chill settled over him as her words sank in.

He had put that detail out there like bait, mainly to make sure she didn't blow off his call later. He hadn't really considered how he'd feel if he found out his hunch was *right*. He hadn't counted on the sharp jab of frustration from knowing that the predator who had eluded him for years was back at work again, and that he'd escalated.

Jack clenched his teeth and looked at the crime scene behind her swarming with cops and CSIs.

Heidi's phone chimed. She pulled it from her pocket and muttered a curse.

"I'll let you get back."

She glanced up. "The thing with the T-shirt. How did you know that?"

"It was a guess."

Her look turned skeptical as her phone chimed again. "I have to go, but call me tomorrow and we'll talk."

"Count on it."

THREE

THE POLICE STATION was buzzing with activity, which Rowan figured was typical for the downtown headquarters. Uniformed officers streamed back and forth through the lobby, mixing with plainclothes detectives and civilians who looked lost. A middle-aged man in a tracksuit approached the reception desk, where a frizzy-haired woman sat at a computer. She made a phone call and then directed him to a bank of chairs near a fake-looking ficus tree before returning her attention to her screen.

Rowan took a deep breath and made her approach.

"Good afternoon," she said with a smile. "I'm here to see Detective Bruner."

The woman didn't look up. "Do you have an appointment?"

"No."

"Detective Bruner isn't in right now."

Rowan rested her elbow on the counter. Still no eye contact. So, was he really not here, or was she getting the brush-off? Rowan knew she should have called ahead, but this stop had been impulsive. One minute she'd been eating a sandwich on a bench in front of the vital records office, and the next minute she was in her car rushing to police headquarters. Until five seconds ago, she hadn't even been sure Jack Bruner worked here and not at some substation. But she'd figured he did because he was in violent crimes.

Rowan put another smile on her face, even though the receptionist wasn't looking. "So . . . do you know if he'll be back later today or—"

"I don't." She glanced up, clearly annoyed. "I only know that he's out. You're free to wait." She nodded toward the chairs.

"Could I leave him a message?"

"Rowan?"

She turned around. Relief flooded her as Jack approached from the glass double doors. No rain-dampened leather jacket this time. He wore a blue dress shirt and a tie, and with his badge and gun on prominent display, he looked like a real detective now.

He stopped in front of her, his gaze intent, and she felt her leverage slipping as he obviously knew why she was here.

"What's up?" he asked.

"Do you have a minute to talk? I've got a question for you."

"Sure." He glanced at the receptionist, who was watching with interest now that it was clear she and Jack were on a first-name basis. "Is Bryan back yet?"

"Haven't seen him."

Jack looked at Rowan, his gaze a mixture of interest and skepticism. "Come on back."

He led her to a closed gray door and paused beside a keypad to enter a passcode. Then they stepped into a sea of gray cubicles where people talked on the phone and sat in front of computers. Except for the squelch of police radios and the occasional uniform walking around, it could have been a regular office.

She followed Jack down a row of cubicles, suddenly second-guessing her decision to come here. She was in her typical research attire—jeans and a sweatshirt—and once again, her hair was pulled up in a scrunchie. She tugged the band loose and ran a hand through her hair. At least she'd showered this morning.

Jack stopped at an empty cubicle and reached over the wall to grab a brown accordion file off the desk. Then he led her to a closed door with a placard beside it. **INTERVIEW 3**, it read. He tapped his knuckles on the door before pushing it open.

The room was dark. Jack switched on the light and set the accordion file on a small Formica table. He gestured to one of two gray plastic chairs.

"Have a seat," he said. "You want anything? Water? Soft drink?"

She stepped into the room and looked over her shoulder. "No, thanks."

What she needed was coffee. She'd been up half the night working, and she was running on fumes today.

"You sure?" he asked. "I'm grabbing a water."

"I'm okay."

"One sec."

He disappeared, leaving the door ajar.

Rowan glanced around before taking a seat on the far side of the table. The room was small and windowless. Nothing on the walls. She glanced up and noted the camera mounted in the corner near the ceiling. Her gaze dropped to the fat brown accordion file he'd left on the table. Just looking at it made her heart rate speed up.

Rowan set her purse at her feet and smoothed her hair as she waited. What the hell was she doing here? She was in the middle of a project. She didn't have time for this detour, and she *definitely* didn't have time for the logistical nightmare that likely would result from it.

But here she was. Once again, she hadn't been able to stay away.

Jack stepped back into the room, leaving the door slightly open again. Was that intentional? Probably. In her experience, men like him did most everything intentionally.

He set a bottle of water on the table and eyed her curiously as he took the chair across from her.

"Did you try calling?" he asked. "I had my phone off all morning."

"Why?"

He smiled. "Why did I have it off?"

"Aren't detectives supposed to keep their phones on twenty-four seven?"

He lifted an eyebrow. "Not if they're in Judge Ferguson's court room. I had to testify in a trial."

He twisted the top off his bottle of water. "So, what brings you by?" he asked, as though he didn't already know.

Rowan pulled her phone from her purse and tapped open the article she'd come across on her lunch break.

"Is this it?" She turned the screen to face him.

His brow furrowed as he read the headline: NEW ASSAULT ECHOES COLD CASES. He glanced up.

"Is that what?"

She rolled her eyes. "The thing you want my help with."

He watched her for a long moment. "Why do you ask?"

"Because." She sighed. "I need to know."

"Need?"

"I want to know." She flipped her phone over, watching his eyes now, even though she was pretty sure she already knew the answer to her question. "You didn't tell me you were investigating the West Campus Rapist."

His jaw tightened as he watched her.

She folded her arms. "Well? Is it him or not?"

He didn't respond. Of course not. Even if he knew for sure, he certainly wasn't going to tell her.

"Do you think it *might* be him?" she asked.

"I think . . ." He studied her face, and she could tell he was deciding whether he could trust her. "I think it's possible."

"So, he's been, what, dormant all this time? I mean, I haven't read anything about WCR in the news in five years. You're saying he's back?"

He watched her, his expression unreadable. She felt self-conscious as she pictured herself through this detective's eyes. When he'd come to her for help, she'd basically told him to take a hike. Now three days later, she'd shown up at his office demanding to know more about the case.

But like most detectives she had worked with, he was stingy with information and unwilling to comment on an ongoing investigation, especially one as high-profile as this one. Now that the media had made the link between the November rape and a string of unsolved cold cases, Jack and his team wouldn't be able to escape the spotlight.

He took a deep breath. "I guess I should have figured you keep up with current events."

"I do, yeah."

She folded her arms. He'd just given her confirmation without really giving it. Very smooth.

And now she was in a quandary—a quandary she'd created for herself by coming over here and asking for info about his case, the same case she'd refused to be roped into helping with only days before.

"I'll do it."

His eyebrows shot up. "You will?"

"You know I will. You knew it the second you saw me here."

He didn't bother denying that.

"Thank you," he said, trying to sound humble. But she doubted that would last long. He wasn't the humble type.

"I have a condition, though."

His eyebrows shot up again, and this time his surprise looked genuine. "What is it?"

"I want the original profile."

"How do you mean?"

"From the DNA lab. I want the raw genetic data."

He frowned. "As opposed to what?"

"As opposed to some other genetic genealogist's report that you want me to *build on* or *extrapolate from.* Or some other half-baked research that you think is going to give me a head start."

"Okay." He sounded wary, as though he didn't see the point of her condition.

"I do my own research," she told him. "And I do it from scratch."

The corner of his mouth ticked up. "You don't trust other people?"

"No." She waited a beat. "Do you?"

"Not really, no."

She nodded. "I have certain methods I've developed, and I don't want to be tripped up by someone else's mistakes. So I start each case from zero. Just give me the data and I'm good to go."

"What about payment? Are you planning to work pro bono?"

She tipped her head to the side. "Nice try."

He smiled.

"I charge by the hour. Some jobs are fast, some aren't, but I work as efficiently as I can."

Damn, she was really doing this. She'd thought she'd gotten away from police work, yet here she was about to take on his case. She picked up her purse and set it on the table. The detective watched her as she unzipped her bag and pulled out a business card.

"Send me an email, and I'll get you my rates and bio," she said, handing him the card.

"I don't need all that."

"No?"

"I already know I want to hire you." He glanced at the card, then slid it aside. "Ric tells me you're a wizard when it comes to genealogy."

"I don't know about 'wizard,' but . . . I have a strong track record. How long until you can get me that info?"

He pulled the fat brown accordion file toward him and unhooked the rubber band holding it closed. She watched with interest as he thumbed through the file and tugged out a slim manila folder.

He pushed it across the table toward her, and she was surprised to see *R. Healy* scrawled across the tab.

She looked up at him accusingly. "You assumed I'd say yes."

He smiled, laying on the charm again.

"I didn't assume—I hoped."

B RYAN WATCHED JACK return to his desk.

"Who was that?" he asked as Jack sat down.

For a moment his partner didn't respond. He seemed deep in thought as he jotted something on a notepad. Then he looked up.

"Rowan Healy."

Bryan frowned.

"The genealogist I told you about."

"That was her? I was picturing an old lady."

Jack scooted in his chair and tapped open his email, clearly not wanting to acknowledge the fact that the pretty young genealogist had come to visit him at work.

"Well, what's the deal? Is she going to help us?" Bryan asked.

"Maybe."

"Why 'maybe'?"

"She agreed to try."

"Which is huge, right? Ric said she's amazing. If she agreed to give it a look—"

"Don't," Jack said.

"Don't what?"

"Get too excited. We've been down this road before."

Well, not "we" exactly. Bryan hadn't been down this road at all. His work on the case had started with a callout to Evelyn Wood's house back in November. The seven other rape cases—all of them stone cold, at this point—had happened before Bryan even got his detective's shield.

But Jack was a different story. He'd been working this thing for years. Of course Bryan was aware of the cases—everyone knew about the West Campus Rapist. Austin was a college town, and the guy's rampage had struck fear in the heart of every woman in the city for two long years. But then the attacks had stopped, and the story faded from the news and drifted from people's minds.

But not Jack's. He was still hung up on the case, to the point that some people said he was obsessed with it.

Bryan hadn't agreed with that take—at least not until recently. His partner seemed so relaxed and laid back, Bryan had a hard time imagining him being obsessed with anything.

But that was before November. From the moment Bryan and Jack set foot inside Evelyn Wood's bedroom two months ago, it was like a switch flipped. Jack's whole demeanor changed as he surveyed the room. He told Bryan later that he'd walked in and experienced a sick sense of déjà vu.

Jack had been fixated on the investigation, to the exclusion of almost everything else, ever since.

Bryan watched Jack now as he scrolled through a police report on his computer. It was the San Antonio homicide from three days ago. Jack believed *that* case was connected, too, although Bryan wasn't convinced.

Jack glanced up. "What?"

Bryan leaned back in his chair. "So, what's her timeline?" he asked, getting back to the genealogist.

"I gave her the file. She's on it."

"Did you tell her we're in a hurry? This isn't just some cold case?"

"She understands."

Bryan studied his partner's expression. "I'm surprised you're not more excited. You've been trying to pin her down for weeks."

"If she delivers? Then I'll get excited."

"Ric said she's the best."

"Yeah, well. Let's see what she does."

FOUR

JACK TAPPED THE brakes as he approached the low-water bridge.

"I just talked to Heidi," Liz said over the phone. "The labs are in on that homicide."

"Already?"

"Yeah, and everything's negative for DNA."

"Nothing at all?"

"Zip."

Jack cursed.

"Tell me about it," Liz said.

Liz Lasco specialized in sex crimes and had interviewed WCR's victims after the attacks, collecting an amazing number of key details. Coaxing information from traumatized rape victims was difficult but necessary. Liz's interview skills were unparalleled, and Jack knew his investigation would be nowhere without her.

"So, no DNA, but same lubricant," Liz continued. "Which means we know he used a condom. That's what we expected though, right? I mean, no prints, either, so we already knew he wore gloves. This guy's meticulous."

A "meticulous" rapist. Given the violence of the crimes, Jack had a hard time accepting it. But the surviving victims all had said he used a condom.

The most recent attack represented a turning point, a critical break in the pattern. Jack had been hoping for a break in his "meticulous" pattern, too, but now the samples collected at the autopsy were telling a different story.

"What else did Heidi say?" Jack asked.

"Not a lot. Seemed like she was in a hurry. She wants you to call her later."

The road curved again, and again Jack tapped the brakes. This place was way the hell out here, and he checked his phone again to make sure he had the directions right. It seemed like he should have been there by now.

"Jack?"

"Yeah, I'll call her and see what else she knows."

"I have to tell you, she sounded skeptical."

"She is."

"Why?"

"Not sure," Jack said, although he could guess.

Heidi, like most detectives, probably didn't want to believe the unidentified subject she was looking for was a transplant from a different location where he'd struck multiple times before. That would make him a serial offender, one who had eluded police for years. Another factor was the jurisdictional headache such a development would create. It would be one thing if police in the other jurisdiction could offer a suspect list, or a giant case file filled with tantalizing clues. But despite years of effort, Jack had nothing close to that.

"So, you'll talk to her?" Liz asked.

"Yeah."

"Good, because it would be nice to get her on board."

"Yeah."

"Adding her case to the mix would get the L-T's attention."

"I know."

Their lieutenant was another skeptic, probably for many of the same reasons as Heidi. If their string of unsolved rape cases turned out to be linked to a recent murder in San Antonio, the result would be a shitstorm—for both departments, but especially for Austin, which had been sitting on the cases for years.

A brown blur dashed across the road, and Jack slammed on the brakes.

"Shit!"

"You okay?"

"Almost hit a deer." He looked at the scrub brush where the buck had disappeared.

"Where the hell are you?"

"West of town. Listen, I'll circle back with Heidi and let you know tomorrow."

"See you then."

Jack clicked off and checked his rearview mirror for headlights, but he seemed to have this windy old road to himself. He pulled onto the shoulder and read Rowan's cryptic message again.

Left on Juniper Rd, go a mile past the bridge until the big cactus on left. U cant miss it

Well, evidently you *could* miss it, because it had been over a mile since he'd passed the bridge, and he hadn't seen a cactus anywhere. He checked for traffic and started to pull a U-turn.

And then he spotted it. A giant brown cactus on the side of the road. It was a saguaro, well over ten feet tall, made of rusted iron. The sculpture was spotlit from the base, and Rowan was right—he should have noticed it. He probably would have if he hadn't been distracted on the phone.

Jack made the U-turn and hooked a right onto the private driveway beside the sculpture. He passed through an open gate and followed a narrow gravel road. Jack checked Rowan's text again as he bumped over the ruts.

Green house on the left after wall.

Jack curved around, and his headlights swept over a tall limestone wall. He spied a clump of oak trees beside a red barn. Tucked beneath one of the oaks was a small green structure that looked more like a shed than a house. A silver Corolla that Jack recognized from the Lucky Duck was parked right out front.

He pulled in next to the Corolla and cut the engine as he looked around.

This place wasn't what he'd pictured. But then, nothing about Rowan Healy was what he'd expected after talking to Ric. His friend had described her as brainy and introverted. Not exactly the type to show up at police headquarters and dictate her conditions for taking Jack's project.

Ric *had* warned him he was going to have to do some convincing to get her to work for him. That part had been right on.

She's best in her field, and laser-focused—but only if you can get her attention. She's not taking many new cases.

Jack shoved open his door, letting in a waft of cold air. He grabbed his file and got out, and his boots sank into the sodden grass. It had been drizzling all afternoon, finally letting up during his drive over here.

He looked at the big red barn again, noting the foggy glass doors with a white glow behind them. Glass doors on a barn. That was a new one. A high-pitched buzz, like maybe a Skil saw, emanated from inside the building.

Jack turned his attention to the little green cottage. Blinds covered the windows, and thin strips of light seeped through the slats. He crossed the weedy lawn, checking out

Rowan's car. Her inspection sticker was three months overdue.

The porch light was out, but he could still make out a brass door knocker in the shape of a disembodied fist. He stared at the fist for a moment before rapping his knuckles on the door.

Jack waited in the wet chill, eyeing the sagging gutters and chipping green paint. The place clearly needed work, but the welcome mat looked new, and the steps were lined with pots of purple and yellow pansies.

The door swung open, and Rowan looked him over. She wore jeans again, along with a gray tank top that left her arms bare. Her hair was damp, as though she'd just gotten out of the shower.

"You made it," she said.

"Yep."

"Damn, it's *cold*." She stepped back. "Come in, come in."

Jack wiped his boots on the mat before entering. Tonight he wore jeans and an APD golf shirt, and Rowan's gaze went to his holster as she ushered him inside.

Her warm living room smelled like pepperoni. A gray cat was curled up on a red velvet sofa that looked like it belonged to someone's grandmother.

"Who's in your barn?" he asked, nodding over his shoulder.

"You mean the studio? That's Skyler. She's the artist in residence."

"Oh yeah?"

"Well, sculptor, to be precise. That's what she's known for. She did the iron cactus you saw by the gate. This ranch belongs to her stepdad."

Rowan turned and locked the door. "Any trouble finding it?"

"Nope."

He gazed down at her, marveling again at her deep blue eyes. It was the first thing he'd noticed at the bar the other night. That and the fact that she was clearly pissed off that he'd tracked her down after she'd spent days dodging his phone calls.

She turned away. "I'm just finishing dinner. You hungry?"

"No," he lied, following her into a tiny kitchen with checkered linoleum flooring. There was a drop-leaf table in the middle and mismatched chairs.

"You sure? I've got extra." She nodded at the old white stove where a pepperoni pizza sat on a baking sheet.

"I'm good," he said.

"How about a drink? I have Coke, Snapple, water."

She leaned back against the counter and crossed her feet at the ankles. She wore brown leather slippers with a fuzzy white lining. He looked up and tried not to get distracted by her breasts in that shirt.

"There's some beer in there, too, I think."

"I'm fine, thanks," he said, even though he would have liked to have a beer with her. But he was here on business.

"I was surprised by your message," he told her.

"Why?"

"I wasn't expecting to hear from you so soon."

She lifted her shoulder. "Actually, I would have been done sooner but I smacked into that wall you mentioned."

Jack's pulse quickened. He hadn't wanted to get his hopes up, but there was no mistaking the flare of excitement in her eyes.

"And?" he asked.

"And come take a look."

She turned and led him into a glassed-in sunporch that seemed to be an add-on to the little house. On the far wall was a table with two computers—a notebook and a desktop with an oversize monitor. Mounted on the wall above the monitor was a pair of copper angel wings. Created by the sculptor in residence maybe? Beside the desk was a green armchair piled with files and paperwork.

Rowan leaned over the keyboard and turned to smile at him. "I managed to break through."

Jack moved closer to look over her shoulder, catching the scent of her shampoo. She tapped the mouse and brought the screen to life, and Jack leaned in to study the columns filled with numbers. He glanced at her.

"Let's back up, though," she said, probably sensing that the information on her screen was Greek to him. "How much do you know about genetic genealogy? In terms of new developments in the field?"

"Not nearly as much as you."

"So, a lot of this goes back to the fallout from the Golden State Killer investigation. Law enforcement uploaded the killer's DNA profile to a public site, and after he was arrested, there was a backlash from privacy advocates—which I get, actually. The site's users hadn't given permission for police to comb through their DNA data. So, anyway, now this site specifically tells people that they permit law enforcement usage—which is good news for cold case detectives."

"It's the best tool we have now," Jack said. "A bunch of cases are seeing the light of day again."

"And despite the initial backlash, plenty of people have no problem with cops using their genetic data to catch rapists and murderers, so the database keeps growing by leaps and bounds." She turned to her computer. "So, these genealogy sites are great, but it's not like they do all the work for you. Basically, they can provide you with a list of 'matches'"— she did air quotes with her hands—"and I hate that term, because it isn't really a *match* but more of an overlap. You get a list of individuals that share your sample's DNA. Of course, it's not a list of names. That would be too easy. People on these sites often use aliases or anonymous email addresses. So part of my work is sorting out who's who. You follow?"

He nodded.

"And there are a lot of clues to work with that aren't about the DNA. We can narrow down possibilities with geography—who lived near the crime? And age—who was alive and physically capable when the crime was committed? And sex—we know the crime was committed by a male. So, all those factors helped me focus my search." She turned to her screen. "I don't know what kind of results you got back the first time, but I got two promising matches. The closer match—or the one with more overlap—was on the mother's side so—"

"How do you know?" he asked.

"That match shares DNA on the X chromosome, which males only get from their mother."

"Got it."

She turned to her computer again. "Sorry." She rolled her eyes. "You probably aren't used to reading these charts. Here." She scooted around him and picked up a large whiteboard propped against the wall. She mounted it on an easel in the corner and turned to look at him.

"This is what I've been working on for three straight days."

Jack studied the diagram. The spreadsheet on the computer meant nothing to him, but this visual, he could read. It was a family tree with what had to be dozens of branches. Colored sticky notes were stuck to different limbs, creating the effect of actual leaves. He tipped his head to the side and tried to decipher some of the scribbled notes.

Henry m. Agnes?? 1894

He glanced at her. "You went back a hundred years?"

"More than that." She shrugged. "I had to. That's how I do it."

"How do you mean?"

She rested her hand on her hip. "Well . . . it's complicated. But suffice it to say, it's easier if you go backward and then work your way down. So, I zeroed in on my most promising match and went back, building a family tree to the great-great-grandparent level. And then I moved down, filling in gaps, using all kinds of research tools. That's called 'descendancy research,' and that's the fun part—using vital records, genealogy websites, even social media to infer the relationships between people."

He raised an eyebrow. "Call me skeptical."

"What, that it's fun? Well, to me it is. Anyway, sometimes I get lucky and catch a break. Like in this case, someone on a genealogy website had publicly posted a family tree recently, so that helped me fill in some blanks in my research. And that's when I homed in on this particular part of the tree."

She turned to her whiteboard.

"Your unidentified subject—or UNSUB in cop jargon—belongs to this branch right here, I'm sure of it." She tapped the whiteboard. "And *that's* when I ran into your wall."

"My wall," he repeated.

"The wall you told me about at the bar."

She smiled, and Jack felt a jolt of warmth. It was the first genuine smile he'd seen from her, and it lit up her whole face.

"I broke through it," she told him. "I think I figured it out."

"And?"

"And your UNSUB is adopted."

FIVE

Jack stared at her. "Adopted."

"That's right. I'm almost certain of it."

She wished she could say she was 100 percent certain, but she didn't like to use numbers like that, especially with cops.

His brow furrowed. "How do you know this?"

"Because"—she gestured to the whiteboard—"it's the only explanation that makes sense."

He turned to the whiteboard and folded his arms over his chest. Rowan tried not to notice the way his biceps bulged. She wasn't used to having a man in her messy home office. Or in her home at all, really. She didn't entertain much, and she sure as hell didn't entertain cops.

"Here's our best match." She tapped a name on a sticky note. "I think this woman is a first cousin of your UNSUB's mother, which would make her a first cousin once removed from your suspect."

Jack stared at the name. "Could he be *her* son? Looks like she has children."

She shook her head. "Not enough DNA overlap. Parent-child is a first-degree match, and this looks more like fourth degree." She tapped again on a different sticky note with the name *Joy Kendall*. "I think this is your UNSUB's mother. Even though according to the family tree posted by one of her relatives, this woman has no children."

He glanced at her. "You're sure about this conclusion?"

"Almost positive." She eased closer and studied the family tree she'd painstakingly constructed over the past three days. "Like I said, there are a few other possible explanations, but I've been doing this awhile, and I tend to go with Occam's razor."

"The simplest explanation is usually the right one."

"Exactly."

She watched his face, looking for clues to his reaction. But he was good at masking. His expression was almost unreadable . . . except for the spark of intrigue in his eyes. He rubbed a hand over the stubble on his chin.

"Interesting," he said, still staring at her board.

"Interesting, as in . . . you buy it? Or you don't believe me?"

He glanced at her. "No, I believe you. You're the expert. I'm just thinking about where we go next."

"We?"

"The investigation. Me and my team."

"I see. Well, my suggestion would be to locate the birth mother. I have no idea what her current address is, but I could find out. You could, too, obviously, and probably a lot faster, given your resources."

He stared at the name on the sticky note, seemingly lost in his thoughts. Maybe the name had some meaning to him. Was it possible he'd come across it during his investigation? Rowan didn't see how. But if there was one thing she'd learned through years of genealogy work, it was that coincidences—sometimes truly bizarre ones—happened a lot.

He looked at her. "Why purple?"

"What?"

"The note here." He gestured to the board. "All your other sticky notes are blue or pink or orange."

"Oh."

Her cheeks warmed as she realized her mistake. She hadn't expected him to pick up on that detail. Then again, he was a detective, trained to look for patterns. And exceptions to patterns.

"No big reason," she said. "The name is important, you know? The culmination of my research, so I wanted to emphasize it."

That explanation was true, as far as it went. What she'd left out was that purple was her favorite color, and she was superstitious. She used purple to reward herself when she unlocked a mystery.

Rowan glanced at him, and he was watching her closely with those sharp brown eyes.

She cleared her throat. "What?"

"Nothing."

He knew she'd left something out, but he let it go.

He turned to the whiteboard again. "You're right. It shouldn't take me long to track this woman down."

"What will you do when you find her?"

"Assuming she's alive, go talk to her."

Rowan had figured he would say that. "You know, you want to be careful there."

"Careful of what?"

Oscar walked over, purring, and rubbed against Rowan's leg. She picked him up and stroked his head.

"Just . . . adoption situations can be sensitive."

The side of Jack's mouth curved up. "I think I can handle it."

"Don't be so sure."

"I've been doing interviews awhile."

"Yeah? So have I." She set Oscar down and folded her

arms over her chest, mirroring his stance. "In particular, I've done a lot of interviews with women who gave a child up for adoption."

He looked genuinely surprised. "Why?"

"Because of my work. I'm a search angel."

"A who?"

"A search angel." She gestured at the wings above her computer. "Only the 'angel' part doesn't really apply to me because I'm not a volunteer. I do it for money. I have a business helping adoptees identify and connect with their biological families."

His eyebrows arched, and she realized this was news to him. She would have thought that as a detective, he would have vetted her background beyond whatever Ric Santos had told him.

"My specialty is cases where the adoption records are sealed, and people have to resort to DNA to find their birth parents," she went on. "It can get complicated. So, in tough cases, people turn their results over to me and I reconstruct a family tree for them."

"They hire you," he stated.

She nodded. "It's a lucrative business. Or, at least, it will be once I get my referral streams going. Right now I've got a couple of family law attorneys that have been throwing business my way when their clients don't want to do the genealogy research themselves. A lot of busy professionals don't have time to spend on it and would rather just hire someone. The other thing is a lot of people prefer to keep some distance. They want a liaison to reach out to their biological parent to see if they're amenable to contact before they initiate communication. It shields them from the trauma of rejection."

"So, you're the middleman."

She nodded. "It can be a sensitive topic, for all kinds of reasons."

Rowan turned and grabbed a printout she'd made for

him showing a snapshot of her research. This version didn't go all the way back—just three generations.

"Here's an abbreviated version of my findings so far to get you started." She handed him the paper. "I'll send you a full report detailing everything, but you said you were on a ticking clock, so I figured you'd want to get going right away."

"I do." He frowned down at the paper, his gaze homing in on the name at the bottom of the page.

"I'm telling you, you want to be careful how you approach her."

He nodded.

"Really, I mean it."

He glanced up.

"I'd be happy to go with you," she said.

"Go with me?"

"To interview her. You plan to go in person, don't you? You'll probably have more luck that way."

She could see he hadn't thought about it.

He folded the paper and checked his watch. "I appreciate the offer."

"But you don't want help."

"Like I said, I've been doing this awhile."

She sighed. As she'd feared, he was going to be stubborn about this, meaning he might blow the interview.

"Thank you for this, though." He held up the folded printout. "This is huge for us."

"I know."

"Really, you have no idea."

JACK LET HIMSELF into his apartment and dropped everything on the bar—keys, phone, mail, along with the warm cardboard box containing his dinner.

He ran a hand through his hair, sprinkling water onto

his tile floor. The rain had started up again the minute he'd left Rowan's house and continued his entire drive home.

His phone buzzed from beneath a pile of junk mail. Jack checked the screen and was surprised to see a San Antonio area code.

"Are you at home?" Heidi asked when he picked up.

"Yeah."

"Same place?"

"Yeah. Why?"

"I need to come by. Be there in five."

She clicked off before he could object. Not that he wanted to, really. But she'd always had a knack for catching him off guard.

Jack's stomach growled, and he glanced at the pizza box. He lifted the lid and grabbed a slice of double pepperoni, chomping into it as he walked into the bedroom. By the time he'd changed into jeans and a T-shirt, Heidi was knocking on his door.

"Sorry to barge in," she said as he ushered her inside.

"You're not."

She wore a black pantsuit and high heels, and she was damp from the rain.

"What's up?" he asked.

"Not too much," she said, glancing around. "Hey, I like what you've done with the place."

She was being sarcastic. The last time she had been here was the summer Jack moved in, and not a whole lot had changed since then.

Jack looked around at his smallish condo, trying to see it through a woman's eyes. The place was minimally furnished but comfortable. It had a brick fireplace and a balcony he never used. Jack had picked the place because of its proximity to work. Over the last few years, the traffic had gotten bad, but Jack had stayed because he liked the neighborhood.

Heidi was looking around, openly taking inventory of his bachelor pad.

"You want pizza?" he asked her. "I just stopped by Home Slice."

"Thanks, but I can't stay. I'll take a water, though."

He led her into the kitchen. "Why are you dressed up?" he asked as he opened a cabinet.

"I was at the funeral earlier. Then I stopped by the police station."

He filled the glass with chilled water from the fridge. "Amber Novak's funeral? They waited this long?"

"Yeah."

He handed her the glass, and she took a long gulp.

"I assume you're aware that her family lives here," she said.

"I know." The connection between the San Antonio homicide victim and Austin had jumped out at Jack as soon as he learned about it.

"Her brother agreed to sit down with me after the wake." Heidi rested the glass on the counter. "We had a long visit. The guy's a software developer here in town."

"You get any leads?"

She sighed and folded her arms. "Not really. Amber had an ex-boyfriend he never liked."

"John Bauer."

She looked surprised. "You've heard about him?"

"You guys have. His name came up in one of the witness interviews I read."

Heidi had been generous enough to give him a look at the paperwork in case anything jumped out at him. But she'd made it clear at the time that she still wasn't persuaded that there was a link between her homicide and their cold cases.

"Anyway, the brother doesn't like the guy," Heidi continued. "Said he was very controlling of his sister."

"Abusive?"

"He didn't know of anything specific but said his sister probably wouldn't have told him about it. Anyway, John Bauer and Amber broke up six months ago."

Typically, an ex-boyfriend—particularly a "controlling" one who raised red flags with the victim's family—would zoom straight to the top of any suspect list.

But this case wasn't typical.

Jack watched Heidi's expression, searching for clues to how she was leaning, but she had a good poker face.

"The evidence doesn't fit with a vengeful-ex scenario," Jack said.

"I'm aware." She sighed. "But that doesn't make it your guy, either."

Jack just looked at her, wondering whether she had something new to tell him to explain why she didn't like his theory.

"So, no DNA. Same condom brand. The choking." Jack paused. "The T-shirt draped over the television."

She frowned. "I know. But all of that's circumstantial."

She was right.

"You're *sure* it's the same guy?" she asked.

"No."

"But you believe it's him."

He nodded.

She sighed again and shook her head.

"You still aren't convinced?" he asked.

"No." She gave a slight shrug. "But I'm coming around."

"You know, Amber Novak grew up in Austin, so they could have crossed paths here," Jack said. "Maybe he's someone from her childhood."

"Gee, that hadn't occurred to me."

"Sorry." Jack combed his hand through his hair. "I sound like a know-it-all."

"Well, you do, but that's why I came here. I want your input. If you're right about the connection with your rape cases, that makes you the expert on this UNSUB. You know more about him than anyone, and I have questions. For example, the T-shirt thing. What's up with that?"

Jack turned and opened the fridge to grab a beer. He offered it to Heidi, but she shook her head.

He twisted off the top and took a sip, then set the bottle on the counter. "You know, five years ago this was the hottest case we had going."

Heidi just watched him. She'd moved to San Antonio by then, but he knew she would have followed the investigation in the news.

"The press was all over us, we were doing briefings all the time," he said.

"And then he stopped."

"That's debatable."

"Five years with no attacks?" she asked. "Sounds like a hiatus to me."

"No attacks that we know of," Jack corrected. He took another sip and set the bottle down. "We had no new reports, but we continued to work the cases hard. We didn't let up."

Jack had remained fixated on the unsolved rapes long after the media had moved on and the public had seemingly forgotten. The brazenness of the crimes had always bothered him, and he'd believed all along the perpetrator was capable of murder. Jack had been determined to track him down before that.

Heidi was still watching him, clearly interested in the background now that it potentially involved her case.

"We had that one DNA sample," Jack said.

"From under the fingernails."

He nodded. "Victim two scratched him. After that, he started wearing long sleeves for the attacks. Of course, we had the sample analyzed and ran it through CODIS. But we didn't have any luck."

He wasn't ready to tell Heidi about Rowan yet, not until he had more to go on.

"Another thing we did around then, we brought in a pro-filer."

She looked surprised. "FBI?"

"Yeah. This guy actually flew all the way down from Quantico, and I drove him to the various crime scenes."

Jack had spent a hot summer day with this guy tromping around the greenbelts and wooded creek beds near the victims' houses. The man had taken photos with his phone and later wrote up a report that came to the same conclusion as Jack—the UNSUB surveilled the victims extensively and learned their routines before every attack.

"Did he come up with anything?" Heidi asked.

"Your basic rundown. White male, twenties to thirties, above-average intelligence, likely history of depression, yada yada."

She lifted an eyebrow. "How informative."

"Yeah, I know. But his take on the blanket thing was interesting."

"Blanket?"

"Blanket, towel, T-shirt, whatever. This profiler said light is important to him. It's part of some need he serves when he's committing the act, part of the script he follows. He wants a dim light source so he can see her, but she can't see him."

"But she can't see him anyway. He wears a ski mask."

"Yes."

She shook her head. "What a freak."

"Yep."

"Well, at least he's a *consistent* freak. Gives us something to go on."

The lighting thing wasn't the only element connecting all nine of the crimes, but it was the most unusual. And it was the reason Jack had taken one look at Evelyn Wood's bedroom and known his UNSUB was back.

"What about the strangling?" Heidi asked.

"That's new."

She frowned. "But I thought—"

"Not completely new. The victim from November, Evelyn Wood, he choked her, too. She said she truly believed he was going to kill her."

He almost had, and Jack couldn't shake the image of the angry red welts around the Evelyn's neck when he had gone to see her in the hospital. After interviewing Evelyn, it was clear to him that their UNSUB had escalated during those missing years. His rage had expanded. He was fighting the urge to kill now, and he was losing.

And then eight weeks later, Amber Novak was raped and murdered, confirming Jack's worst fears.

"So, if you're right, then we're screwed," Heidi said bluntly. "We're wasting our time on the ex-boyfriend, who happens to be our only suspect at this point."

Jack nodded.

"Shit." Heidi tipped her head back. Then she checked her watch. "I need to go. Cora's sitter is going to quit on me."

"Cora is your daughter?"

"Yeah."

Jack felt guilty for not knowing.

"How old is she?" he asked.

"Two and a half." She smiled. "She's a great kid. Willful as hell, but great."

Her voice was tinged with pride, and Jack was happy for her. Heidi had always talked about having a family. Her marriage hadn't worked out, but he was glad to see she'd gotten at least some of what she wanted.

She headed for the door, and he reached around her to open it.

"Keep me posted on the rest of the labs," he said.

"I will. There's not much left to analyze, but maybe they'll come back with something off the clothing. I'll let you know."

"Thanks."

"And same goes for you. If you turn something up, I want to know about it."

"You will."

She stepped through the door and turned around. "I mean it. If you hold out on me, I will seriously cut your balls off."

He winced. "Damn, why so harsh?"

"Because I know you, Jack. And you'd better fucking keep me in the loop."

SIX

WISH I COULD make it," Rowan told Lila over the phone.

"That's okay. We can have Noodle Night without you."

Rowan was supposed to be on her way to Lila's right now to eat Thai food and to hear all about Dara's blind date that had turned into an entire weekend.

"I'll swing by the Duck tomorrow," Rowan said. "You can catch me up."

"Maybe you'll have a story of your own by then."

"This is *work*," Rowan said, regretting now that she'd mentioned Jack's name.

"Yeah, you said."

Rowan got off with Lila and dropped her phone in her purse as she hurried down the sidewalk, scanning faces.

She spotted Jack leaning against a black Jeep. He was watching her, and the intensity in his eyes sent a ripple of warmth through her.

She jogged across the intersection as the **WALK** sign expired. Approaching Jack, Rowan squared her shoulders and tried to appear confident. For once, she looked reasonably put together in black jeans, a pine green sweater, and her favorite heeled ankle boots.

Jack lifted his eyebrow as she stopped in front of him. "You sure you're up for this?" he asked.

"Absolutely."

He turned and popped the Jeep's locks with a chirp.

"We're taking this?" she asked.

He reached around her and opened the passenger door.

"This is me being sensitive," he said. "I didn't think she would appreciate me rolling up to her house in a police ride."

Rowan stepped onto the running board, and Jack touched her elbow to help her into the seat. She nestled her purse at her feet, and he closed the door.

She glanced around curiously as he walked to the driver's side. The Jeep was low-tech but clean, with a pair of aviator sunglasses tucked into the cup holder. On the back seat was a blue mountain-biking helmet and a pair of rubber boots with grass clinging to the soles.

Jack hitched himself behind the wheel and started the engine. Once again, he was wearing slacks and a dress shirt—no tie today—with his badge and gun on his hip. Despite the businesslike clothes, the old Jeep seemed to suit him.

"You mountain bike?" she asked.

"Yeah. You?" He glanced at her.

"Not lately. What are the boots for?"

He turned around. "Outdoor crime scene."

He reached back and tossed the boots behind the seat into the cargo area.

"Sorry for the last-minute notice." He checked over his shoulder and pulled into traffic.

"No problem. I was done for the day."

She didn't mention that she'd had to rearrange her evening. She hadn't even hesitated when he'd called less than an hour ago.

So, does your offer still stand?

His low-key question had prompted her to cancel her plans. She'd told herself it was because he needed help with his case, and he was man enough to admit it. But that wasn't the only reason.

He ran a yellow light and checked the mirror.

"By the way, where'd you park?" He glanced at her.

"The garage by the police station."

"Visitor space?"

"Yeah. Why?"

"They tow."

They neared the courthouse, and he lifted his fingers off the wheel in greeting as they passed a couple of uniformed officers. He downshifted as they turned and cut through a neighborhood where the streets were lined with old houses that had been converted into law offices and accounting firms.

Butterflies filled Rowan's stomach as she looked out the window. She liked the way his car smelled. Something earthy—probably the boots—but with a hint of aftershave. Was there any chance he'd primped before meeting her? This was work. Period. But she'd felt a flutter of excitement when she'd heard his voice over the phone.

He turned north onto Lamar Boulevard.

"So." She glanced at him. "Where does Joy Kendall live, exactly?"

"Pemberton Heights. Shouldn't take us long, assuming traffic's not crazy."

"Nice neighborhood," Rowan said. "What's she do for a living?"

Jack's phone buzzed and he pulled it from his pocket.

"One sec," he said, and then connected the call. "Bruner."

He paused, and Rowan looked out the window at the sidewalks busy with people headed home or going out after work. It was a Thursday, and everyone seemed to be getting a jump on their weekend. She would be, too, but she'd ditched her best friends and dropped everything to help this detective she barely knew. Was this a mistake? Maybe. She could have simply sent him the report he'd paid for and wished him good luck.

But instead she'd allowed herself to be lured in. Violent cases pulled at her, and especially this one. But part of it was Jack.

She glanced at him beside her.

"No," he said curtly, followed by a long pause. "All right, keep me posted."

He clicked off.

Silence settled over them, and Rowan turned her attention out the window. The hike-and-bike trail that paralleled the creek was almost empty tonight, which wasn't surprising given the soggy weather they'd had lately. Rowan spotted a woman jogging alone, AirPods stuffed into her ears. She had a zipper pack clipped around her waist, and Rowan wondered if it contained pepper spray.

"What's wrong?"

She glanced at Jack. "Huh?"

"You look worried."

"Oh. Nothing—just . . . I used to run on this trail all the time. Campus to the lake. Four-point-five miles round-trip."

"You went to UT?" he asked.

"Yep. Graduated six years ago."

She glanced at him, surprised he didn't know this already. Of course, it wasn't one of the facts she included in the short bio on her website. That paragraph purposely omitted personal information and focused on her membership in various professional associations.

"So, you were there for the first attacks," Jack said.

"I was, yes."

She didn't mention that she had lived in a garage apartment just half a block away from Olivia Salter, WCR's second victim.

Rowan also didn't mention that she and Olivia had been friends.

Had been. As in, years ago. But Rowan hadn't seen or talked to Olivia in ages. Rowan had tried to find her on social media but hadn't had any luck, and she felt guilty for letting the relationship slip away.

She glanced at Jack, who was watching the road now with a somber look on his face. She wondered if he was thinking about Olivia, too. And it suddenly occurred to her that he'd probably talked to Olivia way back when. He'd probably interviewed her shortly after her attack, right after her world was shattered by a ski-masked intruder.

The crimes had rocked the campus. The entire city of Austin, really. By the third attack, people were scared. Many women were buying Mace and changing their routines to avoid walking home after dark. By the sixth attack, it was clear WCR's preferred MO was to break into women's homes when they were alone, often through a sliding glass door. People began installing steel brackets on sliders. Some women moved in with boyfriends or tried to get roommates.

A lifelong introvert, Rowan had remained alone in her studio apartment. But the combination of the intensive news coverage and knowing one of the victims personally ratcheted up her stress. She signed up for self-defense classes and installed braces on her windows—despite the fact that she was on the second floor. When neither of those things helped her sleep easier, she bought a motion-sensitive security cam that linked to her phone and sent her alerts—which served only to make her resent the squirrels and other critters that interrupted her sleep several nights a week.

But her resentment wasn't just reserved for nocturnal animals. She started to feel pissed off at the men in her orbit, who seemed to go right along as normal, oblivious to the possibility of waking up in the middle of the night to a masked terrorist.

Rowan had operated in a state of constant vigilance, not letting her guard down until years later when she accepted

Skyler's invitation to come live at the ranch. But even after moving, her anxiety lingered, and to this day, she slept with a can of bear spray under her bed.

They hung a left into a neighborhood with stately houses and giant oak trees. As a college student, Rowan had done a few babysitting jobs over here—mostly professors' families. After hearing they paid well, she had posted her name and number on bulletin boards in several of the academic buildings on campus.

Jack turned onto a curving road and shifted gears as they headed up a hill. Rowan had never been on this street. The lots were getting bigger, and many of the houses were tucked behind vine-covered walls.

"Three-fourteen," Jack said, slowing at an open gate.

He pulled onto a long driveway that curved in front of a redbrick house with black shutters. Neatly trimmed hedges lined a path leading from the driveway to the black front door.

"What did you say she does again?" Rowan asked.

"Works for a software company." He veered around a huge magnolia tree and rolled to a stop beside a black convertible Mercedes. "She's a VP of sales."

Rowan glanced at the convertible. Given Austin's typical sunshine, she guessed the top was down much of the year.

Jack cut the engine.

"So, what's your plan?" Rowan asked him.

"I thought you had one."

"You thought *I*—" She halted, noticing his sly smile.

"Kidding," he said. "I told her I needed to talk to her about an investigation. I was pretty vague, but she seemed open to talking. So, I figured we could play it by ear."

"That's not much of a plan, Jack."

He smiled. "I thought you did this all the time?"

"I do."

Lights flashed behind them as another car came up the

driveway. Rowan glanced over her shoulder as a white Range Rover slid into a space beside the Mercedes.

"Is her husband home?" Rowan asked.

"I don't know. Why?"

She sighed and pushed open her door. "If things get awkward, follow my lead."

They walked over to the Range Rover as the driver's-side door opened and a woman slid out. Petite, midforties. She wore black leggings and a layered blue sports top, and her curly blond hair was pulled up in a ponytail.

"Detective Bruner?" the woman asked, looking from Rowan to Jack.

"That's me. Joy Kendall, I take it?"

"Yes."

A pair of brown Yorkies sprang out of the car.

"Sorry." Joy turned around. "Inside. Both of you." She clucked at the dogs and pointed to the back door, and they scampered away.

Joy looked at Jack, then checked her Apple Watch. "I thought you said five thirty?"

"We're a little early," he said.

"That's all right." She turned around before Rowan could introduce herself. "Come on inside."

Jack motioned for Rowan to go ahead, and she followed Joy down a cobblestone path and into a courtyard where two spiral-shaped topiaries flanked the back door. After letting the dogs in, Joy led them through a sparkling clean utility room and down a corridor into a kitchen.

Rowan stopped short, and Jack bumped into her.

The giant kitchen opened into a great room with a vaulted ceiling and a limestone fireplace. The room was enormous. Skyler's barn-studio could have almost fit inside it.

Joy dropped her keys and purse on a white marble counter. "Thanks for coming, Detectives. Can I get you some water or anything?"

Rowan shot a look at Jack.

"Thanks, I'm good," Jack said. "Ms. Kendall—"

"Call me Joy."

"I'd like to introduce you to my colleague Rowan Healy."

Joy turned to Rowan, seeming to really notice her for the first time.

"Rowan's assisting with the case," Jack said. "She's not a detective."

"Oh." A little line appeared between Joy's perfectly shaped eyebrows as she looked Rowan over. "You're not with the burglary unit?"

"Burglary?" Rowan glanced at Jack.

"Detective Garcia told me—"

"I'm sorry. Armando Garcia?" Jack stepped forward. "He's with our burglary team. Is he helping you with something?"

"Well . . . yes. My case. Isn't that why you're here?"

Rowan looked at Jack, who was frowning now.

"I think there's been a misunderstanding," he said.

"So . . . you're *not* here to give me an update about my car break-in?"

"No." Jack paused. "When was your car burglarized?"

"Last week. My SUV was broken into overnight. Someone stole my iPad and some brand-new Pings."

"Pings?"

"My husband's golf clubs. Detective Garcia came out and took the report."

"I wasn't aware of it," Jack said, "but I'm happy to follow up with him on that. We're here about something else."

Joy glanced at Rowan.

"Mind if we sit down?" Jack asked.

"No. Please." She gestured toward the living area. "Make yourselves comfortable."

Rowan stepped into the cavernous room filled with over-size furniture—all of it white with throw pillows in various shades of blue. Rowan picked the closest sofa. It was too deep to lean back on, so she perched on the edge of a cushion. Jack sat on an armchair and made eye contact with Rowan as Joy bustled around in the kitchen, filling a glass with ice.

A moment later she joined them, trailed by the dogs. They trotted to a pair of beds by the fireplace, and each made a circle before settling down.

Joy lowered herself onto the sofa opposite Rowan and rested a glass of what looked like ice water on her knee.

"So." She turned to Jack with an expectant look. "What is this about?"

"I'm investigating a series of cold cases," Jack said, "and your name came up in the investigation."

"*My* name?" She looked from Jack to Rowan. "What kind of cold cases?"

"I'm not at liberty to discuss the details," Jack said.

Her posture stiffened, and Rowan felt the tension ramping up in the room.

"We recovered DNA from one of the crime scenes," Jack continued. "And we have reason to believe it may have come from a relative of yours."

Her eyebrows shot up. "Of mine?"

"That's correct."

She leaned forward. "An *Austin* crime scene? You're with APD, so am I to assume—"

"Yes, Austin."

She looked flustered now. "But . . . how did you—"

"Excuse me." Rowan glanced at Jack. "If I might step in here?" She turned to Joy. "To give you some background, I'm a genetic genealogist." Rowan smiled. "I know, sounds redundant, right? I use DNA for genealogy research. In this case, to trace a DNA profile to a particular person within a family tree."

Joy stared at her.

"Based on my research," Rowan said, "it appears that the DNA sample in this case belongs to a close relative of yours."

"I don't have a lot of close relatives," Joy said. "My father passed away last year, and my mother lives in Sage Springs."

"This would likely be someone one generation down from you, such as a nephew." Although, according to Rowan's research, Joy didn't have any nephews.

"I'm an only child," Joy replied. "I don't have nieces or nephews."

"Perhaps a son?"

"But I don't—" She stopped short.

Rowan held her gaze, watching her face transform as understanding dawned. Joy's cheeks flushed, and she darted a glance at Jack. The silence stretched out.

Joy leaned forward and placed her drink on the table in front of her. She reached for a coaster and carefully set the glass on top of it. Her fingers were trembling now.

She settled her hands in her lap and looked at Jack. "Exactly what sort of case is this?"

He darted a look at Rowan. "I can't go into specifics, I'm afraid. But I can tell you it's serious. Otherwise, we wouldn't be here asking for your help."

"Let's back up a moment," Rowan said, pulling Joy's attention away from Jack and back to the science side of the conversation. "Are you aware of any one of your relatives who might have done one of those home DNA kits recently?"

"A home DNA kit," she said, looking at Rowan. "Oh my God. Oh no." She put her hand on her stomach. "I always thought he might come looking for me one day, but I never imagined . . ." She buried her face in her hand. "Oh my God. It was so long ago. I was a teenager."

"And you gave the baby up for adoption?" Rowan asked.

She nodded, her face still hidden behind her hand. "My husband doesn't even know about this." Then she jerked her head up and looked at Jack. "What is the crime?"

"All I can tell you is—"

"*No.*" She held up her hand. "Don't tell me. I don't want to know. I need to think about this." She glanced toward the back door. "Michael will be home soon. I can't be sitting here talking about this." She stood abruptly. "I'm going to have to get back to you. I need to think about this."

Rowan stood, and Jack did, too—reluctantly, Rowan thought.

"I'm going to have to get back to you," Joy repeated.

"We understand," Rowan said. "It's a lot to absorb."

"I mean, it was *years* ago."

Rowan nodded. "I realize this probably comes as a shock."

"It does." She darted a desperate look at Jack. "Please understand, you're putting me in an impossible situation here. I want to help you, but . . . I need to think through this."

"We understand," Rowan said, pulling her attention away from Jack before he could object. "When you're ready, you know how to reach us."

Jack shot Rowan a sharp look. Then he pulled a business card from his pocket. "Here's my contact info. My cell is on the back."

"I have it." Joy moved to the kitchen, clearly eager to get rid of them. "I'll be in touch." She corralled them down the corridor as the dogs scurried around their feet.

Rowan stopped by the back door and made eye contact with Joy. "It's a lot to think about, I know."

Tears welled in her eyes. "It is."

"Take your time," Rowan told her. "Call us when you're ready."

JACK GRIPPED THE wheel with frustration as he drove down Lamar. He glanced at Rowan gazing sullenly out the window. She hadn't said a word since leaving Joy Kendall's house.

"Stop giving me that look," she said, still staring out the window.

"What look?"

"That *How could you blow my big interview?* look."

"I'm not giving you a look."

"Right."

"I'm not. I'm just . . . frustrated. I don't understand what just happened."

"What do you mean?" Rowan tore her attention away from the window, finally. "We told her why we were there and asked for her help. Now she has to think about it."

"Yeah, but 'Take your time'? You really think that was the best way to end it?"

Rowan folded her arms, clearly unhappy to have her tactics questioned.

"You can't pressure her. I'm telling you, that could backfire. Then you're looking at a major setback."

Jack was already looking at a major setback. The best lead he'd had in months—*years*—had potentially turned into a dead end.

And if not a dead end, at the very least, a delay.

Rowan pulled her purse into her lap and unzipped it. "She'll reach out. Trust me." She pulled out a roll of Life Savers and popped one into her mouth. "Want one?"

"No."

Jack trained his gaze on the road.

"Relax," she said, swishing the Life Saver around.

He shook his head.

"Seriously, I bet she calls you tomorrow."

"This isn't a family reconciliation we're dealing with, Rowan. I'm on a clock here." He glanced at her. "This guy's out there. And he's dangerous."

"I know, all right!" She tossed her purse to the floor. "But you can't just badger people. Think about what you're asking her to do here."

"I'm asking her to do the right thing and help me take someone dangerous off the streets."

She huffed out a breath. "But you can't just *make* someone do the right thing. I mean, look at it from her perspective.

She thinks you're coming over to update her on a *car burglary*, and suddenly you're sitting there asking about a baby she gave up for adoption when she was a teenager. Because that baby has grown up to be a violent criminal. Geez! Did you see how unnerved she was? Her own husband doesn't even know she had a teen pregnancy."

"Yeah, I caught that. They must be really close. Sounds like a great marriage."

"You're missing the point."

"No, I got it." He changed gears as he neared a stoplight. "I understand you don't want to put pressure on her, and you want to treat her with kid gloves and all that. But in my job, pressure comes with the territory. We're under *pressure* to find this guy before he goes after his next victim."

Quiet settled over them, and he realized he'd raised his voice. Rowan was staring out the window again, ignoring him. Or probably thinking he was an asshole.

Jack took a deep breath. He shouldn't be taking this out on her. She was only trying to help.

A drizzle started up again as they made their way through downtown. The *swish-swish* of the windshield wipers filled the silence as they wended their way back to the police station.

"This is me on the left," she said, grabbing her purse off the floor.

Jack pulled up to the curb in front of the parking garage.

"Well, it's possible you're right." She made eye contact. "Maybe I handled it wrong. But I think your message got through. I really think you'll hear from her in the next few days."

She pushed her door open, and Jack felt a dart of panic as she slid out.

"Wait."

She turned around, a wary look in her deep blue eyes as she stood in the rain. She was pissed at him. And he wanted a chance to smooth things over.

"How about dinner?"

Her eyebrows shot up. "Dinner?"

"Would you like to go get something together?"

"You mean, like, tonight?"

She didn't look even remotely tempted by the invitation.

Jack cleared his throat. "Yeah, we could go grab a bite somewhere. My treat. Consider it a thank-you for helping me with the interview."

A line appeared between her eyebrows. "I thought you said I botched it?"

"The jury's still out on that." He tried to keep his tone light, but she still looked less than thrilled by the prospect of dinner with him. And suddenly he desperately wanted to convince her. If she slammed that door and walked away, he might not ever see her again.

"Come on." He gave her what he hoped was a charming smile. "Say yes."

SEVEN

ROWAN CHECKED HER reflection in the rearview mirror. Her hair was damp and frizzy, and the tip of her nose was pink from the cold. She put on some ChapStick and decided it was hopeless.

"Screw it," she said, sliding from her dry car into the drumming rain. She jogged across the parking lot and hopped over a puddle near the sidewalk.

The inside of the restaurant was warm and dim and smelled of barbecue. Rowan hadn't been here since a disastrous blind date five years ago. This one wasn't off to a much better start.

But it wasn't a date.

She stepped up to the host stand and spotted Jack in the bar at a high-top table. He slid off his stool as she approached him.

"This all right?" he asked, pulling out her chair for her.

Okay, maybe it was kind of a date. His badge and gun were no longer on display, and he looked like a civilian now.

"Sure." She hung her purse on the back of the stool and sat.

"The dining room had a half-hour wait," he said.

"Must be good."

"Best brisket in town."

That was saying a lot, given their location, but Rowan wasn't much of a barbecue connoisseur.

She was hungry, though, and she grabbed the menu tucked behind the condiment bottles. It gave her a distraction as she felt Jack's gaze on her.

He kept watching her, and whenever he did, she felt a warm glow. He rested his arms on the table, and she was acutely aware of his closeness as he read his menu. Jack was attractive. She couldn't pretend otherwise.

Which made it all the more annoying that she was ticked off at him for questioning her judgment.

A server walked over. Rowan ordered a local beer they had on tap and Jack did the same.

Yet another sign that this dinner was more personal than business.

"And are y'all eating tonight?" the server asked.

"I'll have the wings," Rowan said. "Extra ranch, please." The woman turned to Jack.

"Brisket sandwich, please. Chips instead of coleslaw."

She jotted it down and walked away. Rowan looked at Jack. He'd rolled his sleeves up, and his arms were tan, probably from mountain biking.

"So, what did you think?" he asked.

"Of?"

"Joy Kendall."

Rowan tipped her head to the side, debating how much to tell him. She had a lot of thoughts about Joy—most of them conjecture—and she didn't want to share them with Jack at this point.

"I think we rattled her."

He nodded. "I expected that. What else?"

"I think . . . she really didn't want us inside her house once she knew why we were there."

"She didn't want her husband seeing us. What do you think that's about?"

"I have no way of knowing."

"Yeah, but what do you *think*?"

He held her gaze, and she felt the power of it. He had a strong personality, and he was used to persuading people. Right now he wanted her opinion, and he wanted her to feel flattered that he wanted it.

She understood what he was doing, but knowing she was being manipulated didn't keep her from falling for it.

"I think she's got a tough decision to make," Rowan said. "And she may or may not decide to bounce it off her husband."

Jack just watched her, obviously picking up on her evasiveness.

"You know from my report that they've only been married three years, right? And this is his second marriage."

"What are you suggesting?" he asked.

She shrugged. "I don't know. She kept her name when she got married. I wouldn't be surprised if she keeps her finances separate. Maybe she keeps parts of her past separate, too."

"Like I said, I don't think they're close."

"Not everyone is a love match."

Rowan's parents certainly hadn't been. They had divorced when she was fourteen and barely spoke anymore.

The server was back with two beer glasses filled to the brim.

Rowan took a sip, hoping to settle her nerves. It wasn't just that Jack was a cop that was getting to her. He had a way of questioning her that made her feel like he was reading between the lines of everything she said, gleaning information that she hadn't intended to share.

Jack sampled his beer and set the glass down. "So, how'd you get into this work?"

Rowan smiled. Was he really interested or was this more flattery?

"What? Why is that funny?"

"Nothing," she said, deciding to go along with it. "I guess you could say I have my mom to thank."

"Is she a genealogist?"

"She's a court reporter."

He lifted an eyebrow.

"I majored in biology in college," she said. "My goal was to work in a research lab, help find a cure for cancer and genetic disorders."

"Lofty goal."

"I was an idealist." That was before she got involved with police work.

"Past tense?"

It was, but she didn't want to talk about that, either.

"That kind of work requires grad school," she said, "so I took a job as a lab assistant and started applying to programs. That's when I got sidetracked. I was working in the state crime lab in their DNA section."

He nodded. "They're always slammed over there."

"Always." She took another sip. "Anyway, when I signed on, they were just ramping up their genetic genealogy work. I had a knack for it right off the bat, and pretty soon, I was inundated with cases. See, the DNA analysis is only part of it. A lot of scientists are good at that. But there's also the traditional genealogy piece, and that's where some people get bogged down."

"Not you?"

She shrugged. "I really like the research. You know, public records searches. Death records, marriage records, that kind of thing. My mom worked in a courthouse for years, and I grew up comfortable in that setting. Combing through public records and requesting access to stuff came naturally to me. Plus now, there's so much you can track down online."

"If you know where to go."

"Yeah, but I mean—that's the fun part. Knowing where to look and then *finding* that one key kernel of information than unlocks a mystery." She watched him, gauging his reaction. Some people's eyes glazed over at the mention of public records searches, but Rowan thought it was fascinating.

"You sound passionate about it," Jack said.

"I am."

"So, why'd you stop? Some people go their whole lives without doing something they're passionate about."

The server arrived with their food, giving Rowan a chance to get her thoughts together. The plate she put in front of Rowan was piled high with chicken wings.

"There's no way I can eat all this," she said when the server was gone. "These portions are crazy."

"You were saying? About why you stopped?" He picked up his sandwich, undeterred by her pathetic attempt to change the subject.

"I didn't, really." She dunked a wing in ranch dressing. "I still do what I did—using DNA to trace things—just not for police investigations."

The wings were hot and sticky, and she dabbed her mouth with a napkin as Jack watched her.

"Police work didn't hold your interest?" he asked.

"It wasn't that." She sipped her beer, stalling for time. "If anything, I had the opposite problem. I was immersed. I was working evenings and weekends and holidays. I was always in the lab, and everything started to feel out of whack."

"Burnout."

Crime labs were known for it. Constantly working around rape kits and bloody clothing took a toll on people.

Rowan had done it for only a few years, but she'd felt like the walls were closing in on her.

She focused on her food, dipping a celery stick in dressing. She wasn't comfortable talking about this with him, but she didn't know why. Cops knew all about burnout.

Maybe she was worried he'd have the same reaction she'd picked up from her coworkers when she'd quit—that she was too young to understand burnout. That was for people fifteen or twenty years in.

"So, how'd you get into adoption work?" Jack asked.

Why was he so stuck on this? She couldn't remember the last time she'd been out with a man and he hadn't wanted to talk about himself the whole time.

She smiled, trying to lighten things up. "Why are we so focused on *me*?"

"I'm interested."

A tingle went through her. His voice sounded sincere, and the steady look in his eyes made her think he meant it. But, again, he was a detective, clearly skilled at drawing people out. She needed to remember that.

She finished off a wing and wiped her hands on her napkin. "Well, you met my friend Lila. The bartender at the Duck?"

He nodded.

"Lila's adopted, and a while ago she bought one of those DNA kits. She asked me to take a look at her results and help her find her birth parents. So I did. She was able to reconnect with her mom and also locate a half brother she never knew about."

"Instant family."

"Sort of."

Lila and her birth mother didn't get beyond a few stilted encounters. But Lila and her half brother had hit it off, and now she did stuff with his family. For someone who had been a loner most of her life, just having that one familial connection had made a big impact. Rowan felt good being a part of that.

"Anyway, it's rewarding," she said now because Jack was still at least pretending to look interested. "I like re-uniting families. And there's a lot more of that happening now that DNA kits have become so popular."

"So, I'm guessing you've mapped out your own ancestry?"

She shrugged. "No."

"No?" He smiled. "Why not? I would have thought you'd have traced your family back to the *Mayflower* or something."

Despite his smile, he was watching her closely, and she tried to seem nonchalant.

"Well, I have some reservations about putting my profile out there."

"Oh yeah?"

"It's a privacy thing," she said. "Plus, I've been so busy with other people's projects. Lila put me in touch with a couple of online groups, and I started helping more and more adoptees. It began consuming so much time, I decided to quit my day job and make a consulting business of it, and I've been building up my network ever since, getting referrals and recs from people."

"Sounds like it's really getting off the ground," he said. "Guess I'm lucky you made time for my case."

"Of course."

"Not 'of course,'" he said with a smirk. "You dodged my calls for more than a week."

"I didn't know it was about WCR. You should have led with that."

His brow furrowed as he set down his sandwich. "You know, WCR is a misnomer."

"How do you mean?"

"The first two cases happened on the west side of campus, yes, but the other seven happened elsewhere."

"The other seven?"

Something flickered across his face—just for an instant—and then it was gone.

"The other day you said *eight* cases total. Has there been another one?"

Jack held her gaze, and she got a knot in the pit of her stomach.

"How come it wasn't on the news?" she asked.

He watched her, and she could see his wheels turning as he probably debated how much to tell her.

"Off the record?"

She rolled her eyes. "I'm not a reporter. Who would I tell?"

He picked up a chip and seemed to consider that.

"Well, this depends who you ask," he said, "but there's a recent San Antonio case that may or may not be connected."

The knot in her stomach tightened.

"What do *you* think?" she asked.

"I believe it's linked, but I'm pretty much alone with that take."

"Why do you think it's connected?" she asked, knowing he probably wouldn't tell her. But she was burning to know, and she had to at least ask.

"A hunch."

"A hunch? That's it?"

He nodded. "I've been investigating this UNSUB for years. In some ways, I feel like I know him."

His eyes were dark and serious now, and she could tell he didn't like having some sadistic psycho stuck in his head. Working a serial case for years had to be its own kind of torment.

They ate without talking for a few moments, letting the bar's bluesy music fill the silence.

"So, what about *you*?" she asked, deciding to turn the tables. "You've been doing this awhile now. Do you ever feel burned out?"

He waited a beat.

"I try to focus on the positive," he said, not really answering the question—which she supposed was answer enough.

"Which is?"

"I try to get to the facts," he said. "When I meet people, often they've just been through the worst experience of their life. They're shaken up. They want answers." He looked grim now. "Doesn't bring their loved one back or undo a sexual assault. But it helps hold people accountable."

Guilt gnawed her. She used to feel that way about her work, too. But she'd traded a deep-rooted sense of mission for a chance to get some semblance of balance back in her life.

A phone dinged beneath the table. Jack dug his cell from his pocket, and his expression tensed as he checked the screen.

"Need to go?" she asked.

"Yeah." He looked up. "Sorry."

"No problem."

He signaled the server, and they paid the bill. Less than three minutes after someone had pinged him, they stepped from the warm restaurant into the cold night air. The drizzle had stopped, but the slick sidewalks told her it had been raining while they ate.

She glanced at her car.

"This you?" Jack said, stepping off the sidewalk. She was parked on the opposite side of the lot from him, but he walked her to her car anyway, and she felt a flutter of nerves again.

A giant pickup had wedged itself into the space beside hers. She stopped at her bumper and turned to him.

"Thank you for dinner."

The corner of his mouth lifted. "Why? You didn't let me pay."

"Well, thanks for the invitation." She glanced over her shoulder. "I like this place."

She looked up at him in the glow of the security light two rows over. His eyes looked black and serious. She needed to go, but her feet wouldn't move as he stared down at her, and the moment stretched out.

She wanted to kiss him. The urge came out of nowhere. He might reject her, but still she felt the impulse to try.

His phone dinged again, and he pulled it from his pocket.

"You'd better get that." She slid into the narrow space between her car and the truck. "Good night, Jack."

JACK WATCHED HER pull out of the parking lot. Then looked down and read the text from Bryan.

Did you talk to Heidi?

Jack reread the text Heidi had sent a moment ago telling him to contact her ASAP. Jack called her.

"What happened?" he asked when she picked up.

"Jack, we got it."

His pulse jumped. "Got what?"

"A profile."

"You're talking about Amber Novak?"

"Yeah, they lifted something off her clothing. A tiny drop of blood. I figured it was hers but—"

"You *knew*?"

"Yeah, but I didn't want to get my hopes up. Jack, it's a match. The profile matches your UNSUB."

EIGHT

BRYAN HARDLY RECOGNIZED Evelyn Wood when she opened her front door. She wore paint-spattered overalls and had her hair pulled back in a red bandanna.

"Morning, ma'am. I'm Detective Bryan Hunt, with Austin PD." He flashed his badge and handed her a business card. "We met back in November?"

"I remember you." She held the card in her paint-speckled hand and frowned down at it. "Liz isn't coming?"

"Detective Lasco had a callout, so she asked if I could swing by." He paused. "Assuming that's all right with you."

"No, that's fine." She looked past him at the unmarked police unit parked by the curb. "Come on in. Please."

The smell of paint fumes hit him as he stepped into a living room that looked nothing like the last time he'd seen it. Cardboard boxes filled the center of the space, and a stack of framed pictures was propped against the wall.

"'Scuse the mess," she said, stepping over a rolled-up rug.

"No problem. Doing some painting?"

"And packing."

She led him down a hallway lined with more boxes and stopped beside a room where Lady Gaga crooned from a portable radio. The floor was covered in plastic sheeting, and swaths of pale gray covered the bubble gum–pink walls that Bryan remembered from last time.

"My Realtor suggested neutrals," she said, bending down to switch off the radio. "Not everyone wants a princess castle mural in their bedroom, apparently. Excuse me."

He moved out of the doorway, and she scooted past him. "Come on back. It's in here."

She led him into the primary bedroom, where a pile of furniture had been shoved into the center and draped with drop cloths. More cardboard boxes lined the wall beneath the large window covered in plantation shutters.

The same window, according to Jack, where Evelyn's attacker had watched her from the cover of a mulberry bush prior to the crime. Shoe impressions—Adidas sneakers, size twelve—had been discovered on the ground beneath the windowsill.

"I would have called sooner, but I didn't realize it until just last night." She glanced over her shoulder as she stepped into a walk-in closet and switched on a light.

Bryan stopped beside the doorway, not wanting to crowd her.

"And what exactly was it you realized?" Bryan asked, wishing Liz had given him more detail. All she'd said on her voicemail was that he needed to stop by Evelyn Wood's residence to take a statement about something she had suddenly remembered about her attack.

"Sorry." Evelyn turned and hung a plastic-covered batch of dry cleaning on a hook on the wall. "It's tight in here. What was that?"

He cleared his throat. "What was it you realized? Detective Lasco was a little vague."

"Oh. Well, it's weird." She turned and sighed, folding her arms over her chest. She wore a loose T-shirt beneath the overalls, and the red welts he had observed on her neck the night of her assault had long since healed. "So, when Liz interviewed me the first time, she said not to be surprised if things came back to me in waves. She said it happens sometimes."

Bryan remembered that Liz always told victims to call her by her first name. She said she liked to keep their conversation as relaxed as possible, so they'd feel more comfortable recounting things that were hard to talk about.

"I understand," Bryan said, still not really understanding at all.

"So, I was in here packing." She gestured to a pile of sweaters on the floor beside an unzipped duffel bag. "And I came across my jewelry box. I suddenly remembered my silver locket was missing."

Bryan nodded.

"I thought my husband took it."

"Your husband?"

"*Ex*-husband, as of next week. Sorry." She gazed down at the floor, which was blanketed with shoes and piles of clothing. "I'm not making any sense, am I?" She looked up at him, and her green eyes welled with tears. "Sorry." She put her hand over her mouth.

"It's fine. Take your time."

She looked at her feet again and took a deep breath. "The week before it happened, I noticed my locket was missing. It's a silver locket that my ex-husband gave me for Mother's Day. It has my daughter's picture in it."

Bryan felt a knot in his gut as he started to see where this was going.

"This would be the week of November twelfth," he stated.

"Yeah, sometime in there. Anyway, it's my favorite piece of jewelry, and I thought Drew had taken it just, you know, to be vindictive because we were in a dispute about money. We were working with a mediator at the time, and things were getting pretty contentious." She rolled her eyes. "Anyway, I noticed it missing. I mentioned it to my sister that very *night*, the night of the attack. And then later, with everything, I totally forgot about it. Then yesterday I was in here packing, and I saw my jewelry box, and it suddenly hit me. So I called Drew, and he swears he didn't take it." She turned to Bryan. "And I believe him."

Bryan stared at her. "You're suggesting—"

"Drew didn't take it. He swears. And he can be a real jerk sometimes, but I believe him about this." She paused. "I think *he* was in here." She stepped aside and motioned to a shelf.

Bryan studied the shelf, which was about her shoulder height. Beside a line of perfume bottles was a white heart-shaped box.

"That's your jewelry box?" he asked.

"Yes. I don't keep much in there anymore, but I always put my locket in it."

"Mind if I . . . ?"

"No. Please." She scooted past him, brushing against his arm. "I haven't touched it in weeks. As soon as I remembered about the locket, I called Liz and told her."

Bryan pulled a pair of latex gloves from the pocket of his pants. "Have you noticed anything else missing?"

"No. Nothing besides the locket. But I remembered Detective Bruner telling me there was evidence he'd been in my yard in the days beforehand. And he even said it was possible he'd been *in the house* before that night. So, you know, when I remembered the missing locket, I suddenly thought maybe that was him."

The UNSUB had a history of slipping into women's homes while he was stalking them. Jack believed it was reconnaissance. The guy would learn the floor plan and familiarize himself with points of exit ahead of time—sometimes even unlocking back doors to give himself multiple escape options. He would peek in windows and go through garages and trample flower beds, all in his effort to gain information about the scene of his next attack. Bryan believed there was more to it than reconnaissance, maybe some sort of power trip about sneaking into his victims' homes when they weren't there.

Evelyn was watching him carefully, her face a mix of dread and stoicism.

He motioned to the shelf. "Is it okay if I—"

"Go ahead."

Bryan lifted the porcelain lid. Inside the box were a pair of small hoop earrings and a delicate gold chain.

"That's where I keep it. *Kept* it."

He replaced the lid. "And you're sure you didn't leave it somewhere, or possibly misplace it, back in November?"

"Positive."

Bryan believed her. In addition to his recon missions, the UNSUB made a habit of stealing items from houses. He'd taken jewelry, underwear, cash. His first victim even reported that he'd taken the car keys sitting on her kitchen table. But—unfortunately for investigators—he hadn't taken her car, which would have made him easy to track down.

"We'll probably need to send a CSI out to fingerprint this." He turned to Evelyn.

"That's fine. Or you can take it with you. Whatever."

"Do you mind?"

"No." She gestured at it. "Take it."

"I'll need to get an evidence bag from my car."

She stepped out of the doorway. "Sure. Do what you need to do."

Bryan retraced his steps out of the house, noting the pink Big Wheel sitting on the porch. He retrieved an evidence envelope from his trunk and then returned to the bedroom, where Evelyn stood by the closet, reading her phone.

She glanced up. "Is there anything else you want in there?" She gestured toward the racks of clothes.

"Not at this time."

Bryan photographed the box and carefully bagged it, folding the envelope so the contents wouldn't get jostled around in transit. Then Evelyn led him past her daughter's bedroom to the front door, where Bryan paused to write out an evidence receipt.

He felt her gaze on him as he stood beside the door. He looked up. "So. Where are you and your daughter moving?"

"South of the lake, near my sister. Hannah's been great, but I'm sure she's sick of us being on her sofa bed." She glanced over her shoulder at her living room. "I found an apartment over near Zilker Park. It's expensive but—" She looked at him. "At least it's not here."

Guilt needled him. Of the eight Austin victims, six had moved. Seven now, including Evelyn. Bryan hated that they had had to uproot their lives, but he didn't blame them. He couldn't imagine how they felt living in the same house, sleeping in the same room, where they'd been assaulted.

"So . . . you think there's a chance his prints are on it?" she asked.

"We'll find out."

She looked away, and he felt another pang of guilt. Here they were two months later, and the guy who'd attacked her was still out there. Bryan wished like hell he could tell her they had made an arrest, or even that they were close to making an arrest, but they still hadn't even identified a suspect, and it had been seven long years since the original rape. He glanced at the line of moving boxes behind her, and frustration filled his chest.

He handed her the receipt.

"Thank you," she said. "And thanks for coming out."

"We'll get this back to you." He held up the envelope.

"Take your time. Or you know what? Keep it."

"Keep it?"

"Keep all of it. Even the jewelry." She shuddered. "If there's even a chance he touched it, I never want to see it again."

J ACK HAD NO trouble spotting her. Joy Kendall sat at one of the umbrella tables, two Yorkies at her feet, peering down at her phone from behind a pair of oversize black sunglasses.

Jack approached the café, sidestepping a tourist on an electric scooter. It was the first sunny day in weeks, and the sidewalks were crammed with people eagerly taking advantage of a break in the rain.

"Joy?"

Her head jerked up. "Hi." She looked around. "I hope you don't mind. They were so crowded, I went ahead and jumped in line."

"No problem." Jack pulled out the chair across from her. "May I?"

"Of course. Don't you want anything?"

"I'm good."

He lowered himself into the chair and the dogs scurried over. He reached down to pet them as they sniffed at his shoes.

"Boys, *no*." She gave their leashes a tug.

"They're fine." He looked up, and she was watching him from behind the eyewear equivalent of a Cadillac Escalade with black-tinted windows. Jack was good at reading faces, but that was going to be tough with this particular interview.

"Did I catch you after a run?" she asked.

"Before."

"Sorry to sidetrack you."

"No problem." Jack leaned back in the chair, trying to keep things casual. When she'd called him twenty minutes ago, she'd made it clear she didn't want to come to the police station and instead suggested a downtown coffee shop. Jack wasn't sure what she was worried about. He was in sweatpants and sneakers, so no one passing by would have reason to think she was talking to a cop. Then again, maybe she was worried about someone spotting her with a man who wasn't her husband.

She reached for her cardboard coffee cup but didn't take a sip. "I've hardly slept in two nights." She blew out a breath. "This whole thing really . . ." She trailed off, seeming unsure of how to get around to the topic she'd come to discuss.

He waited.

"Those damn DNA kits." She shook her head. "I've been dreading this for years. I always thought I might get a phone call. Or maybe a knock at the door. I never dreamed it would be a homicide detective."

Jack watched her, keeping his face blank. She'd jumped to homicide—which maybe wasn't surprising given that he'd told her his investigation was serious, or he wouldn't have involved her. She had no way of knowing he was investigating a string of unsolved rape cases—cases she'd no doubt heard about. Every woman living in Austin back then knew about WCR. The man's rampage had dominated the news for two long years.

Jack could have clarified things with her, and if she had said something Thursday at her house, he might have. But as of his phone call with Heidi, Jack now knew that the link between his cold cases and the recent San Antonio homicide was real. The UNSUB was active again and he'd escalated to murder.

Joy broke off a chunk of muffin and held it under the table for the dogs. "Sorry." She broke off another chunk. "This is harder than I thought."

Jack nodded, wishing Rowan were here. So far, her instincts about this woman were right on.

She wiped her hands on a napkin. "It's just a lot, you know?"

"I understand."

She took another deep breath. "The thing is, when all this happened, I was so young."

"How old were you?"

"Sixteen. I was scared to death. I had no idea what I was going to do. And then my mom found out." She shook her head. "My parents are very religious. They pulled me out of school and made me break up with my boyfriend. My dad was—" She shook her head again. "Well. He blamed my mother."

"He blamed your mother that you were pregnant?"

She pursed her lips. "They didn't have the healthiest relationship. It was a division of labor. Basically, he brought home the bacon, and my mom was in charge of everything else. Screwed up, I know. I vowed never to even *get* married. Yet here I am."

Finally, she took off the sunglasses. Her eyes were puffy and bloodshot, and he doubted that was only from lack of sleep.

"Michael doesn't know about any of this. Or that I've ever been pregnant. We never wanted kids together. We got married late, and he already has two from his first marriage."

Jack waited, struggling not to seem impatient as he hung on her every word.

She folded the glasses and set them beside the coffee cup.

"What happened after they pulled you out of school?" he asked, knowing she had to have finished. According to her online profile, she had an MBA.

"I went to live with my aunt in Beaumont. And then my parents got me in touch with Bethany House."

"Bethany House?"

"An adoption agency. It's private."

Jack kept his face neutral, but he was vacuuming up every word in case she suddenly shut down on him. Joy

Kendall was forty-five years old, and based on what she'd just told him, he now knew his UNSUB was twenty-eight or twenty-nine, depending on how old she'd been when she gave birth.

She picked up her coffee cup, then set it back down again. "Bethany House is a Christian agency. And it's known for its discretion. Both those things were important to my parents. If it weren't for all this genealogy stuff—" She halted. "Well, I guess all that's good, from your perspective." She closed her eyes and rubbed the bridge of her nose.

Again Jack wished Rowan were here. She'd no doubt have something to say, and she'd say it in that empathetic voice that was sure to draw the witness out.

He leaned forward, resting his elbows on the table. When Joy opened her eyes, he gave her his most direct look.

"You were saying about Bethany House? Is that in Beaumont?"

Jack would have no trouble finding out, but he wanted to get her answering his questions.

She cleared her throat. "Houston."

"And do you know the names of the adoptive parents?"

She nodded.

"And do you know *his* name?"

She nodded.

Jack's pulse quickened. He stared at her, this conflicted, puffy-eyed woman who held the key to everything.

"Will you tell me?"

BRYAN STRODE INTO the bullpen and spotted Jack at his computer with a stack of files beside him.

He grabbed his desk chair and rolled it over. "We got a print."

Jack didn't look up. "On what?"

"The jewelry box. From Evelyn Wood's closet. We got his *fingerprint*." Bryan sank into the chair and rocked back.

"How do you know it's his?"

"Because. Well, we don't for sure. But it's not hers. Or her ex-husband's or any of the other prints we took for exclusion purposes. I really think it's *him*."

He leaned forward, watching Jack, who remained unnaturally calm.

"Jack? Are you getting what this means? If we ever get a suspect, we can put him *inside her house*."

"We've got one."

"What?"

"The UNSUB. I have a name."

Bryan stared at him. "Bullshit."

Jack finally made eye contact, and Bryan could see it wasn't bullshit at all.

"Rowan came through."

"Rowan?"

"Rowan Healy. The genealogist." Jack pivoted in his chair. "She was right, the guy's adopted. So, I tracked down the birth mother, and she gave me his name."

"When?"

Jack checked his watch. "Three hours ago."

"Who is he?"

Bryan's pulse picked up as he watched Jack's face. Something was wrong, he could tell.

"Guy's name is William John Anderson." Jack handed him a spiral notebook. "Twenty-eight years old."

Bryan looked at the name scrawled across the page and underlined. Then he looked at Jack. "This is great. What's the problem?"

"He's not in the system."

"Which one?"

"All of them. No address, no phone number, no current driver's license—here or out of state. No passport, no military record. I can't even find a fucking water bill for this guy."

"Okay. But that's got to be a common name."

"It is." Jack raked a hand through his hair. "That's part of the problem. I found 116 William John Andersons in Texas alone. Three of them in Beaumont."

"Why Beaumont?"

"That's where he was born."

"What about the adoptive parents?"

Jack nodded. "Gale and Philip Anderson of Round Rock, both deceased."

"Round Rock?"

"Yep. Interesting connection, I know—a suburb of Austin. But I couldn't find him there, either. There are eleven William John Andersons here in Travis County, but they're all completely the wrong age."

Bryan glanced down at the notebook page where the name APD had been after for years was written in Jack's handwriting.

"And are you sure this is legit?" Bryan asked.

"The name? Yeah."

"You're sure."

"Hundred percent."

Bryan looked at him. "So, what do we do now?"

"Now, we get to work."

NINE

SKYLER LINED UP a bank shot. "Did either of you meet this guy?"

"I didn't," Rowan said.

Skyler sank the nine ball and looked at Lila. "You?"

"Briefly." Lila sipped her ginger ale. "Nice shot."

"Thanks." She scooted around the table and leaned over.

Rowan noticed the trio of men watching from a nearby high-top. Auburn-haired Skyler in a scoop-neck sweater always attracted attention.

"All I know is he works at a startup, and Dara says he's some tech genius." Lila darted a skeptical look at Rowan.

"Does he have any money?" Skyler asked, probably because Dara's last boyfriend had been a deadbeat who ran up her credit card.

"No idea," Lila said.

Skyler glanced at Rowan.

"Don't look at me. I've never even laid eyes on him."

Skyler took her shot and missed, then sauntered over and handed Rowan the cue.

"Okay, break's over," Lila said. "Damn. Why are we so busy on a Tuesday?"

Lila headed back to the bar as Rowan rounded the table, scoping out her next move.

"Red in the corner," Skyler said.

"Yeah, right."

"What? You can make it."

Rowan shook her head. "No way."

"Put a little backspin on it."

Shaking her head, Rowan leaned over the table. She took the shot and ended up scratching.

"See?" She looked up, but Skyler wasn't watching. Rowan turned and saw that her attention was fixed on a man who'd just entered the bar.

Jack's gaze locked on Rowan, and a jolt of heat went through her. He made his way through the crowd and stopped in the doorway leading to the pool room.

"Hi," he said.

"Hi."

"Thought I might find you here."

They stared at each other, and butterflies swarmed inside her as she remembered the last time she'd seen him. It had been five days ago—not that she was counting.

"Uh, Rowan?"

She looked at Skyler, who had a smirk on her face now. "You want to finish this?"

"Oh. Yeah." Rowan handed her the cue.

"Better yet, why don't you two finish?" Skyler handed back the stick and picked up her glass from a nearby table. "I think I need a refill."

"Wait. Skyler, this is Jack Bruner. Jack, this is my friend Skyler Shaw."

"You're the sculptor."

She smiled, obviously charmed. "That's me." She shot a look at Rowan, clearly assuming Jack had been out to the ranch. Which he had, but not under the circumstances she thought.

"Very nice to meet you, Jack. Don't let her hustle you." Sklyer gave Rowan a wink and walked off.

Rowan turned back to Jack. He was watching her, and she couldn't read the look on his face. He had a slight smile, but his eyes looked serious.

He stepped closer, and the warmth inside her started to spread. He was dressed in jeans and the black leather jacket that reminded her of the first time he'd come here. Only this time, there was a spark of heat in his eyes that hadn't been there that night.

"What brings you here?" she asked.

"You."

Her heart gave a little lurch, but she managed to keep her face neutral. "Oh yeah?"

"Yeah." He glanced over his shoulder at the bar. "They're busy tonight."

"Yep."

"You want to finish your game?" He nodded at the table.

"Depends." She paused. "Did you want to talk about work or—"

"No."

It was a definitive *no*, and it piqued her curiosity.

"Let's start over then." She leaned the cue against the table and turned to retrieve the balls from the pockets.

He grabbed the triangular rack from a hook on the wall and collected the balls inside it, quickly arranging them in the proper order. Rowan's pulse sped up as she watched him move. There was an edge to him tonight, and she wondered what it was about.

He gave the rack a brisk jolt and lifted it. "Your break."

"All right."

She took the cue and turned away. From the corner of

her eye, she could see Skyler at the bar, probably talking to Lila and getting the gossip on Jack.

Rowan rounded the table and thought about her technique. She wasn't exactly a powerhouse, and she didn't want to embarrass herself.

Jack hung his jacket over the back of a stool. He wore a plain black T-shirt, and she tried not to think about how nicely it stretched over his pecs as he crossed his arms.

She positioned the cue ball and leaned over the table.

Crack!

Relief flooded her as the balls flew apart. The fourteen dropped into a corner pocket with a *thunk*.

"Stripes."

Jack nodded.

She walked around the table, keeping her distance for now. She pretended to study the layout as she mentally berated herself for going with a boring gray turtleneck instead of the snug black sweater she'd almost worn tonight.

She leaned over the table and took another shot, missing this time.

Jack selected a long cue from the rack on the wall and chalked the tip.

"How's your week been?" He leaned over the table.

"Busy. You?"

"Same."

And yet he was here. There had to be a reason. She got the feeling he didn't make a habit of driving out to dive bars on the outskirts of town on a typical weeknight.

He sank the seven with a surprisingly soft tap and walked to the other end.

"So, Skyler's your friend and not just your neighbor?" He leaned over the felt again.

"We went to high school together."

"Where?"

"Austin High."

"Oh yeah?" He glanced up.

"Go, Maroons."

He smiled and took aim at the five. This time he missed. Rowan studied the layout.

"I was living in the city after graduation," she said, "but I got priced out of my apartment. Skyler's stepdad had the creek cottage for rent, so I decided to move there."

"It's kind of far out. You like living there?"

"Usually. I'm not crazy about the traffic, but a lot of my work can be done online, so it's not like I have to drive in every single day."

She lined up a bank shot and tapped the cue ball, managing to sink the twelve. A little thrill went through her.

"Nice," he said.

"Thanks."

She tried for another bank shot and totally whiffed it.

"Yikes."

Jack didn't comment, just chalked his cue.

"So, you were right." He leaned over the table.

"About?"

He smacked the white, which sent one of his solids sailing into a corner pocket.

"Joy Kendall." He straightened. "She called me over the weekend, just like you predicted."

"Yeah?"

His brow furrowed as he studied the table.

So, Joy had reached out over the weekend. Had she given Jack a name? Rowan had been following the news religiously, but if there had been any major break in the case, the media didn't have it yet.

Jack made a combination shot and sank two balls. He moved around the table, and Rowan watched him, brimming with impatience.

"So, did she provide you with a name?"

He didn't look up. "Yeah."

"And?"

"And I'm working on it."

Rowan frowned. "What's that mean?"

"We're having trouble locating him."

"You're kidding."

"Nope."

He stepped around the table, brushing past her as he lined up another move.

So Jack now had a name. But not a location.

Somehow, she thought that must be even more frustrating.

She watched his sharp focus as he took another shot. He straightened and watched the ball glide into the pocket. Despite the casual clothes, there was a tension about him tonight. He carried it in his chest and shoulders as he moved around the table, sinking balls one after another with ruthless efficiency.

He'd come here to see her. He could have called or texted, but instead he'd come in person.

He looked at her. "Your shot."

"Mine?"

"I missed the six."

"Oh. Right." She looked at the table and tried to decide which of her unlikely shots was the least unlikely. She went for a combination and didn't even come close.

Jack sank the six this time and then leaned over the table and took aim at the eight.

"Side pocket," he said.

She watched him, annoyingly impressed by his broad shoulders and lean waist. She knew pool could be sexy, but she'd never felt it as much as she did tonight.

He sank the eight with a hard *thunk*.

"Congratulations." She rested her cue on the toe of her boot and looked at the table. It was a decisive victory. But it left her floundering for something to say now.

He stepped over and gazed down at her, not gloating even though he could have.

"Can I buy you a drink?" he asked.

"I think I'm supposed to buy *you* one. Especially considering the crappy week you're having."

His expression clouded, and she regretted saying anything. He took the cue from her hand and replaced them both in the rack on the wall. Then he grabbed his jacket, and they stepped over to the bar, where a pair of seats had just been vacated.

Rowan scanned the room for Skyler, but she wasn't in sight.

"Lila, have you met Jack?" Rowan asked when Lila put coasters in front of them.

"Good to meet you." Lila smiled and pretended she knew nothing about the mysterious detective she had been teasing Rowan about for days. "What would you like?"

"A Shiner Bock, if you have it."

"Bottle okay?"

"Sure."

"Rowan?"

"Diet Coke." She looked at Jack. "I'm the driver tonight."

He didn't seem to mind her order, but when she reached for her wallet, he waved her off and handed over his card.

Lila slid their drinks in front of them, and Rowan pivoted on her stool to face him. He seemed uptight still, despite walloping her at pool. She sipped her drink and watched him.

He looked good, and she felt a ripple of excitement that he'd come here to see her. Even if he'd come to talk about the case, she was still glad to see him.

"You know, I might be able to help," she said, setting her glass on the coaster.

"With what?"

"If you give me the name, I could do some research for you."

"Research?" He tipped his beer back.

"It's what I do."

"Thanks for the offer."

"But you're not interested."

"No." He set the bottle down. "But thanks."

She tamped down her frustration and stirred her drink with the straw. Was he being stubborn because he didn't want to reveal the suspect's name? Or because he didn't think she could help? Either way, it irked her. If she hadn't run up against the adoption issue, she would know the name now anyway. So why did it matter if he gave it to her?

"So, how's the search angel business going?" he asked.

"Good. Great, actually. I'm swamped."

He sipped his drink, watching her.

"I just got a referral from a former client," she added, since he seemed interested.

"You're making a name for yourself."

"Finally. Seems like it's taken forever."

"Another adoption case?"

"This one's a little different. It's a guy who's been estranged from his family for quite a while. But now he needs a bone marrow transplant, and he's looking for relatives."

"'Estranged' like a deadbeat dad?"

"I don't know the full story, but I get the impression it's something like that. His grown kids want nothing to do with him, for whatever reason. So now he's looking for other potentially eligible relatives."

"Doesn't sound like a joyful family reunion."

"It's not. And to be honest, this guy strikes me as kind of a jerk. But his situation is pretty dire, and if he can find someone willing to help him, it might save his life."

He nodded. "Noble work you're doing there."

She rolled her eyes. "I wouldn't call it that. It's not like I'm helping him for free." Although, she was giving him a discount because she felt bad about his situation. So many of her clients had deep regrets, for one reason or another, about losing touch with their families. Rowan wasn't close to her family, either, and sometimes she wondered whether she'd look back someday and wish she'd done things differently.

"Still, you're helping him," Jack said. "Sounds like more than his kids are doing."

"I don't fault the kids, really." Rowan sipped her drink. "Sounds like he's the one who broke off contact when they were little and needed him. Now they're grown and they've moved on with their lives. That's what people do."

Jack pulled his phone from his pocket and muttered a curse. Rowan hadn't heard a ringtone, so it must have been on vibrate. His brow furrowed as he read the message.

"You need to go?"

The look in his eyes answered her question.

"Sorry," he said, tucking the phone away.

"No worries."

Lila had stashed his card and receipt in a glass in front of him. He signed the tab, leaving a big tip.

"Sorry," he repeated.

"It's fine. I need to get back to Skyler, anyway." She glanced around the bar. "I'm her ride tonight."

"She left, I think."

"What?"

"She went outside with someone ten minutes ago." He slid off his stool.

Rowan caught Lila's gaze as she poured vodka with an elaborate flourish.

"Hey, did Sky leave?" she asked over the noise.

"Yep."

Rowan glanced at Jack. "Guess I'm out, too, then."

"You sure?"

"Yeah, it's late anyway. Catch you later, Lila."

"Later, babe."

Jack stood beside her as she slid off the stool and grabbed her purse. He steered her through the crowd, making a path for them without touching anyone. They stepped through the doors into the cold air, and Rowan wished she'd brought a jacket.

She glanced across the parking lot and noticed the black Jeep beside her car.

Hugging her arms to her body, she set off across the lot.

"I meant it about my offer," she said. "If you want to give me the name, I really think I could help. Or you could give me the adoptive parents' names, and I could find them."

"Thanks, but I'm fine."

They stopped at her bumper, and she looked up at him with impatience. He wasn't *fine*. Clearly, he was frustrated.

"I do this for a living, Jack. I'm good at it."

"I know."

She huffed out a breath.

"I'll handle it," he said.

"Suit yourself."

She glanced up, and he was gazing down at her with a look she couldn't read. She hugged her arms closer, studying his bottomless brown eyes.

"What?" he asked.

"I'm trying to understand you. If you really didn't want my help, why'd you come all the way out here?"

The corner of his mouth ticked up. "You haven't figured it out?"

"No."

He leaned down and kissed her.

It took her off guard—so much that she kept her arms clamped around her body. His mouth was warm and seeking, and soon she melted into him. His arms came around her, pulling her against the solid heat of him and lifting her to her toes.

She slid her hands over his shoulders and combed her fingers into his thick hair. His body was like a heater, dispelling the chill around her as he pressed her against him and explored her mouth until her limbs melted and she started to feel light-headed. The kiss went on and on, and her body began to pulse.

He eased back, holding her in his arms, as she blinked up at him in the dimness.

"I'd like to see you again," he said.

She stared up at him, still absorbing his warmth.

His phone buzzed. He stepped back and pulled it from his pocket, and a chill wafted over her as he connected the call.

"Hey, I'm on my way." Pause. "Yeah, I got it. Gimme fifteen."

He pocketed the phone, and Rowan looked down at her feet. Obviously, he was rushing off to some crime scene. This was the problem with police work—or one of the problems. It never stopped.

He took her hand and gently squeezed it. "Can I call you?"

She looked up at him, her lips still numb and tingly.

"I want to see you again."

She cleared her throat. "Maybe. I don't know." Her brain was scrambled. "Let me think about it."

He smiled and dropped her hand as he stepped away.

"Think about it."

TEN

J ACK GRABBED HIS keys off his desk and checked his watch. "You coming?"

His partner's gaze remained glued to his screen.

"Bryan, we're late."

Bryan turned and checked the clock on the wall. Then he stood and snagged his jacket off the back of the chair.

"We need to stop at the corner," Bryan said.

"No time."

"I need food, man. I skipped breakfast."

Jack crossed the bullpen, trying to ignore the grumbling in his own stomach. His breakfast had consisted of stale coffee from a hospital cafeteria after he'd been up all night canvassing a neighborhood and then waiting for a gunshot victim to wake up from surgery. And even after the victim woke up, he'd claimed to remember nothing about his assailant—not even the car the man had been in when he rolled up and shot him.

Not yet one day in, and Jack could tell it was going to be

one of those cases where everyone lied and no one knew anything, even when they did.

They crossed the lobby and pushed through the double doors. Jack stopped and zipped his jacket.

"Seriously, I'm on empty," Bryan said, casting a longing look at the food truck on the corner.

"Five minutes." Jack checked his watch. "We're already going to hit traffic."

"You want anything?"

"No."

Bryan rushed off, jogging right past Rowan.

Jack's heart gave a kick as he watched her stride up the sidewalk. She made a beeline for the door, not noticing him at all.

"Rowan."

She whirled around. "Oh. Hey." She smiled, and Jack's shoulders relaxed for the first time in hours.

She walked over and stopped in front of him. Today she wore a puffy blue coat with jeans, and her cheeks were tinged pink from the cold.

"Hi," she said, looking at the keys in his hand. "Heading out somewhere?"

"I've got an interview."

Her eyebrows arched.

"Different case."

The hope in her eyes dimmed, and he felt a pang of guilt. The same guilt he'd been feeling for seven long years, every time someone brought up his cold case.

Not that it was his only cold case, but it was the one that hounded him every damn day.

"What's up?" he asked.

She bit her lip, looking uncertain now that she'd bumped into him unexpectedly on the street. Maybe she was thinking about that kiss last night. He'd been thinking about it for hours. It had kept him awake and alert during the endless stretch in that hospital waiting room.

She stepped closer and looked up at him. Yep, he was right—she was thinking about it.

"I stopped by hoping to catch you," she said.

"I'm glad you did."

"Do you want me to walk with you to your car or—"

"I'm waiting on my partner."

"Oh." A lock of dark hair blew against her cheek, and she peeled it away. "So, I've been thinking about your problem."

"Which problem is that?"

"Locating your suspect." Her brow furrowed. "Assuming you haven't found him yet, that is."

When he didn't confirm or deny that, she dug into her purse and pulled out a folded slip of paper.

"What's that?" he asked.

"A reference for you. This is my friend Dara, a local PI. I've used her on some of my cases when the biological parents have been hard to track down. She specializes in locates."

Jack didn't take the paper.

"She's expecting your call," Rowan said.

"You told her—"

"I didn't reveal what it was about. You can tell her as much or as little as you want. She owes me a favor, and she's willing to help you pro bono." She pushed the paper toward him. "You may as well call her since you're striking out."

"What makes you so sure I'm striking out?"

"Well, aren't you?"

He gazed down at her, strangely turned on by the impatient look on her face.

"I don't need a PI."

"It's just a resource, like anything else." She held the paper out again, determined for him to take it. "Don't be stubborn, Jack."

He smiled. "*I'm* stubborn?"

"Yes."

She glared up at him, and he felt a warm shot of lust. He hadn't expected to see her today, and now she was standing here picking an argument with him outside police headquarters.

He took the paper and slipped it in his pocket. "Thank you."

"Will you call her?"

"Possibly."

"You won't be sorry, trust me. She gets results."

Pedestrians streamed around them as she stared up at him, cheeks flushed. She looked cold again, even though she had a jacket, and he had the urge to pull her close and warm her up. She was wearing the same cherry ChapStick she'd been wearing last night, and he wanted to taste it again.

"Hi."

They turned to see Bryan walking over.

"Got you a taco." Bryan handed Jack a white paper bag, but his attention was fixed on Rowan.

Jack sighed. "Bryan Hunt, this is Rowan Healy, the genealogist who is helping us."

"Rowan." Bryan tucked his bag of tacos under his arm and offered her his hand. "Very nice to meet you."

"You too."

"You knocked it out of the park with that DNA thing. Wow. Very impressive."

She smiled. "Glad I could help."

"We need to get going," Jack said, and Bryan tore his eyes off Rowan. "The interview."

"Right."

"Nice meeting you." Rowan looked at Jack as she took a step back. "Let me know how it goes."

"I will."

She turned and walked away.

"How what goes?"

Jack glanced at Bryan. "Nothing." He checked his watch again. "Let's go."

ROWAN TURNED ONTO the driveway and studied the two-story house. With its neatly trimmed hedges and traditional architecture, it had that all-American look of one of those homes in a John Hughes movie. As a girl, Rowan had always thought about living in a house like that, but those daydreams seemed unimaginable now. Sweet, yes, but almost laughably out of reach.

Once again, the black Mercedes was parked near the back door. No Range Rover this time, but maybe it was inside the three-car garage at the end of the driveway.

Rowan parked and got out, casting a baleful look at her dinged Toyota. Her tires were bald, and she desperately needed to get the oil changed, but she hadn't had the funds to devote to auto maintenance lately.

With any luck, this meeting would help.

She cast a glance at the back courtyard but this time followed the cobblestone path around to the front entrance. The glossy black door had cut glass windows on either side and stone pots filled with carefully manicured topiaries. Did Joy do her own gardening? Somehow Rowan doubted it. As a tech executive with no kids, she could probably afford a fleet of domestic helpers.

Rowan squared her shoulders as she stepped up to the door. In contrast to Rowan's severed-hand door knocker, courtesy of Skyler, this knocker was a traditional brass lion. Rowan gave it a double tap, setting off a flurry of yips inside the house. A moment later, a blurry figure appeared at the glass and the door swung open.

"Thank you for coming," Joy said.

"No problem at all."

Joy ushered her inside. As opposed to the last time Rowan had been here, her hostess was immaculately put together in pants, riding boots, and caramel-colored cashmere sweater. Her highlighted blond curls spilled loosely over her shoulders.

"Come in. Please." She ushered Rowan through the foyer. "Boys, no."

The dogs scampered around her, and Rowan bent down to pet them as they sniffed at her shoes.

Joy led her through the enormous living room where she and Jack had been just the other day. What would he think if he knew that she was here right now? She had a feeling he wouldn't like it.

"Can I get you anything?" Joy asked over her shoulder. "Water? Coffee?"

"I'm fine, thanks."

Joy walked through a hallway with French doors that opened onto a brick patio, then stepped into a spacious office.

The room had a vibrant colored rug and a corner fireplace. But it was the floor-to-ceiling bookshelves that took Rowan's breath away.

Gaping, she stepped through the doorway. The shelves occupied three of the four walls, leaving the fourth wall open for a huge window with a cushioned seat. Rowan felt a wave of reading-nook envy.

Joy gestured toward a pair of brown leather chairs. "Please. Make yourself comfortable."

"I love your library."

"Thank you."

The dogs trotted over to a pair of plaid pillows in front of the fireplace and did their circle dance.

"They have beds in every room?"

"Almost." She rolled her eyes. "They're spoiled rotten, I know."

"And what are their names?"

"Sam and Frodo."

Rowan smiled. "You're a Tolkien fan."

"Yes.

Rowan rested her elbow on the arm of the chair, getting comfortable without leaning back. "So. What can I help you with?"

Joy took a deep breath. "Well, as you obviously know, your visit the other day came as a shock."

"I'm sorry about that."

"Not your fault." She paused. "You do these a lot?"

"These?"

"Visits with family members." She motioned back and forth between them. "Meeting with people you've traced through DNA."

"I do some." She tried to choose her words carefully. "But not very many with police detectives anymore. Lately, I've been focused more on my consulting business."

"I visited your website."

Rowan nodded. She was proud of the website, and she'd invested a lot of money into it. Skyler had created a logo for free—the same angel wings Rowan had hanging above her computer—but Rowan had hired a web design firm for everything else.

"It's a fascinating business, tracking down birth families," Joy said. "Do you like doing it?"

She hesitated. "Most of the time I do. It can be rewarding."

"But . . . ?"

Joy's gaze was direct, and for the first time Rowan could see the edge that probably propelled her to the top of a software company filled with tech bros.

"But . . . not every adoption story has a happy ending," Rowan said. "Some birth mothers don't want to be found."

"True."

Rowan waited, trying to read her expression.

Joy folded her hands in her lap. "I think I might like to hire you."

Her pulse picked up. She nodded.

"I'd like to learn more about my family history, but we're not exactly tight," Joy said. "There are some . . . rifts here and there."

"I understand."

She heaved a sigh. "I'm embarrassed to say I can't even tell you the names of all of my grandparents."

"That's more common than you might think."

She lifted an eyebrow. "Is it?"

Rowan nodded. "Have you ever looked into it before? Gone on any genealogy sites?"

"No." She looked down at her hands. "I never took the time. And, to be honest with you, with the adoption situation, I just . . ." She sighed. "I haven't wanted to go there. It's something I haven't given much thought to in years, but then when my father died . . ." She shook her head. "It made me think about everything differently. Death has a way of crystalizing things."

Rowan didn't respond, sensing she had more to say.

Joy picked some lint off her pants. "To give you some background, I lost contact with my dad's side when I went to live with my aunt, and I pretty much decided good riddance. I never wanted to see anyone again, especially my father. He was—" She looked out the window, her expression tight. "Well. Let's just say he was a piece of work."

A tense silence hung in the air, and Rowan didn't fill it. She'd learned not to rush people grappling with a painful past.

Joy looked at her and seemed to shake off the moment. "So, what do you think?"

"There's a lot we can learn through DNA. It's a useful tool for people whose family ties aren't necessarily intact."

Joy laughed. "That's one way of putting it."

"Are you willing to do a DNA kit?"

"I haven't decided." Her brow furrowed. "I want to know whether I can keep my results private. Is that even possible now?"

"Depends on what you mean by 'private.' But generally speaking, there are some things you can do."

Joy looked down at her hands. "In that case, Rowan, I would like to hire you."

B RYAN WATCHED THE fence posts rush by. "I think we should try it." He looked at Jack. "What do we have to lose?"

Jack kept his focus on the road. He wore his mirrored shades, but Bryan had no trouble reading his reaction.

It had been twenty-four hours since Rowan Healy had shown up at the police station with the name of some crack PI she knew who was supposedly good at skip tracing. But Jack didn't want to bring in another outsider. Maybe he was worried about the media fallout if this thing leaked to the press.

"It's been almost two weeks," Bryan said, meaning since Amber Novak had been murdered.

Jack knew exactly what he was referring to, and he also knew the implication—that not only was the trail getting cold, but William Anderson might be zeroing in on his next target by now. Yet still, Jack wouldn't budge on using outside help.

Jack checked his phone. "This is it," he said, swinging a right onto a narrow road.

Shaking his head, Bryan looked out the window at the scrub brush. They'd driven north of town to talk to a retired fire chief, which—as far as Bryan was concerned—was a big waste of time. Until and unless they got a bead on William Anderson, anything else was pointless.

They passed a few spread-out houses and then Jack slowed

beside a mailbox. He checked his phone and turned onto a gravel driveway leading to a modest one-story. An old white pickup was parked near the detached garage, and Jack pulled their unmarked police unit into the space beside it.

"I think we're wasting our time here." Bryan pushed open his door. "We should try that PI."

"If this doesn't work, maybe we will."

Bryan slid from the car and looked at Jack over the roof, surprised. Maybe he was finally getting through.

Jack glanced at the front door but then looked at the garage, where country music drifted from an open door.

"He said he was home working on something." Jack crossed the driveway toward the garage, and Bryan followed him. Suddenly, the music was drowned out by the buzz of a power tool.

They stepped into the garage, where a white-haired man was bent over a worktable with a sander in his hands. The air smelled of sawdust and mineral spirits.

The man glanced up. Straightening, he put the sander aside and switched off the radio.

"George Ackerman?" Jack asked.

He tugged a red bandanna from the pocket of his jeans and wiped the sawdust off his face. Then he came around the table, and everyone exchanged introductions.

Bryan glanced around the garage, where the only vehicle was an ancient riding mower and the rest of the space had been converted into a workshop. Along the back wall was a wooden shelf filled with toolboxes. On the wall above the shelf hung a fire helmet and a plaque.

"Thanks for making the time for us," Jack said, turning to the freshly sanded swing in the middle of the table. Some of the slats looked old while others appeared new.

"You building or repairing?" Bryan asked.

"Building." He wiped off his dusty arms. "My wife's family's got a farm in Brenham, and the wood's salvaged from their old barn. She's been after me for years to make her a swing for the porch."

Jack nodded. "Sounds nice."

"Ah, not really. It's hot as hell in the summer and you get eaten alive by mosquitoes." He tossed the bandanna on the table and turned to face them. "So, what can I do for you? You said something about a cold case?"

"We had some questions about the Anderson case," Jack said. "Gale and Philip. They died in a house fire."

The man nodded. "That was about five years ago."

Five years and a half, but Bryan didn't correct him.

"What can you tell us about it?" Jack asked. "I understand you were on the scene that night?"

He nodded again. "They were out in Whitewing Grove, if I remember right. You been out there?"

Jack shook his head.

"One of those stamped-out subdivisions built in the eighties. Five floor plans." He stepped over to a dusty minifridge and opened the door. "Water?" He looked at Bryan.

"No, thanks."

He looked at Jack.

"I'm good."

He took out a bottle of water and twisted off the top. He took a long sip and rested the bottle on the table.

"This was back in the summer, I remember. Middle of the night. A fire tore through the house, and they never woke up. Died in their bed."

"Smoke detector?" Jack asked.

"Dead battery." He took another swig.

"We took a look at the report," Jack said. "It says the point of origin was the water heater?"

"Yeah."

"The report says the fire was ruled an accident." Jack paused. "Do you agree with that assessment?"

"I wrote the damn thing."

Jack darted a look at Bryan. There was definitely something in his tone.

"But you initially investigated it as a possible arson," Jack stated.

"That's right." He shook his head. "To me, the whole thing smelled funny."

"Accelerants?" Jack asked.

"No, I mean the scene, the circumstances. The two of them never woke up. Died of smoke inhalation."

Bryan glanced at Jack, then looked at the retired fire chief. "Any suspects?"

"None we could label that way. But we looked around."

"Did you look at the son?" Jack asked.

He nodded. "Will Anderson. We looked at him pretty hard."

Bryan's pulse quickened. "Did you interview him?"

"Not me—one of the police detectives. But I remember him from the night of the incident. He and his older sister— Melissa?"

"Marissa," Jack said.

He nodded. "They both showed up while we were putting the fire out. One of the neighbors called them. We took a look at both, but they had alibis. The sister was at home across town with her husband and baby."

"And Will?" Jack asked.

"He was working the night shift at one those twenty-four-hour call centers."

A night shift. Bryan and Jack exchanged another look. They had discussed the possibility that WCR worked nights and had a reason to be out on the prowl on a regular basis.

"I know what you're thinking," George said. "I thought it, too, at the time. But a detective vetted the kid's alibi. He went over there and talked to his boss in person."

Jack didn't comment, but Bryan knew what was on his mind. Someone needed to take a look at this case again.

And Will Anderson wasn't a "kid." He was a serial rapist by that point, becoming bolder—and more sadistic—with each new attack.

"Hell of a case." George shook his head. "We tested carpet samples, brought in a canine team, everything. No pour trails, no trace of accelerants. But I never liked that faulty water heater. Combined with that dead battery and the son not being home? Damn case always bothered me. Couldn't get it out of my head."

"I've got a few like that, too," Jack said.

The man leaned on the worktable, and Bryan's gaze settled on the red bandanna. He thought of Evelyn Wood with her hair pulled back, painting a house she couldn't stand to live in anymore. Her entire life had been blown apart, and so far the police hadn't done anything to help her.

"You know, before I retired," George said, "I went back and took a fresh look at some of the old ones."

"Old cases?" Jack asked.

George nodded. "I tried to look up the son. I wanted to see if he'd got himself in any trouble since the fire."

"And?" Bryan asked.

"Couldn't find hide or hair of him. No current driver's license, no current address. No arrest record—which was the main thing I was looking for."

"We can't find him, either," Jack said.

"You try his sister?"

"She's still in Round Rock," Bryan said, "but she said she hasn't seen him in years."

"Oh yeah?"

"She said he's been out of touch since they settled the estate."

Quiet filled the room as they looked at one another.

Bryan felt wired now, with impatience and excitement pinging around inside him. Any shred of doubt he'd had that they had the right suspect was gone.

Now they just needed to find him.

"So, tell me." George folded his arms over his chest. "What is it you want him for?"

"Homicide."

Bryan glanced at Jack, startled by the answer. He hadn't thought Jack was ready to reveal that yet.

"You don't look surprised," Jack said.

"Wish I could say I was." George shook his head and looked down at his dusty work boots. "Damn case has been eating at me for years."

ELEVEN

SKYLER LAY SPRAWLED on the rug with her feet propped on an old camp trunk. Rowan stepped over her legs.

"Want another mojito?" Rowan asked her.

"Sure."

She held up her glass, and Rowan grabbed it as she went into the kitchen. Lila stood by the sink, where she'd converted the one square foot of counter space into a bar. She'd brought her favorite cocktail shaker and was using a special tool to make spiral-shaped lime peels.

"These are good," Rowan said.

"Too strong? I'm experimenting with a new recipe."

"They're perfect."

Lila refilled drinks as Rowan cut the last half of the pizza into squares and slid them onto a plate.

"Want some?" she asked.

Lila made a face.

Rowan returned to the den with the plate balanced atop the glasses. "Last of the pizza," she announced, setting everything on the camp trunk that she used as a coffee table.

Skyler sat up and plucked a pineapple chunk off the top of a piece. "Good thing Dara's not here. More for us."

"I don't know how y'all eat that." Lila sank down on the sofa beside Oscar. "I can't stand sweet pizza."

Rowan settled on the floor by the table and grabbed a piece.

"Am I the only one who's worried about her?" Skyler asked, snagging another pizza square.

"No. I am, too," Rowan said around a mouthful of food.

"What's to worry about?" Lila asked.

"We've barely *seen* her in two weeks," Skyler said. "And she only just met this guy."

"Oh please. She's a freaking PI." Lila reached for the Cheetos bowl. "She runs criminal background checks for a living."

"So?" Skyler asked.

"So, I'm sure she scoped him out."

"Okay, but how'd she miss that other one? Trevor?" Skyler rolled her eyes. "What a douchebag."

"She didn't," Rowan said.

Skyler frowned. "What do you mean?"

"She knew he had a history of forged checks when she went out with him."

Skyler's jaw dropped open. "Why the hell did she go out with him?"

Lila shrugged. "Because he was hot?"

"Not *that* hot."

"No?" Lila looked at Rowan. "What did you think?"

"He was okay."

"Hey, speaking of hot guys." Skyler nudged Rowan with her foot. "I want to hear about Jack."

"What? I did a project for him."

Skyler grinned. "What else did you do for him?"

Rowan reached for her mojito. "Nothing."

"Right."

"Oh, come on." Skyler looked at Lila. "Now, *that* man I'd do in a heartbeat."

"Sky!"

"What? Wouldn't you?"

Lila looked at Rowan. "Maybe."

"Look, we're pissing her off." Skyler poked Rowan with her foot again. "I knew there was something going on there."

Rowan got up and grabbed the Cheetos bowl. "Anyone want a refill?"

Skyler laughed. "I told you. Did you see her face?"

Shaking her head, Rowan retreated into the kitchen, where she opened the fridge and stared at the contents. She didn't mind the teasing, but she wasn't ready to talk about Jack yet, even to her closest friends. She was too confused.

So far, she liked everything she knew about Jack. *Except* for his job. It was a major sticking point. She'd worked with cops for years and even dated one once, and she'd made a promise to herself—never again.

Of course, she hadn't been thinking about that promise when she kissed him in the middle of the Duck parking lot.

"Hey."

She turned around, and Skyler was standing in the doorway with Oscar in her arms. "You know I'm kidding, right?"

Rowan closed the fridge.

"I would never do your boyfriend."

"Yeah, duh. But he's not my boyfriend." Rowan refilled the Cheetos bowl and returned to the den.

Lila looked up from the phone on the table. "Sky, what's this? Are you getting a new tattoo?"

"I'm thinking about it." She put Oscar down on the rug. "What do you think?" She picked up her phone and showed Rowan an intricate tattoo of a cross.

"Hmm."

"What?"

"I don't know." Rowan tilted her head, studying the picture. "Too Celtic."

"What? I can do Celtic. I'm a natural ginger."

Rowan glanced at Lila.

"I think what Rowan means is, you're not ready for religious ink."

"What? Why not?"

"Sky, you change religions on an annual basis," Lila pointed out.

"Oh, whatever." Skyler threw a Cheeto at her.

Oscar jumped into Rowan's lap and rubbed his head against her stomach.

"What happened to the peacock feather you wanted?" Rowan asked. "You had it all sketched out."

"I decided it was trite. Feathers are everywhere."

Lila snorted. "As opposed to crosses?"

A rap sounded at the door, and everyone froze.

Skyler jumped up and rushed to the window. Parting the blinds, she peered outside.

"It's Jack," she whispered, and tipped her head back. "I *knew* it."

Rowan transferred Oscar to the floor and stood up. She glanced down at her sweatpants and dusted the crumbs off her shirt as she stepped over to check the peephole.

A flurry of nerves hit her as she saw Jack standing on her doorstep. He wore jeans and his leather jacket, which probably meant he was off duty.

"Open it," Skyler hissed.

Rowan smoothed her T-shirt and pulled open the door. "Hi."

"Hi." His gaze went past her, and something flickered in his eyes. "I probably should have called."

"It's fine."

Rowan opened the door wider and stepped back as Skyler walked up beside her.

"Hello, *Jack*. So good to see you again." Skyler smiled, and Rowan noticed the car keys in her hand.

"Hi." Jack nodded at her, then at Lila.

"We were just heading out." Skyler leaned over and gave Rowan an air kiss.

"You guys don't need to—"

"Bye!" Skyler stepped onto the porch, followed by Lila.

"Call me tomorrow," Lila said.

Rowan glared at her.

"Bye, Jack." Skyler waved over her shoulder and hurried down the steps.

Rowan watched them cross the lawn to the barn, where Lila's pickup was parked.

"Didn't mean to interrupt," he said. "I didn't see her car."

Rowan took a deep breath, trying not to think about the state of her hair or the fact that she hadn't showered in almost forty-eight hours.

"No problem." She forced a smile. "What's up?"

Jack gazed down at her. A ripple of heat went through her as he reached up and touched her lip.

"Doritos?"

"What?"

He showed her the orange crumb on his finger.

She licked the side of her mouth. "We were just finishing dinner." She ducked past him. "Would you like a drink?"

She padded into the kitchen, snatching up her glass on the way.

He followed her and leaned against the doorframe. "I'm sorry to break up the party."

"No party." She checked the drink shaker. "Just Lila's night off. We do this every week. When the weather's nice, we sit outside around the fire pit, but it's been too wet lately." She took a Star Wars glass down from the cabinet and poured the remainder of the cocktail into it, then crossed the kitchen and handed it to him.

He took the glass and sniffed it. "Mai tai?"

"Cherry mojito."

He made a face.

"Try it."

She turned away, catching her reflection in the microwave as she headed into the den. God, she had a scrunchie in her hair again.

"You know, you really have a talent."

He followed her into the den. "For what?"

"Nothing. Have a seat." She sank onto the sofa, trying to act totally comfortable even though her pulse was racing now.

Jack was in her house.

He'd been here before, but that was business. And that was before the kiss. Now all she could think of was how tall he was. And whether his feet would hang off the end of her bed.

He stepped over an empty plate on the floor.

"I should have called but—" He lowered himself onto her armchair, and she felt a twinge of disappointment. His gaze met hers. "—I didn't want to make it weird."

"Weird?"

"I have a proposition for you."

TWELVE

HIS WORDS SENT a jolt of nerves through her.

"What sort of proposition?"

"You can say no, obviously. But I'm hoping you won't."

Now she was more intrigued than ever.

"Does this proposition involve your case?" she asked. Part of her hoped it was personal, and part of her was unnerved by the idea that he'd come over here and proposition her about anything after that kiss the other night. Her gaze drifted to his mouth, and she felt heat rippling through her.

"Yes," he said. "But not the one you're thinking."

She focused her attention on his eyes—which didn't really help. They were deep and dark, and the intensity in them put a flutter inside her. She liked that intensity. But it worried her, too, because she was starting to realize it applied to everything he did. His work, his cases, his relationships. His whole low-key demeanor was an act. Or maybe not an *act*, but a layer that most people didn't see past. He only *seemed* low-key and *sounded* low-key. But in reality this man was super focused on getting what he wanted.

She cleared her throat. "So . . . not the case I've been working on?"

He shook his head, still watching her closely. "This is a cold case. As in ice-cold."

"Tell me more."

The second the words were out, she felt a twinge of panic, and the feeling was only reinforced when she saw the flare of triumph in his eyes.

"I'm not saying I'll do it," she added. "I just want to know what it is."

"Fair enough." He rested his forearms on his knees, Mr. Casual, and she knew that was an act, too. Whatever this was was important to him.

"Eight years ago I got a middle-of-the-night callout to a park on the east side of town," he said. "Ashland Park."

"Over off Manor Road."

"You know it?"

"Sure, I used to have a friend who lived over there. That was before the area got gentrified and all the rents went up."

"Someone called 911 about a body in one of the bathrooms. Hispanic male, probably early twenties. He'd been bludgeoned to death with a blunt object."

She shuddered. "How horrible."

"No ID."

Dread started to sink in as she realized where this was going.

"You want me to identify him? Using DNA?"

"We did, actually," Jack said. "That's where it gets even worse. Turns out, this victim was only seventeen years old. He'd been arrested before on drug charges, and his prints were in the system. Ramon Huerta."

The way he said the name, she could tell it had significance to him.

"Did he have any family or—"

"He'd been in foster homes since he was six. Mom was a junkie, Dad was nowhere. By the time this kid died, he was basically an addict who'd been getting by on the street. It was one of those cases. I've seen it so many times, but . . ." He shook his head. "This time was different."

"Why?"

He looked down and rubbed the back of his neck. "I found the brick."

"The brick?"

"The murder weapon. Someone smashed his skull with a brick, and I found it by the playscape right there in the park." He paused. "I mean, this victim was still pretty much a kid himself, and someone—maybe his dealer or someone who stole his stash from him—bashed his skull in." Jack leveled a look at her. "I've never been able to stomach it."

"How he died, you mean?"

"That, yeah. But also not being able to figure it out." He shook his head. "This was my first homicide case, and we never arrested anyone. We never even had a damn suspect."

Rowan's chest tightened as she watched him. Clearly this case, and his inability to solve it, had been weighing on him for years.

"So . . . you're opening the case again?"

"It's never really been closed, just de-prioritized."

She caught the bitterness in his voice.

"In other words, the victim was a junkie, so your limited resources got channeled elsewhere," she said.

His jaw tightened. "That's the way it works. Budgets are strapped, and the squeaky wheels, the high-profile cold cases, get the grease. But I've never been able to let this one go."

She watched him, trying to read whether this case haunted him because it was his first and he'd failed to solve it. Or because he truly cared about a seventeen-year-old whom society considered a lost cause before he even hit adulthood. Based on what she knew of Jack, she figured it was both.

"What do you have?" she asked.

"Touch DNA," he said. "Off the murder weapon."

"The brick."

He nodded. "Skin cells. It was a spur-of-the-moment crime, we figure. Whoever killed him didn't wear gloves."

Rowan watched his face, easily reading that look in his eyes. He was determined, once again, to convince her to help him.

And once again, she wanted to turn him down flat. She was done with police work.

Except for that one case for Ric, which was supposed to be a one-off.

And then that one case for Jack.

And now another case for Jack again.

What the hell was she doing? She'd gotten herself out of this. *Disentangled* herself from all of it and lost the respect—not to mention friendship—of her former co-workers in the process. She'd broken free of all of it, but then this dogged, stubborn cop walked into her life and lured her back in again, and now she felt worried because she could feel her resolve slipping.

What if she threw everything away—her business, her clients, the network she'd been so diligently building— what if she threw all of it away and just went back to helping detectives track down rapists and murderers?

And what if everything up to now—the dinner, the drinks, the kiss in the parking lot, the *I want to see you again*—what if all that was just him laying the groundwork to get her to help him again?

He stood up. "Think about it."

She blinked up at him. "What do you mean?"

"I know this isn't what you do anymore, so . . . take your time deciding. If you're not up for it, I'll understand."

Not up for it. That annoyed her, which was probably his point.

"If you're up for trying, I can put in a request to have the sample analyzed."

She glared up at him. "So, that's it?"

"What do you mean?"

"You want me to agree to help you, and then you'll run it up the flagpole and—what?—try to scrape up some budget to hire me?"

"Basically." He paused. "I told you what I want. It's up to you to decide."

She stood and put her hands on her hips. He was just going to show up here and dump this request in her lap and then take off?

He moved for the door.

Evidently, he was.

She followed him across the room. She couldn't pinpoint what, exactly, she was so upset about, but her chest was tight.

He pulled the door open and turned to face her. "Sorry to interrupt your thing with your friends."

"They were leaving anyway."

He gave her a look that told her he knew that wasn't true.

He rested his hand on her shoulder. "Thanks for hearing me out."

Then his hand dropped away, and he walked out the door.

THIRTEEN

W HAT ARE YOU doing down here?"
Jack glanced up from a file to see Bryan in the
doorway.

"Looking for inspiration," Jack said.

Bryan was dressed up today in a button-down shirt and
tie, and Jack remembered he'd been scheduled to testify.

"How'd it go?" Jack asked, leaning back in his chair.

"Big waste of time. I waited around all morning, and
they didn't call me."

Bryan stepped into the windowless space known as
the "reading room," which was really just a vacated storage
closet where detectives sat at a table to review evidence. He
eyed the carton at Jack's feet, then stepped over to read
the label on the box beside him.

"Shana Klein?"

"I'm impressed you know the case number," Jack said.
"That was before your time."

Bryan tapped the lid. "Mind?"

"Sure." Jack reached for the shelf behind him and handed over a box of latex gloves.

Bryan pulled on a pair and then removed the top of the banker's box.

Jack had memorized the contents long ago and wasn't surprised when the first item to catch Bryan's attention was a ziplock bag containing a student ID card.

"She looks so young," Bryan said, studying her photo through the plastic.

"Yeah."

Shana had been nineteen years old when a masked intruder broke into her ground-level apartment in the middle of the night and raped her at knifepoint.

Now she was twenty-six.

Bryan replaced the bag in the carton. "You go through these a lot?" he asked.

Jack picked up on the curiosity in his voice. It was one of the reasons he liked working with the guy. He was open to learning from older detectives instead of being defensive.

"I like to look at the physical evidence from time to time, see if anything jumps out." Jack paused, watching Bryan comb through the box. "Every now and then, you see something in a new light."

"Why is her student ID in here?"

"We found it on the sidewalk just outside her place. At the time, we figured he took it with him as a souvenir and dropped it, so we ran it for fingerprints."

"Gloves, though, right?"

"Yeah."

Bryan replaced the lid and peered down at the box on the floor, tilting his head to read the case number.

"Olivia Salter." Bryan looked at him. "Why these two?"

"They were the first. I figure maybe he made a mistake early on, we just haven't caught it yet."

Jack stood up from his chair. He moved Shana's box to the

floor and then hefted Olivia's onto the table. Hers was heavier because it contained a pair of ten-pound hand weights.

Jack removed the lid and slid the box toward Bryan. "Take a look. Tell me if anything jumps out."

Bryan reached for a file folder that contained the crime scene photos. As he slowly sifted through them, Jack used his gloved hand to pick up the bag with one of the hand weights.

Olivia's attacker had surprised her in her bedroom after she stepped out of the shower. They'd struggled on the floor, and he'd grabbed the hand weight from under her bed and hit her in the face with it, knocking out a tooth.

Like Shana's ID card, the hand weight had been sent to the lab, but no prints or DNA from the UNSUB had been recovered.

Jack replaced the weight and picked up an envelope containing a carpet sample. He remembered standing in that bedroom as a crime scene tech used a utility knife to carve out the square.

"Where'd the blood on the carpet come from?" Bryan asked.

"Olivia."

"No, I know. I've read the report. I meant was it from when he hit her?"

"Yeah. He knocked her tooth out."

Jack glanced at the photos in Bryan's hands and saw that he'd come to the picture of the faint shoeprint from the kitchen floor near the back door.

"Size twelve, right?" Bryan held up the photo.

"Yeah. Different shoe than the recent one."

At Evelyn Wood's house back in November, he'd been wearing size twelve Adidas sneakers.

Jack studied the photograph. The dirty shoeprint had prompted detectives to search the creek bed near Olivia's house, where they'd discovered a hide. It was a carefully selected spot, camouflaged from view but offering an unobstructed line of sight to Olivia's back porch and her bed-room window.

"He watched her," Bryan muttered.

"Every time. That's his MO."

Bryan frowned down at the photo. Then he flipped back through to the shoeprint on the kitchen tile.

"Where do you think he finds them?" Bryan asked.

Frustration needled Jack. "I wish I knew."

For years, Jack had been trying to figure it out. They'd compared the victims' daily routines, hoping to discover a connection. But they hadn't come up with anything. All the victims—with the exception of Amber Novak in San Antonio—lived in what could loosely be called "central Austin." But Jack hadn't been able to find a place where their paths intersected. They didn't frequent the same gym or grocery store or coffee shop. Two victims were students, the others were young professionals. Some were single, some had boyfriends, one had a husband.

In each case where there was a man in the picture, the attack had occurred when he was out of town.

Which told Jack he didn't just watch the victims. He *surveilled* them. He followed them and studied them and conducted elaborate reconnaissance. He figured out when they left for work and came home and liked to exercise. He slipped into their homes when they left doors unlocked—possibly even while they were there—and gathered infor-mation. He learned floor plans. He unlocked seldom-used doors to make entry easier. He picked up spare keys and collected souvenirs—lingerie, jewelry, photographs. What-ever caught his interest, he helped himself.

Jack had no doubt that right now, to this day, he had a stash somewhere, a collection of mementos from the women whose lives he had shredded. And he probably went through it from time to time.

Just like Jack came in here and combed through these boxes over and over.

"He's sick, you know." Bryan held up the picture of the creek bed behind Olivia's place.

"I know. And I don't give a shit."

"You don't care that he's probably a mental case?"

"I only care about finding him."

Shaking his head, Bryan flipped to another picture. This one was a crime scene photo showing a Polaroid that Olivia had had taped to her refrigerator. The snapshot showed Olivia and her boyfriend, both in Hawaiian shirts and leis at a luau-themed party, smiling for the camera and holding up red plastic cups. Her attacker had removed the picture and left it sitting on the kitchen table.

Combing through the crime scene photos, the FBI profiler had locked on the kitchen table shot. In his report, he'd concluded that the Polaroid had been placed there as some kind of message.

Jack was no profiler, but he'd understood that the instant he saw it. It was a taunt.

"The victims don't look alike," Bryan said, shaking his head. "Blond hair, dark hair. Short, tall, different body types. What do they have in common?"

"They're shorter than he is," Jack pointed out. The surviving victims all described their attacker as at least six feet tall.

"You think that's important?"

"He hasn't used the knife yet, except as a threat. He holds it in his teeth and controls them with his hands."

"The choking, you mean."

Jack nodded.

But just because he hadn't used the knife yet didn't mean he wouldn't. Mutilation might be coming. Slowly but surely, he was losing control of his urges.

Bryan flipped to another picture of the creek bed.

"Let me see that one." Jack held out his hand, and Bryan passed it over.

Jack studied the photograph showing the wooded area

under the harsh glare of the CSI's portable light. The creek ran through central Austin, and Oliva's apartment backed up to it. A hike-and-bike trail paralleled the waterway, and Olivia had frequently used it for runs.

So had Rowan.

Seven years ago, Rowan had lived less than a block away from WCR's second victim. Jack had looked it up after their conversation. And Rowan had used the same jogging trail that ran along that creek.

Frustration churned inside him. Had Rowan crossed paths with WCR, too? Had she caught his attention? Jack's gut clenched as he thought about how close she might have come to ending up in a killer's sights.

Jack handed the picture back to Bryan, who was looking at the crime scene photo of Olivia's back porch.

"He stalks them," Bryan said. "He's patient, too. He probably sat out there for hours."

"I know."

Bryan shook his head. "It's like he's a hunter."

"Not like. He *is*."

B RYAN CROSSED THE park, skimming his gaze over the rainbow-colored playscape. He spotted Evelyn at the base of a yellow slide. A little girl with wispy pigtails slid down and landed at her feet. Smiling, Evelyn scooped the girl into her arms.

Bryan's chest squeezed as he watched her swing the toddler upside down and then set her on her feet as she squealed with glee.

Evelyn glanced up and spotted him, and the light went out of her eyes. She whispered something in her daughter's ear that sent her scampering back up the playscape.

Bryan trudged over, getting sand in his dress shoes. In a suit and tie, he stood out with all the kids and caregivers. Evelyn sat down on the bench beside her stroller. Today she wore a fleece pullover and black yoga pants, like many of the other moms and nannies out here.

"Hi," he said, stopping beside her. He tucked a hand in his pocket, making sure the other side of his jacket covered his holster. He hadn't really thought about how conspicuous he'd look at a playground.

"Thanks for coming." She held her hand above her eyes to shield her face from the sun.

"No problem." He glanced at the kids on the slide.

"We always come here on Fridays. I get the day off."

"And what is it you do?"

Bryan didn't know why he asked. He knew exactly what she did for a living. Just like he knew where she bought groceries and gas and that she'd canceled her gym membership six months ago. He knew that her ex was a product manager for a computer company and that he had a condo on Lake Austin, where he lived with his girlfriend.

"I manage a dental office," Evelyn said with a smile. "We're closed on Fridays."

Bryan nodded. "Mind if I sit?"

"Sure."

He sat on the other end of the bench and watched as she reached for the stroller and pulled an overstuffed black bag from the bottom of it.

"It's in here somewhere," she said, rummaging through. She pulled out a magazine.

"What is this?" he asked.

She handed it over, and he saw that it wasn't a magazine but a glossy catalog.

"This came to the apartment with my forwarded mail. I marked the page there."

Bryan opened it to the page with an orange sticky tab.

"That's my locket."

Bryan studied the necklace on the model's smooth ivory neck. An image flashed into his mind of Evelyn in the hospital with a ring of red welts around her throat.

"See?"

He glanced up. "This is it exactly?"

"I confirmed it with Drew. I wanted you to see what it looks like in case you ever, you know, find it in his possession. When you find him, that is."

When not *if.*

"Mommy, I'm hungry."

He glanced up from the catalog as Bella ran over and buried her head in her mother's lap.

"I know, sweetheart, and we're going home for lunch soon."

Bella looked up at him with wary green eyes. She turned to her mother. "Can I have Goldfish?"

"No more Goldfish."

"Please?"

"We'll have some with lunch. Two more slides, and then we'll go, all right?" She planted a kiss on her daughter's head. "I'll watch you."

Bella ran off.

"This is helpful, ma'am. Thank you."

She rolled her eyes. "It's Evie. Please. You don't have to ma'am me."

He nodded. "Thank you, Evie. We appreciate this."

"No problem." Her brow furrowed as she turned to her bag again. "There was one other thing."

Bryan caught the tension in her voice and watched with a feeling of dread as she poked through the bag again. She took out a sippy cup and a tattered pink blanket. Then she pulled out a gallon-size ziplock bag and handed it to him. Inside was a folded yellow flyer.

"That was under my wiper blade yesterday."

He read the flyer through the plastic. It was an ad for a pizza restaurant with a coupon at the bottom. WELCOME TO THE NEIGHBORHOOD was scrawled beneath the coupon in green block letters.

He glanced up.

"It's probably nothing." She waved her hand. "Maybe I'm being paranoid but . . . I don't know." She leveled a look at him. "It gave me the creeps."

He nodded, not sure what to say.

"None of the other cars had them, and that restaurant isn't anywhere near us. So I picked it up with a tissue and put it in the bag. But . . . I don't know. It's probably nothing, don't you think?"

"I'm sure you're right."

He instantly regretted the words. But he couldn't take them back, so instead he tucked the ziplock bag into the jewelry catalog—right beside the picture of the locket that some sadistic dirtbag had stolen from her house.

Bella ran back as Bryan stood up.

"Mommy, I want *lunch*."

"We're leaving, sweetie. Look, here's your juice." She handed her the sippy cup and then stood up.

"Thank you," Bryan repeated.

"Let me know if anything comes of that." Her brow furrowed as she nodded at the items in his hands.

"I will."

She picked up Bella and balanced her on her hip as she grabbed the blanket off the bench. Bryan reached for the big black bag and handed it to her.

"Thanks," she said, hitching the strap onto her shoulder.

"Again, we appreciate the call, Evie. If you think of anything more, don't hesitate to reach out."

"I won't." She gave him a somber look. "And keep me posted about everything else, too."

FOURTEEN

JACK'S PLACE SURPRISED her. Not only that it was in a trendy part of town but that he'd lived here for years.

Rowan checked the address on her phone screen and eyed the glowing window on the building's second floor, three in from the corner. She was pretty sure that one was his. She had counted the units, plus whoever lived there stored a mountain bike on the balcony.

Rowan dropped her phone into her purse and got out. Once again, she was dressed in a sweatshirt and jeans, but for once she didn't care how she looked. She glanced up at the building as she locked her car, hoping she had the address right.

"Hi."

She turned around.

Jack walked across the parking lot toward her. He wore shorts and running shoes, and his long-sleeved gray T-shirt was soaked with sweat.

He stopped and frowned down at her, hands on hips. "Everything okay?"

"I need to talk to you."

"Come on up."

He gestured for her to go ahead of him.

She stepped onto the sidewalk in front of his building where yuppie-looking people with computer bags were getting their mail from a wall of postboxes.

"This way," he said, leading her to an outdoor stairwell. They walked up in silence and reached an open breezeway that looked out over a landscaped courtyard. A woman stood beside a fountain reading her phone as her little dachshund strained against his leash.

Jack stopped beside a door and untied a key from the drawstring of his running shorts.

"You want something to drink while I grab a shower?" He held the door open, and she stepped inside.

"I can't stay. I'm meeting a prospective client for dinner." She turned around as he switched on the light in the foyer.

"Can you at least sit down?"

Ignoring the question, she turned and surveyed his home. The place had a slanted ceiling with exposed rafters. A counter divided the kitchen from the living area, where an oversize leather sofa faced a brick fireplace and a coffee table blanketed with paperwork. The place was tidy, but minimalist, and she wondered if a woman had ever lived here with him.

"What's on your mind, Rowan?"

She set her purse on the counter and turned to face him.

"I was researching William Anderson today, and I came across something disturbing."

He frowned. "Why are you researching William Anderson?"

"It's a follow-up for Joy."

"What kind of follow-up?"

"She hired me for help constructing her family tree. He's part of it."

He just looked at her, and she sensed he didn't approve of this development for some reason.

"What did you find out?" he asked.

"Gale and Philip Anderson—William's adoptive parents— died on the *same exact day* five years ago. I found a news article about it. The story said it was an 'accidental' house fire but—" She halted midsentence, seeing his reaction. "You knew."

He nodded.

"William Anderson isn't only a sexual predator, Jack. He's also a murderer."

He nodded again, and she felt a rush of disbelief that he was standing here calmly confirming her bombshell.

"This guy killed *his own parents*!"

"We don't know that for sure."

"But you said . . ." She trailed off as she watched the look in his eyes. Her stomach twisted as she put it together. "There's another victim?"

"Yes."

It was like a punch in the gut.

Rowan turned away. Tears burned her eyes. She had worked as fast as she could, and still it hadn't been fast enough.

"This was in San Antonio." He stepped over to the coffee table and picked up a newspaper. He handed her the folded A-section.

She looked down at the article. A photo at the top showed a smiling young woman. Dread filled her as she read the caption: **AMBER NOVAK, TWENTY-NINE, WAS FOUND DEAD IN HER QUAIL GROVE HOME.**

She skimmed the first few lines of the story and glanced up. "She was strangled?"

Jack nodded.

Rowan continued reading, feeling sicker with every paragraph.

Jack stepped into the kitchen. He grabbed a dish towel and wiped his face.

Emotions swirled inside her as she set the newspaper aside. "You *knew* all this? This is what you meant by your 'ticking clock' when you tried to hire me back at the Duck?"

"No." He tossed the towel on the counter. "I met you before I found out about Amber Novak, before we linked the cases with DNA." He folded his arms over his chest. "At the time we met, I suspected but I didn't know."

She searched his face, unsure whether he was being straight with her. "You *suspected*."

"I had reason to believe he was escalating, shedding his inhibitions and becoming more dangerous. That's why I wanted your help so bad."

She stared at him, feeling queasy all over again. He'd come to her for help, and she'd waited days to get back to him with an answer.

"It was that night, the night we met for the first time at the bar," he said. "Remember that call I got?"

She stared at him, visualizing the calendar in her mind. What would have happened if she hadn't dragged her feet? Maybe if she'd responded to his very first phone call, Amber Novak might be alive right now. She should have responded the instant Jack called the first time. She should have dropped everything.

She turned away as a wave of anxiety crashed over her. Her palms were clammy. She felt herself being pulled right back into the vortex, the same powerful vortex she'd been trying to extract herself from for years. Years ago, it had taken over her life. She hadn't been able to escape the violence, the depravity, the sick images swirling through her mind every night as she tried to go to sleep.

He stepped closer. "Hey."

She shook her head.

He touched her chin, gently turning her face to look at

him. "You didn't do anything wrong, Rowan. You're *helping* us here. Without you, we still wouldn't know his name."

"Have you called my friend Dara?"

His hand dropped away, and she felt a rush of anger.

"Oh my *God*. What is it going to take—"

"I called her today," he said.

"You did?"

"She agreed to help. We've reached out to the marshals, too. They'll find him."

"Dara will find him first."

He lifted an eyebrow skeptically.

"I told you, she's good." Rowan looked down at her feet, only slightly comforted by the thought of Dara's help. So much damage had already been done, so many lives impacted. And it was irrevocable.

She thought of the newspaper picture she'd come across today of that burned-out house. She closed her eyes.

Jack took her hand. "Hey."

She looked up, and he was gazing down at her with those deep brown eyes. A ripple of awareness went through her as he lifted his finger and traced it under her jaw. She held his gaze as he leaned down and kissed her.

It was soft this time. Slow, patient. She was the one who reached up and pulled him against her. He felt warm and solid again, and his arms wrapping around her made her feel grounded in a way that put a pang in her chest.

She fused herself against him, absorbing the warmth of his mouth and the solid feeling of his body against hers. She combed her fingers into his damp hair.

He leaned away. "I need to shower."

She pulled him back. She didn't care that he was sweaty—she liked him this way. He was real and raw, and she liked that she'd caught him off guard by coming here. And she liked that he kissed her in a way that made her know he'd been thinking about her since the last time.

How had she gotten herself into this? She'd promised

herself that first kiss was it—no more. It was a temporary lapse in judgment. She'd told herself she was going to keep her distance from him *and* his cases *and* that penetrating look in his eyes that she couldn't resist.

His hands slid over her hips, and her entire body started to thrum as she felt his heat seeping into her.

Finally, she eased back.

"What?" he asked.

"I have a meeting to get to. And even if I didn't . . ."

His eyebrows tipped up. "Even if you didn't, what?"

She shook her head. "I can't get involved with you."

"Why not?"

"Because." She stepped back. "It's too hard. Everything you represent."

He frowned. "What do I represent?"

She stepped back again, frustrated. "What I *should* be doing if I wasn't such a chickenshit."

He blinked at her. "I'm not following."

"Police work. Investigating." She looked away, wishing she hadn't brought it up. "I'm good at it, Jack. But I can't do it again. I won't. The nightmares, the paranoia. I felt like I was losing it!"

Quiet settled over them as she looked at his coffee table covered in paperwork. Case files. Of course. He brought his work home with him. He was a dedicated detective, and his job no doubt dominated his life.

Rowan glanced up, and he was staring down at her with a wary look on his face, like maybe she was crazy. Embarrassment flooded her, and she grabbed her purse.

"Wait."

"I have to go." She moved for the door.

"Just—*wait*. Look at me."

She looked up.

"This type of work isn't for everybody," he said.

"I'm aware of that, thanks."

"It can be dark. Depressing. Hell, half the cops I know are battling booze and burnout."

"I *know*, all right? That's exactly my point."

"Don't be so hard on yourself."

Something about his tone irked her. Like he knew he was stronger than she was. And it was true—he was! But she'd made a decision to step away years ago, and she didn't want to go back. Not even when he was standing there giving her his reverse psychology, trying to make her *think* it was her decision, when really he was just laying a guilt trip so she'd help him with another cold case.

"I have to go." She checked her watch. "I'm going to be late."

He opened the door for her. "Thanks for telling me what you found."

"Why? You already knew." She stepped out and paused by the door. "How come I haven't seen this in the media? The link between the San Antonio homicide and WCR?"

His expression darkened. "They haven't caught wind of it yet. It won't be long, though."

She turned away, but something in his tone made her look back. "You think he's trolling for another victim? This soon?"

The look in his eyes answered her question.

"I know he is."

J OY STOOD AT the back door, peering through the glass. She stared at the gazebo at the center of her yard, but all she could see was that charred black skeleton that had once been a house.

The blaze was determined to be an accident.

Her stomach knotted as she replayed the words, over and over, as if replaying them in her mind would somehow make them true.

Twenty-eight years.

How many times had she thought of the Andersons during those years? In her mind, they were fixed in time, along with her baby. It was easier that way. It kept things in the past. But in reality, Gale and Philip Anderson had been *dead* for five long years now.

Because they'd adopted a psychopath.

Someone who had the capacity to kill not just strangers but his very own parents.

Scritch-scratch.

Joy jumped, startled, as Sam pawed the door near her feet.

She turned the bolt and opened the door, and he darted outside.

"Hurry up, Sam. It's cold."

She started to close the door, but then Frodo was there, wanting to go out, too.

"Chop-chop!"

He dashed out, joining Sam on the edge of the patio. Together, they ventured into the strip of grass beside the pool.

Joy locked the bolt and grabbed her glass from the coffee table. It was empty again. Funny how that happened so much when Michael wasn't around to notice. She padded across the kitchen, enjoying the cool tile floor on the soles of her feet. She had come straight home from work and kicked her Louboutin pumps into the corner, then changed into her oldest, comfiest, unsexiest pajamas, which she kept in the back of her closet for nights when Michael wasn't around.

Joy plunked her glass on the bar and poured another glug of Grey Goose. Two glugs. Then she added the last sip of cranberry juice.

The blaze was determined to be an accident.

"Determined by who?" she murmured, stepping on the pedal for the trash can. The stainless steel lid popped up, and she dropped the plastic jug into the bin. "Or determined *by whom*?" She sipped her drink. "*Who* set the blaze? No one did. But! The blaze was determined to be an accident by *WHOM*?"

Joy pictured her freshman English teacher, Mrs. Perkins, diagramming that sentence. And another one: *WHO brought the child into the world? Joy did. Joy to the world!* However: *The child who murdered his parents was brought into the world by WHOM?*

Mary Perkins was a stickler for grammar, and her students scored high on the SAT. They got scholarships, and went to college and grad school, and *went on to do big things*!

Joy stumbled, slamming her toe into the chair, and caught herself on the dining table.

"Shit!" She set her drink down. "Shit, that *hurt*." She sank into the chair and stared down at her toe. It was going to bruise. Badly.

Scritch-scratch.

She got up and hobbled over, taking her drink with her. She undid the bolt and opened the door. Frodo scurried into the house.

"Where's Sam?"

She looked outside.

"Sam?"

Joy peered into the yard, trying to penetrate the shadows along the fence line. A gust of cold air blew the door against her.

"Sammy?"

Sighing, she set her drink on a side table and stepped out, pulling the door shut behind her.

The patio felt like ice beneath her feet, and she crept toward the pool. Sam wasn't in the patch of grass. Or the flower bed. Or sniffing the rosebushes around the gazebo.

She ventured to the edge of the patio and looked around the corner to the courtyard off the bedroom where she and Michael had imagined having breakfast on Sunday mornings—Belgian waffles with bacon, fresh-squeezed orange juice, the works.

They'd lived here two years, and they'd never done it once.

"Sam!" she trilled, not giving a damn if she woke up her neighbor now. He'd fired up his Ferrari on Saturday mornings more times than she could count.

A wind whipped up, and Joy clutched her arms around herself as she walked back across the patio. Where the hell was he? She picked her way across the flagstones that made a path to the herb garden, which was nothing more than a sad mound of dirt at the moment.

He wasn't back there. She looked around the side yard, even glancing at the inky darkness of the pool.

Squeeeeak-bang!

She jumped as the gate slammed shut beside the garage. Alarm filled her as she followed the flagstone path around the corner. Damn it. How had that gate gotten open? She kept it closed, always, because if it was ever left even slightly ajar, the dogs would make a run for it.

"Sam! Come here right this minute!"

Her stomach clenched. She'd had way too many vodkas to go driving around looking for him.

A thick tangle of vines covered the narrow passage behind the garage. She ducked under the branches, barely able to see anything. Nearing the trash cans, she smelled garbage and the faint trace of skunk.

"Ouch!" She snagged her sleeve on something and jerked it free. "Damn it." She clutched her hand to her shoulder and felt a tear in the fabric. Great. Now she had not only a stubbed toe but a cut arm. And a hole in her favorite pj's.

She emerged from the viny tunnel into the side yard, where a floodlight illuminated a pair of trash cans.

The gate blew open with a *squeak* and smacked against the fence.

Fear gripped her as she jogged past the trash cans. She

rushed through the open gate and looked down the long driveway. But she knew it was hopeless.

Sam was gone.

J ACK CAUGHT BRYAN'S attention as he entered the bar.

"Spurs are up," Jack said as Bryan pulled out the empty stool beside him.

"Sorry, I'm late. They were packed tonight."

"Where were you?"

"The Octagon."

Bryan took jujitsu at a gym on the south side of town, and he'd been asking Jack to join him for more than a year.

"You should come sometime."

"Maybe I will," Jack said, although he doubted it. He preferred solo sports like running and mountain biking.

Not that he'd been on his bike lately. It had been weeks. But biking was time-consuming, and it was easier just to throw on his shoes and pound out a few miles.

The bartender put a pint-size pilsner in front of Bryan, and he thanked her with a nod.

"So." Bryan took a sip. "How's it going with Rowan? I thought maybe she'd be here tonight."

"Why?"

"Aren't you seeing her?"

"No."

Bryan lifted an eyebrow, clearly unconvinced.

Jack turned his attention to the game as the Spurs hit a three.

"She seems smart," Bryan said.

"She is."

"You should talk to her about the Huerta case."

Jack looked at him.

"She nailed it on the WCR thing," Bryan continued. "Who knows? Maybe she could turn up something new with that, too."

Jack gave a noncommittal nod.

"I know it bothers you."

He sent him a sideways look. "Why do you say that?"

"I've seen your name in the log."

Jack checked the case out every year, hoping maybe at some point he'd see something he missed. He hadn't known anyone had noticed.

"So, you think you'll talk to her?"

Jack looked at his partner.

"I know you've at least thought about it," Bryan said. "Could generate a breakthrough."

"She's focused on her day job."

"Oh yeah? What's that?" Clearly, Bryan wasn't aware that Rowan didn't do forensic work full-time. And why would he be? He had only just met her.

"Genealogy consulting. She helps people find their birth parents. Or track down relatives for medical reasons, that kind of thing."

Bryan's brow furrowed. "I thought Ric Santos recommended her?"

"He did," Jack said. "But she doesn't do police work anymore. Or not often. This case was an exception."

Bryan sighed. "Too bad, man. She's good."

Jack watched the game, annoyed tonight for reasons he couldn't pinpoint.

Well, besides Rowan showing up at his place earlier and then rushing away.

I can't get involved with you.

Since the moment they'd met—hell, since the whole week before that—Jack had sensed her wariness. Ric had flat out told him Rowan was out of police work and that Jack was going to have to do some convincing if he wanted to get her help.

And Jack had been up for the challenge. He'd welcomed it, really. He was good at convincing people to do things for him, and the need to identify WCR was a major motivator for him to pull out all the stops. He'd do damn near anything for a lead in that case—especially now.

But what Jack hadn't counted on was persuading Rowan to help him and then getting to know her and then her specifically *not* wanting to get involved with him on a personal level.

Most women liked him. It was a fact. It was usually a case of them pursuing him, and *him* being reluctant to get too involved because he didn't have the time and wasn't willing to make it. Of the two serious relationships Jack had been in during the last five years, both had ended with his girlfriend pushing for more time and attention than he had to give, and with him trying to explain the demands that came with his job.

But Rowan knew all about that. And she wanted no part of it. She was intent on setting a new path for herself, and she would probably be a healthier, happier person for it.

So, who was he to try to drag her back to something she didn't want?

And it wasn't just his work, it was him, too.

Everything you represent, she'd said.

She knew all about his hours and his workload and the shit that kept him up at night, and she wanted no part of any of that, either.

Who could blame her? As far as personal relationships were concerned, his job sucked. And it was the defining feature of his life, so there was no getting around it.

"Jack?"

He glanced at Bryan, who was watching him with a concerned look.

"Yeah?"

"You want another one?" He nodded at the bartender, who was standing there looking at him expectantly.

"Thanks, I'm good." Jack picked up his glass, then put

it down. It was almost empty, and the game still had a quarter to go.

"You okay, man?" Bryan asked.

"Yeah. Just tired. It's been a long week."

What was Rowan doing right now? She'd gone to the trouble to track down his home address—not that it was all that hard for someone who knew a thing or two about online research, but still. She'd shown up at his place, and the instant he'd seen her, he'd felt a punch of desire. He had been sweaty and smelly and in desperate need of a shower, and there she was, gazing up at him with those big blue eyes. And he'd wanted nothing more than to take her upstairs and pull her into that shower with him.

But then almost as quickly as she'd appeared, she was gone again, leaving him restless and edgy and wishing for more.

Again.

He couldn't get her out of his mind. When they'd first met, it was her eyes. And later it was her stubborn streak. Then, as of the other night, it was the way she kissed, like she wanted to inhale him. She'd done that again tonight, too.

And then she'd freaking left.

So, was she home from her client dinner by now? And was this new client a man or a woman? It was none of Jack's business, but he'd been picturing her in a cozy booth with some guy pouring his heart out and asking her to help him track down his long-lost family or some crap, and Jack couldn't stop thinking about calling her after the game ended just to say hi. Or better yet, dropping by her place.

Dropping by, like it was five minutes away instead of thirty.

"That's you, man." Bryan nodded at the bar, and Jack flipped over his phone and saw the area code.

"Shit," he muttered.

"What?"

He connected the call. "Bruner."

"Jack, it's Heidi."

He could tell by her tone it was bad.

"What is it?" he asked.

"Where are you?"

"At the Icehouse. Why?"

"You need to get down here."

FIFTEEN

JACK PULLED UP to the curb and parked behind a black SUV. Bryan could tell it was a police unit from the antennae on the back.

Bryan glanced up and down the block. "You know what this reminds me of?"

Jack shoved his door open. "Evelyn Wood's neighborhood."

"Yeah. How'd you know that?"

"They're all the same."

Bryan got out and followed Jack up the sidewalk. It was a one-story house with a freshly mowed lawn and a garage that dominated the front. No bikes or skateboards or Big Wheels in the driveway. The lights were on in the front room, but the blinds were closed tight. Other than the one unmarked unit, Bryan saw no other official vehicles.

Jack knocked, and the door swung open almost immediately.

"What took you so long?" a woman whispered. She wore a brown barn jacket and had her hair pulled back in a tight bun.

"Wreck on the interstate," Jack said. "Heidi, have you met my partner?"

Her glare disappeared as she turned to him.

"Bryan Hunt," he said with a nod.

"Hi." Her gaze snapped back to Jack. "They're in the TV room in back. Here, grab some booties."

She gestured to a piece of butcher paper on the floor beside the door, and Bryan and Jack stopped to pull paper covers over their shoes. Heidi led them into the dining room, where, at the end of the table, a laptop computer was open beside a coffee mug.

As he left the foyer, Bryan glanced over his shoulder and noticed a hallway, presumably leading to the bedrooms. He heard the murmur of voices and the faint *click* of a camera.

"Crime scene is still here?" Jack asked. "I didn't see their van."

"They're in an unmarked tonight."

She led them through a kitchen with a sink full of dishes. It smelled like chicken noodle soup, and Bryan noticed the saucepan on the stove. They passed a kitchen table covered with folded laundry and walked into a TV room.

"Detective Green?" Heidi said. "Mind if we step in?"

"Not at all." A woman with curly dark hair stood up from her spot at the end of a sofa.

Jack and Heidi moved out of the way, and Bryan got a look at the other sofa, where a young woman sat clutching a man's hand. The woman had long auburn hair and freckles. Her eyes were bloodshot, and the end of her nose was pink.

The man beside her surged to his feet. He wore business clothes—a dress shirt and slacks—but his hair was mussed. With his short, stocky build and scowling expression, he reminded Bryan of a bulldog.

"How long is this going to take?" he asked, looking from Heidi to the other detective. "She's tired."

"I'm fine."

He turned to his wife. "It's almost midnight, Maura. You need to—"

"I'm *fine*." She reached up and took his hand. "Let's just get this over with."

"We'll try to be quick," Heidi said pleasantly. "We understand this is hard. Does anyone need a drink? Maybe some water?"

"No," the man practically growled.

"Jason, how about we step into the other room?" Detective Green suggested. "It might be easier for Maura to get through this with fewer people in here."

He turned to his wife, and they exchanged a few muffled words. Then he turned to Jack and Bryan with sharp look.

"Keep this quick, all right? She's had enough."

He brushed past them, and the other detective followed him into the kitchen.

"Maura, these are the investigators from Austin I told you about, Detective Bruner and Detective Hunt."

"Thanks for making time for us," Jack said. "We understand it's been a long night."

She nodded, watching them warily. "You can sit down."

Jack took the ottoman near the door, and Bryan sat on the opposite end of the sofa from Heidi, directly across from Maura Mooney. He smiled and nodded, taking care not to encroach on her physical space as he mentally reviewed what he knew about her. Maura Catherine Mooney, thirty-one. She was a paralegal at a San Antonio law firm, and her husband was a sales rep for a local pharmaceutical company. Heidi had given Jack the basics over the phone during their drive down here.

"Like I mentioned," Heidi said, "these detectives are investigating a similar crime in Austin, and they just wanted to get your take on what happened. I filled them in on the basics already."

Maura pulled a green throw pillow into her lap and nodded. "All right."

Jack gave her his relaxed *forget I'm a cop* smile. "Sometimes it's easier for us to get details from a conversation instead of a report."

She nodded again. "Sure, okay. You want me to just—"

"Why don't you start with the garage door?" Heidi suggested.

Maura took a deep breath and blew it out. "Okay, well . . . it was broken. It's *been* broken. For the last few days, my remote hasn't worked, and I'd been meaning to get a new battery. It takes those specialty ones, and I don't have any around. Anyway, I got home from the store after work—"

"Do you remember what time that was?" Bryan asked.

"Yeah, around seven thirty," she replied. "I had to stay late because my boss wanted me to help with something. Anyway, I noticed the door was up a couple of inches off the ground, and I thought I'd closed it all the way when I left this morning. But I didn't think much of it. So I just grabbed my groceries off the seat and went into the house."

"Which door did you use?" Jack asked.

"The front. I parked in the driveway, because I didn't want to get out and open the garage manually when I had all the bags to deal with, so I just got my stuff and went inside and made dinner."

Bryan took a spiral notebook from his pocket and caught Maura's eye. "Do you mind if I take a few notes?"

"Go ahead."

"Did you do anything before dinner?" Jack asked.

"No. I just got the soup going. Jason had texted me earlier to say he had dinner in the airport before his flight, and I didn't really want to cook anything elaborate, so I just opened a can."

"Sorry, okay if we back up?" Heidi asked. "Did you say you went into the bedroom when you first got home?"

"Oh. Yeah, right." She pulled the pillow closer to her body. "I went in and changed clothes. I put on yoga pants and a T-shirt."

At the moment, she was wearing jeans and a turtleneck sweater.

She took a deep breath. "I ate in here with the TV on," she said. "I watched a little of the Spurs game. Then I—" She stopped abruptly and looked down. "Sorry."

"It's okay," Heidi said. "Take all the time you need."

Another deep breath. "I went to take a shower. Jason was coming home, and I haven't seen him in three days. I was in there awhile, shaving and whatever. Then I turned off the shower, and that's when I thought I heard something. A noise."

"While you were still in the shower?" Jack asked.

"Yes. But, again, I didn't think anything of it."

"What was the noise like?" Bryan asked.

"I don't know." She bit her lip. "Maybe a raccoon in the trash can or something? It was in the backyard. At least, I thought it was. Anyway, I put on my bathrobe and dried my hair with the hairdryer. That took about five minutes. I flipped my head down to dry the bottom, you know, like you do"—she looked at Heidi—"and then when I flipped back up, I saw him in the mirror." She put her hand to her chest as her eyes filled with tears. "He was right there behind me with the ski mask," she said softly.

Jack nodded. "What did you do, at that point?"

"I screamed. And he came up and hooked his arm around my neck and put his hand over my mouth and started dragging me backward, into the bedroom. I tried to fight him off and kick, but he was really strong and a lot bigger than me, and then he dragged me to the ground, and all the air went out of my lungs."

"You mean, from the force of him putting you on the ground," Bryan asked, "or from fear or—"

"The force of it," she said. "He, like, slammed me to the floor on my back, and it knocked the wind out of me." She paused. "And then I was fighting, trying to push him off me, and then he put a knife against my neck and told me not to scream. He said, 'Don't scream, Maura, or I'll have to cut you.'"

Bryan glanced at Jack.

"He said your name," Jack stated.

She closed her eyes and nodded.

Quiet settled over the room. All three detectives stared at her, waiting, and she kept her eyes shut tight.

She took a deep breath and opened her eyes. "And then he put the knife in his teeth, and he started choking me. And I was thinking, *I'm going to die, oh my God, I'm going to die.* And then suddenly he was gone."

"Gone?" Bryan asked.

"All of a sudden, he just jumped up and ran out, and I was on the floor gasping and coughing. Then I heard noises in the kitchen and realized that Jason was home."

"Did your husband confront him?" Bryan asked.

"He didn't even see him. He must have got out the back or something, because Jason walked into the bedroom and found me there on the floor."

Someone coughed, and everyone turned around.

A crime scene tech in a white Tyvek suit stood in the doorway. "Pardon me." He looked apologetic. "Detective Rollins, we're about to head outside now."

Heidi gave a brisk nod. "Fine."

Jack caught Bryan's eye and gestured toward his notepad. Bryan nodded.

"Excuse me one moment." Jack stood up. "I'll be back."

THE REASON MAURA Mooney's neighborhood looked familiar was because it was.

Jack stepped through the gate at the end of the cul-de-sac and followed a narrow trail down an incline into the woods. Like Amber Novak's neighborhood and Shana Klein's and all the others, this one backed up to a wooded area, and the victim's house was directly adjacent to a ravine.

"There's a second access point right next door to the house," the CSI told him.

"Any shoeprints?"

"Yeah, plenty. It leads to a hike-and-bike trail, so it's pretty heavily trafficked."

No usable impressions, then.

The CSI swatted at branches as they made their way through the brush.

"Here," he said, pointing his flashlight to the ground as they emerged onto a gravel trail. "This parallels the west side of the neighborhood and connects with a park near the entrance."

"Sunny Hill Park?" Jack had seen it on the way in.

"Yeah."

Jack pulled out his mini-flashlight and shined it over the path. The CSI was right. Shoeprints galore.

Jack glanced over his shoulder and counted the rooftops to Maura Mooney's house. The trail curved left, leaving a gap between the houses and the trail. Jack walked four houses in and then stepped into the brush.

"There's a drainage ditch over there," the CSI told him.

Jack stopped and looked back. "Where's your camera?"

"Our photographer has it. She's finishing up back at the house."

"Tell her to come out here."

The guy paused a moment, probably wondering whether he needed to take orders from some dick down from Austin. But then he trudged off without comment.

Jack pointed his flashlight at the woods. A carpet of leaves covered the ground. Jack ducked through the tree branches and tried to keep his steps to the leaves. If there was a decent shoeprint to be found out here, he didn't want to mar it.

Slowly, carefully, he made his way through the thicket until he reached the space behind the Mooney residence.

The ground made an incline, and the slope was a muddy tangle of vines and exposed tree roots. Jack looked at the house. The TV room's window was illuminated, and Jack pictured Maura Mooney still sitting in there with Heidi and Bryan, clutching the green pillow like a security blanket. The house had a U-shaped floor plan, and the master bedroom was on the opposite side, facing the fence.

From this vantage point, Jack saw only the fence.

He turned around and pointed his flashlight at the ground. Behind him was a sycamore tree with brown streaks on the bark.

"Son of a bitch," he muttered.

Stepping over, he shined the flashlight on the tree and followed the trunk to the first limb, about eight feet off the ground. He stared at the branch, then looked at the Mooneys' yard. Anyone up there would have a perfect view into the house.

Taking extra care now, Jack stepped from leaf pile to leaf pile and made his way closer to the tree. Near the mud-streaked tree trunk was an impression in the dirt.

Pulse racing now, Jack took out his phone and snapped a photo of the shoeprint. Size twelve Adidas, he'd bet his badge on it.

Jack snapped a shot of the tree bark, too, and glanced around. Where the hell was the photographer? It was supposed to rain tonight, and when it did, all this evidence would be long gone.

Scanning the ground carefully, he repositioned himself on another pile of leaves and took another picture.

A breeze kicked up, and some of the dead leaves fluttered on the ground. Something white caught his eye. A cigarette butt? Jack had no indication this guy was a smoker. Crouching down, he picked up a stick and moved the leaf aside.

It was a gum wrapper. He glanced up at the limb above his head.

Snick.

He turned around and caught movement in the shadows.

Jack switched off his light. The CSIs would be coming from the opposite direction.

Jack's pulse picked up again. Slowly, silently, he rose to his feet and unholstered his pistol.

A shadow moved.

"Halt. Police."

The shadow darted into the brush.

"Stop!" Jack yelled as he took off after him.

Branches snapped at him as he plunged into the trees, swiping at leaves. The ground sloped down, and Jack nearly lost his footing as he slid to the bottom of the ravine. It was clearer there, and the shadowy figure sprinted ahead through the tunnel of vines and limbs.

"Stop! Police!"

Jack's toe caught on a root, and he pitched forward onto his knees. He surged to his feet and ran, gripping his weapon as he tried to keep sight of the dark figure ahead of him. It was a man—tall, fast, wearing all black. As Jack sprinted after him, he leaped sideways. The man grabbed a vine and pulled himself out of the creek bed and dove into the trees.

Jack raced after him, heart thundering. It was *him*. He knew it in his bones. But he'd disappeared into the woods. Jack scrambled up the side of the creek, grabbing branches with his free hand to haul himself up. Then he was in the thicket again, and thorns snagged his arms as he swiped at branches. He plunged through the brush, following the *swish* of leaves ahead of him while branches thwacked him in the face. Adrenaline pumped through him as he barreled through the darkness after the target that had eluded him for years. Jack had never been this close, so close he could smell the man's sweat.

Batting at branches, Jack plowed through the thicket. His breath was coming hard and fast as he strained to catch up, but he couldn't even see the guy. Frustration burned inside him, spurring him on, but the noise faded and then disappeared. Jack moved faster, desperate to catch up. Where the hell had he gone?

He stopped and went still, straining to listen.

No sound. No movement.

Nothing but the crazy galloping of his own heart.

Snick.

Jack whirled around. A shadow moved behind him. Jack lunged after it, grasping at the darkness.

Pain lanced up his arm. A sharp blow to his back made him pitch forward onto the ground. Gripping his weapon, he scrambled to his feet and charged after the man. But where the hell was he? Jack ran along the uneven terrain, holding his hand out in case he ran straight into a tree.

Jack heard rustling in the distance. He jumped back into the creek bed and sprinted toward the sound as it faded away. Turning on his flashlight, he shined it ahead at the tangle of vines and leaves.

But there wasn't a sound. Or even a shadow.

Jack switched off his light to make himself invisible and once again strained to listen. Nothing. Just thick, heavy darkness all around him.

Pain pulsed between his shoulder blades. A warm trickle of blood slid down his arm and dripped off his fingertips. Anger washed over him as he stood in the creek bed and did a slow 360.

In the distance, a car door slammed and then an engine roared to life. Cursing, Jack ran toward the sound, but it was pointless. The engine gunned and then the noise faded until it was gone.

SIXTEEN

ROWAN POUNDED DOWN the trail, trying to find her rhythm as she scanned the path. In the muted winter sunlight, everything looked familiar, but not. The mile markers were new. Ditto the solar-powered trail lamps. But the trees looked the same, and Rowan instinctively ducked her head as she came to the thick, gnarled oak that dipped low over the path. She set a brisk pace, alert for anyone who made eye contact too long or who looked out of place with all the Saturday runners in body-hugging Spandex.

Rowan stopped as she neared a fork. Stepping out of the traffic flow, she pretended to do side stretches as she checked behind her for anyone suspicious.

She hadn't done this in years, but it all came back to her, pure muscle memory. It was like swimming the breaststroke. Or balancing on a skateboard. Jogging while remaining hypervigilant was a skill like any other, but Rowan was out of practice.

She veered left at the fork, taking the proverbial road less traveled, which in this case traveled directly past

Olivia's old apartment. Rowan scanned the brush, wondering if any of the cottonwoods or sycamores had provided Will Anderson cover once upon a time. It only made sense. He'd been here. Logically, she knew it, but she still found it hard to believe that she might be walking in his footsteps.

Acid filled her stomach as she neared a familiar bend in the path. Rowan eyed the cut-through—a shortcut created by countless impatient college students who couldn't be bothered to walk the extra eighth of a mile to the gate at the end of the street.

After another glance over her shoulder to make sure she wasn't being followed—although, who knew, really?—she took the shortcut. Only a few paces in, she spied the familiar back porch and halted.

It was just like she remembered it. The porch consisted of a concrete slab with a balcony overhead that protected it from the elements. It looked exactly the same, except there was one of those hanging hammock chairs where Olivia's wind chimes had been.

Rowan remembered the chimes and the whisper-soft tinkling they all used to listen to while passing the bong around. So many lifetimes ago, back when highs came as easily as falling asleep.

Rowan stared at the hammock. Navy blue. Maybe it was a man's hammock, and she hoped so. She hoped a woman wouldn't be careless enough to rent a first-floor unit with a sliding glass door.

She thought of Jack, with his solemn brown eyes as he talked about the victims. Jack was committed. Tenacious. This case needed someone like him, and she was glad he was on it.

But there was more. Something about him pulled at her. He was a gravitational force drawing her into his orbit, and she couldn't move away. Or didn't want to. She'd driven by his place last night after her dinner ended, but his light had been out, and she had resisted the temptation to stop.

I can't get involved with you.

He'd looked surprised. And disappointed. But then he'd looked determined, and she knew she was in trouble.

Leaves rustled behind her, and she whirled around. A squirrel skittered across the path like it was made of hot coals and then raced up a tree.

Rowan picked her way through the overgrown foliage. She passed the side of Olivia's building and came out near the familiar parking lot where the lines were painted too close together and door dings were rampant.

As she paused to look around, a white van with a satellite dish on top turned into the lot.

"Crap," she muttered.

The van made a slow pass, oozing down the row as the driver searched for a space. He rolled to a stop in front of a pair of blue dumpsters and parked directly in front of a **NO PARKING** sign.

The van's side door slid open, and a woman jumped out. She wore a miniskirt and heels, and had a scarf looped around her neck. The thick white scarf contrasted with her wavy dark hair, and Rowan knew that was intentional. This was her winter look. *Coming to you live from the scene of WCR's second attack . . .*

A man climbed out behind her and hefted a camera onto his shoulder, and Rowan got a sinking feeling inside her.

Once again Jack was right, and she should not have been surprised.

THE MEETING WAS already underway by the time they showed up.

"Traffic," Bryan said to Heidi as he took a seat beside her at the conference table. Jack took the last remaining chair on the end in front of a huge screen where a balding man with glasses was saying something about police reports.

Bryan leaned close to Heidi. "Who's this?" he whispered.

"FBI profiler. His name's Skinner."

Bryan looked down the table at Jack. This was the guy who had created the original profile of the West Campus Rapist. Jack had met the man personally and taken him to some of the crime scenes, but all that had happened before Bryan was on the case.

"Agent Skinner is joining us from Quantico. He was just filling us in on his updated profile," the lieutenant at the end of the table said, looking from Jack to Bryan. This would be Heidi's boss, Lieutenant Hood, who—as of bright and early this Saturday morning—had officially created the multiagency task force that Jack had been asking for for years. Bryan knew Jack welcomed the task force but wasn't at all happy about the fact that San Antonio PD was running it.

"Hi, Jack. As I was telling the group, the profile's been updated in light of the new case," Skinner said, addressing his webcam.

"Which new case?" Jack asked.

"Amber Novak of San Antonio."

Bryan glanced around the table, trying to put names with all the faces. Besides Heidi and her boss, there was Liz Lasco, who had driven down from Austin in her own car, as well as Detective Green from last night. Bryan hadn't caught Green's first name. So a lieutenant, five detectives from two different agencies, plus a fed. Not bad, given how shorthanded most departments were these days.

"Give us your bottom line," Hood said from the end of the table. "What makes him stand out?"

Bryan caught the impatience in the guy's voice. The lieutenant was heavyset and had a white buzz cut. Bryan pegged him for ex-military and already knew from Jack that the man had originally resisted any connection between the San Antonio murder victim and Austin's serial rapist. But DNA didn't lie, and now it seemed Hood was on board.

"I was just getting to that," Skinner said, and Bryan shifted his attention to the screen. With his pasty skin and glasses, the man looked more like a college professor than an FBI agent. But he didn't come across as stuffy, and Bryan was glad to see he was on a first-name basis with Jack.

"Let's start with some background," the profiler said, and his display went to a split screen with a photograph of the suspect appearing on the right side. "This is William John Anderson."

"Where'd we get this picture?" Heidi asked. "He looks like a kid."

"This is his yearbook photograph from high school," Skinner said. "It's the most recent one we have. His last known driver's license photo is six months older than this."

Bryan studied the photo. The guy had sandy blond hair and brown, deep-set eyes. His expression was sullen, but Bryan figured that wasn't remarkable for an eighteen-year-old with a skinny neck and bad acne.

"He's been linked to eight separate sexual assaults and one rape-homicide," the profiler went on. "Plus the attack just last night."

"Three homicides," Jack said.

"What's that?" Hood's gaze swung to Jack.

"We can link him to *three*, including his parents, who died in a fire five years ago."

"Is that confirmed?" Skinner asked.

"As of now, Round Rock Fire is standing behind their original arson investigation," Hood said. "Until that changes, let's keep it to one homicide."

"All right," the profiler said. "And here's our most recent driver's license photo."

A new photograph appeared on the screen, and the guy's skin looked even worse. Anyone with skin like that probably had issues in high school.

"No current DL. No current address," Skinner said. "But we can conclude he moved back to Central Texas because of the three separate attacks in the past nine weeks."

"Moved *back* to Central Texas?" Liz asked. "Do we know he ever moved away?"

"Not definitively, no," Skinner said. "But when a violent serial offender stops, it's usually a case of him being incarcerated, dead, or he's moved out of the area. Or—in rare cases—he actually stops."

"How do we know he didn't stop?" Liz asked.

"We don't for sure. But it's uncommon."

"I think he got spooked and moved," Jack said. "He dropped off the radar not long after his parents died and he came under suspicion. I think that's what made him pull up stakes and leave the area."

"How would he know he was under suspicion?" Heidi asked.

"We talked to the fire chief up there in Round Rock," Bryan said. "He told us they went and interviewed Anderson's boss at the time to vet his alibi. Chances are, he knew he was a suspect."

"So he decided to move away for a while and fly under the radar," Jack said, pointedly contradicting Hood's stance that until they knew otherwise, Anderson was linked to *one* homicide and not three.

"Where are you on your search efforts?" Skinner asked.

"We've got the U.S. Marshals involved," Hood said. "Plus our efforts, along with APD. We'll locate him, it's just a matter of time."

Bryan glanced at Jack. He doubted the head of the task force knew that APD's efforts involved Jack enlisting the help of a private investigator. A PI recommended by Jack's girlfriend, no less.

Or sort-of girlfriend. Jack still wasn't admitting that he and Rowan had a thing, but Bryan could tell from the way he talked about her.

Knowing Jack, he hadn't mentioned to Hood or anyone else that he'd enlisted the help of a PI. When it came to seeking permission from higher-ups, Jack tended to go with a less-is-more philosophy.

"So, what's your bottom line on this guy?" Hood asked for the second time.

"Well, you're dealing with a highly organized sexual predator," Skinner said, unfazed by Hood's obvious impatience. "He plans his crimes, carefully selects his targets, and conducts research beforehand. And afterward, he covers his tracks. As you're also aware, this individual is escalating."

Jack shot a look at Bryan. He'd been saying that since November. *This fucker's escalating. Won't be long before he strangles someone.* It was the first thing he'd said to Bryan when they'd left the hospital after interviewing Evie Wood.

Bryan thought of her in the park yesterday handing over that glossy catalog. *It's Evie. Please. You don't have to ma'am me.* Ever since she'd said that, he'd been trying—and failing—to think about her as simply Evelyn Wood, a woman whose case he needed to solve.

But his brain kept coming back to *It's Evie. Please.*

"Something else to point out," Skinner continued, "is that his period between crimes is shrinking—another indication that he's escalating."

"Just what I wanted to hear," Heidi muttered beside him.

"Mind if we back up a sec?" Detective Green asked, chiming in for the first time. "When you say 'organized,' do you mean when he's carrying out the attacks? Or that he has a target list, or what?"

"Good question. It's possibly both. One thing we know about most organized attackers is that they plan. They prepare. They develop contingencies."

"Like the doors," Jack put in.

Hood looked at him. "Doors?"

"In four of his eight crimes in Austin," Jack said, "we know that he slipped into the homes beforehand and unlocked secondary doors, ones that weren't often used. That way he had a backup route to flee the scene if he needed it."

"Contingencies," Skinner repeated. "Organized attackers also tend to be intelligent. In this case, highly intelligent."

Skinner paused to make sure it sank in that they were dealing with a smart adversary, as if they didn't already know. Over and over, he'd shown police that he had a cold, calculating mind.

"We know he had an academic scholarship to UT, but he dropped out during his freshman year and moved back home with his parents. This would have been a pivotal time for him, by the way. A blow to his self-esteem." The profiler looked down and seemed to be consulting his notes. "Also, we know from his sister that he suffered from depression in high school. I wouldn't be surprised to learn that he exhibited other warning signs, such as cruelty to animals, setting fires"—Skinner glanced up and looked directly at Jack at the mention of fire—"and also bed-wetting at a late age in childhood."

"The homicidal triad," Heidi murmured.

Liz heard Heidi's comment and rolled her eyes. "Dr. Skinner—with all due respect—I appreciate the psychological analysis. It's definitely interesting. But what I really want to know—what all of us really want to know—is what can you tell us that's going to help us catch him? Is there anything in his profile that gets to that?"

"I was just coming around to it." He didn't seem miffed, and Bryan figured he was used to dealing with impatient cops who tended to be action oriented. "I would say the most useful tool you have at your disposal is geography."

"Geography," Liz stated. "You mean, like, predicting where he'll strike next?"

"Most geographical profiling is based on probability.

You start with the assumption that he avoids killing in his own backyard in order to avoid drawing attention to himself—that's what's known as a buffer zone. He doesn't want to risk doing it too close to home. If you look at the locations of his crimes *outside* the buffer zone, you may find some overlap. This method was used extensively in an effort to apprehend the Golden State Killer."

Bryan again looked at Jack. That method hadn't worked. What had ultimately brought down GSK was someone like Rowan, who analyzed a sample of the killer's DNA and used it to create the guy's family tree.

"In this case, I think Anderson is showing similarities with that case in that he's using geography to select his targets. You may have noticed that the victims don't share much in common in terms of physical appearance."

"You're saying he picks where they live?" Heidi asked.

"I believe he selects a neighborhood that meets his needs," Skinner said. "Something backing up to a greenbelt or a park or maybe a creek bed where most of the houses are one level, and then he trolls for targets from there. The location is more important than the individual target."

"What do you mean by 'his needs'?" Heidi asked.

"He watches."

All eyes turned to Jack.

"That's what gets him off." Jack glanced at Skinner. "Right? He stakes them out, hides, watches their windows."

"Correct."

"He gets to know their routines, watches them coming and going, then when he feels comfortable, he slips into their houses and does his recon," Jack said.

"Recon?" Hood asked.

"He checks the layout, pockets spare keys, opens doors for himself. Sometimes he grabs personal items he likes—snapshots or jewelry. Hell, one woman even swears he swiped an energy drink from her refrigerator."

Everyone focused on Jack, probably digesting just how sick this guy was. And also, how obvious it was that Jack had far more knowledge about Anderson than anyone else in this room, and Austin PD should have been leading up this task force instead of San Antonio.

But politics were politics, and SAPD had landed the job.

"Speaking of snapshots, that brings up my next point," Skinner said.

Anderson's driver's license photo disappeared from the screen. The image that took its place put a sour ball in Bryan's gut. It was the Polaroid of Olivia Salter and her boyfriend dressed for a luau with leis around their necks.

"After his second attack, he left his victim in the bedroom, and she reported hearing him moving around in her kitchen, opening drawers," Skinner said. "He took this snapshot off her refrigerator and left it on her kitchen table on his way out."

Heidi made a disgusted sound. "Why?"

"It's a type of power trip," Skinner said. "He's saying, 'I was here. Your boyfriend wasn't. He didn't protect you.'"

"He's taunting them," Heidi said. "What an asshole."

"Exactly. Just his presence in the house before the crimes is also a taunt. In addition to the surveillance, as Jack said."

"So, he picks his neighborhood and does his surveillance," Green said. "The question is, Where is he going to strike *next*? The same neighborhood as last night?"

"I haven't had a chance to be briefed on last night," the profiler said, "so I don't know the specifics of that location."

"It fits the pattern," Heidi said. "Backs up to a creek bed *and* a park."

"We discovered his hide there behind the house," Jack said. "He was using a tree for surveillance. From ground level, he couldn't see over the fence, but from the tree limb, he would have been able to watch her bedroom window as she got out of the shower or changed clothes or whatever."

"I don't think he'll go back there," Heidi said. "Not after a direct confrontation with a cop."

Skinner frowned. "He actually confronted someone?"

"I heard him in the woods and tried to chase him down," Jack said. "He nicked me with his knife."

It was more than a nick. The gash in Jack's arm had bled all over his Jeep and required a trip to the ER. But whatever.

"Any idea why he went back?" Skinner asked.

"Maybe he was worried he'd dropped something," Jack said. "Otherwise, why risk sticking around as the cops showed up?"

Bryan gritted his teeth as he thought of the missed opportunity. If he'd been out there, things might have gone down differently. Jack was in good shape, yeah, but he was thirty-eight and a runner. He wasn't experienced at hand-to-hand combat. If Bryan had been in that creek bed, he would have had the guy in a headlock in no time, and they probably wouldn't be having this conversation right now.

"I assume you combed the area?" the profiler asked.

"We did," Hood confirmed. "We didn't find anything promising. Just some litter in the woods. We *did* get a shoe-print near the tree he was hiding in. Our CSIs made a cast of it, and we'll see if it's a size twelve."

"Well, like I was saying, his strict adherence to his MO may be your best advantage," the profiler said. "I would scope out neighborhoods like this one, likely in the greater San Antonio area."

"What about Austin?" Liz asked.

"He's got ties there, too, but I think that's because it was his original stalking grounds," the profiler said. "He revisited there in the fall—probably after some triggering event that set him off after his five-year hiatus. Maybe he lost a job or had a breakup or some other kind of setback, and he went back to his old comfort zone. But with the two most recent attacks being in San Antonio, I think it's likely he's living here now."

"So neighborhoods that back up to parks or greenbelts. Or creek beds or woods or utility easements." Heidi tossed her pencil on the table. "Great. That narrows it down."

"You've also got his early warning signs," Skinner added. "Don't ignore reports of prowlers or burglars or women calling in saying they got home and the back door was open—even if someone didn't steal anything."

"We need to have a press conference," Hood said.

Bryan was surprised by the suggestion. His lieutenant in Austin hated press conferences and did his best to avoid them. But maybe Hood was one of those who liked to look in charge in front of the cameras.

Heidi's phone vibrated on the table beside him. She flipped it over and checked the screen, then pushed back her chair.

"Excuse me," she said, slipping out of the room.

"We need to let people know, without causing a panic," Hood said, "that they need to report any break-ins, even if valuables aren't taken."

"When we did that in Austin six years ago, we were inundated with calls about footprints in the backyard and noises at night," Jack said. "We were getting called out for meter readers and pool guys and possums in trash cans."

"Better than *not* getting called out," Liz said. "I've been saying for years we can't blow off women who report stuff."

"Since when do we blow off women who report stuff?" Jack asked.

"*You* don't, but try talking to Property Crimes. They don't give a damn about panty raids and Peeping Toms. I mean, *wake the fuck up*. These guys are sexual predators sitting there jerking off and working up to the big event."

"I'll get with our public information officer," Hood said.

"We need to come up with a message that gets our point across and puts people on alert *without* causing a panic like they had six years ago."

Jack lifted his eyebrow, and Bryan knew what he was thinking: *Good luck with that.*

"I agree, we need a press conference," Liz said. "Like Dr. Skinner pointed out, he's escalating. And he didn't get what he wanted last night, so he's probably already trolling for his next victim. We need a joint press conference, and we need it soon, before the media gets wind of the story and we lose control of the message."

"Too late."

Everyone looked at Heidi as she stepped back into the room. She held up her cell phone.

"That was a reporter. The press already has it."

J ACK WALKED INTO the bullpen and went straight to the break room. He hadn't eaten in hours, and the protein bar he'd scarfed after the task force meeting wasn't cutting it.

"Jack."

He turned around to see Bryan making a beeline toward him.

"Did you hear?"

His shoulders tensed. "What now?"

"You've got a visitor in Interview Three." Bryan nodded toward a closed door. "And she does not look happy."

Jack looked at the closed door. Was Rowan here again?

"It's Joy Kendall," Bryan added. "She specifically asked for you and said it was urgent."

"Shit," Jack muttered.

"Isn't that the mother?"

"Birth mother, yeah."

"Well, what's she doing here? Why would she be involved now that we have the name?"

Jack didn't know, but he was about to find out.

"Let me talk to her alone," Jack said. "She's a little uncomfortable with detectives."

"Sure, whatever. Text if you need me to join."

Bryan headed back to his desk, and Jack walked over to the closed door. He took a moment to comb his hands through his hair, then tapped on the door with his knuckles before opening it.

Joy Kendall looked up from her phone. Her face morphed into a scowl, and Jack immediately knew Bryan was right. She was definitely pissed off.

"I want answers," she said flatly. "I'm not leaving here until you tell me what's going on."

"Ma'am?"

Her cheeks flushed, and Jack regretted the tactic.

"Don't pull that clueless crap with me. Sit down." She pointed to the empty chair in front of her. "I answered your questions, now it's your turn to answer mine. What did he do?"

Jack pulled the chair out and sat down, stalling for time. He looked Joy over. Today she wore a black cashmere sweater and tan suede boots that looked like they cost a fortune.

"Don't even think about lying to me," she said. "I saw the news conference this afternoon."

Jack scooted his chair in and leveled a look at her. "What exactly do you want to know?"

"William Anderson. My son." Her lips tightened and she glanced down at the table. Then she looked up at him again. "Is *he* the one you're looking for? The one who raped all those women and murdered someone in San Antonio?"

Jack just looked at her, wishing Rowan were here to help him navigate the conversation.

She leaned forward. "Answer me, Detective."

"Our investigation is ongoing—"

"Don't give me that—"

"I *am* investigating those cases," he interrupted. "And William Anderson is currently a person of interest. You're correct. But that information has not been made public."

The color in her cheeks faded, and she sat back in her chair.

"Shit," she whispered. Her eyes welled with tears, and she glanced down.

Jack watched her, caught off guard by her response. All that fury seemed to have evaporated.

"Shit," she said again, and looked up at him.

"That information is not public," he reiterated. "Do you understand? I'm not authorized to share that with you, and if you repeat it to anyone, it could compromise our investigation."

"So, you haven't found him yet?"

"No."

She looked down at her lap and bit her lip.

"Is there anything you know about him that might help us—"

"No." Her head snapped up. "Nothing like that, I was just . . . I was thinking, How is that possible? You're the police, right? Can't you just track him down digitally?"

"We're working on it," Jack said.

"I mean, someone tracks me down if I get a freaking *parking ticket* in another *state*. Don't you have databases and phone numbers and . . . and what about the FBI? Shouldn't they be involved if you're looking for a serial killer?"

"We're working on it," he said again.

She shook her head and looked away. "Sorry, I'm just . . . This is all very upsetting."

"You need to understand what I said about his name being confidential. It's critical that you not—"

"I won't tell anyone."

She pushed back her chair abruptly and stood. "He killed his parents, too. In their own house. You know that, right?" She hitched her purse onto her shoulder. "What am I saying? Of course you do." She reached for the door. "Thank you for meeting with me."

"I need to reiterate—"

"I *won't* tell anyone. Don't worry about me." She jerked open the door. "Just focus on finding him."

SEVENTEEN

Rowan watched in her rearview mirror as the black Jeep pulled up behind her and parked. She slid from her car, and nerves flitted in her stomach as Jack approached her.

"What happened to your face?" she asked, eyeing the scrape on his chin.

"Nothing."

"Nothing?"

"I tripped at a crime scene."

"What crime scene?"

"Don't worry about it."

He turned to look at the small gray bungalow where Dara rented an office. It was one of the many downtown houses that had been converted to commercial use.

"I'm surprised she works Sundays," Jack said, obviously changing the subject. But his evasiveness made Rowan only more curious.

"Dara keeps odd hours."

"How long has she been doing this?"

"About five years." Rowan turned to look at the house.

"This office space is new, though. She moved in here over the summer. I helped her move her stuff in." She looked at Jack. "Thanks for asking me to come."

"She's your contact. I figured you'd want to be here."

He gestured toward the sidewalk, and she walked ahead of him.

"Have you met her in person?" she asked.

"Not yet. I hired her over the phone. I filled her in on some basics, and she said she'd take it from there."

"Did you explain the case you're working on?"

"No. Just told her I needed a locate and that you recommended her."

"Well, did you tell her it was urgent at least?"

"I think she got the idea."

Rowan hiked up the wooden steps to the wide front porch. On either side of the door were clay flowerpots filled with wilted geraniums. She saw Jack noticing them.

"It's a shared workspace," Rowan said. "They're not real big on amenities."

Rowan opened the door, and they were greeted by an electronic bell as they stepped into a waiting room furnished with faux leather chairs.

Dara stuck her head out of an office down the hall.

"Oh, hey." She smiled. "You're here."

She stepped into the hall and strode over. Dara had a petite build and dark hair, and people sometimes mistook her and Rowan for sisters. Today she wore her typical hoodie, jeans, and combat boots.

"Detective Bruner." Dara thrust her hand out. "Nice to meet you." She turned to Rowan. "Glad you could come, too."

"Sure."

They exchanged a look loaded with communication. Rowan hadn't seen Dara since the start of her whirlwind romance with the software guy. And Dara had no doubt heard about Jack from Skyler and Lila.

"You guys want some coffee or anything?" Dara asked, motioning to the Keurig in the waiting room.

"No, thanks," Jack said.

"Rowan?"

"No."

"Come on back, then. I'll show you what I found."

They followed her down the hallway past a closed door, where a man could be heard talking on the phone. That would be the personal injury attorney, one of her two office mates. The other one was a female accountant.

"Forgive the mess," Dara said as they stepped into her office.

The room was spacious, but most of the area was taken up by an enormous desk made from an unfinished wooden door. On the desk were Dara's three computers—two notebooks and a desktop.

"I've been camped out here all day," Dara said, tossing a Starbucks cup into the trash. "I've got a report due to a client Monday morning."

"Thanks for making the time," Jack said, and Rowan caught the hint of sarcasm in his voice.

"Sure. Have a seat." She gestured to a pair of side chairs. Rowan took the seat closest to the door so Jack could have a better view of the computer screens.

"I have to tell you, this was a tough one," Dara said, sitting down at her desk. "This guy's really good. Too good, in fact."

"How do you mean?" Jack asked.

"Well, this guy's way beyond the techniques of your average Joe. It was clear from the start that he'd either hired a professional to help him—someone like me—or he'd had some sort of job that gave him special knowledge. Turned out, it was the latter."

"The call center." Jack looked at Rowan. "When he lived here, he was working at a twenty-four-hour call center for a credit card company."

"Precisely," Dara said. "Part of his job included taking calls from people who had been victims of credit card fraud and identity theft. I'm sure he heard every possible story from people whose purses or wallets had been stolen. I think he used that knowledge to help him execute his plan."

Rowan's stomach filled with dread.

"Also, he's very smart." Dara looked at Jack. "But I'm sure you're aware of that."

Jack didn't comment, but Rowan could see the tension in his face.

"It's not easy to disappear successfully," Dara said. "Assuming a new identity is difficult, and most people who try to do it have some compelling motivation. Often, they're on the run from the law or a spouse or someone they owe money to. But a key step that many people overlook is disinformation. It works best to lay a false trail so that when someone goes looking, they waste a lot of time and resources." She sighed. "I spent two full days following his bogus trail."

Rowan glanced at Jack, who looked impatient, and she knew he was eager for Dara to get to the bottom line.

"But let's back up," Dara said. "You mentioned his last known point of contact in town was his sister four years ago, so I started with her."

Jack's eyebrows arched. "You talked to her?"

"Of course."

"What did you—"

"Relax, I used a pretext," Dara said. "I said I was a friend of Will's from UT. I told her I'd just moved back to town and was looking to get in touch with some college friends."

"Did she buy it?" Rowan asked.

Dara shrugged. "Seemed to. She talked to me over the phone for a while. She said she hadn't heard from Will in four years and that they didn't keep up. She told me he moved west after their parents died."

"That's what she told me, too," Jack said. "She said the last time she saw him in person was when they went to the bank and deposited a check from the insurance claim."

"What insurance claim?" Rowan asked.

"The fire. The house was the bulk of their parents' estate, and Will got half," Jack said. "He was making regular withdrawals from his bank account for a while, but then he stopped. The last withdrawal from the account was three and a half years ago at an ATM machine in Bozeman, Montana."

"That fits with what she told me," Dara said. "She said Will called her from Montana four Christmases ago, and that was the last time she heard from him. And that's not the only clue that points to Montana." Dara turned to her computer and tapped the mouse. Her screen came to life, displaying a background image of a beach at sunset.

"Will Anderson filled out a lease application for an apartment in Missoula." Dara tapped the mouse and opened a document. It was a form filled with messy block print.

Jack leaned closer to see the screen. "How'd you get hold of this?"

"Another little pretext." Dara smiled. "But we don't need to talk about that. You can see he lists an employer here, University of Montana. He said he worked in food services on campus."

"So . . . he's been living in Missoula all this time?" Rowan asked. "Looks like he filled out this form in person."

"He did. I talked to the leasing office," Dara said. "He was up there. But he never occupied the apartment. And this employer—the university—says they never heard of him."

"Then why—"

"Disinformation," Dara told her. "The lease application generated a credit check in Missoula. He was laying groundwork here. Really, he put a lot of thought into this plan."

Rowan heard the admiration in Dara's voice.

"Missoula's not far from the border," Rowan said, looking at Jack, who seemed to be transfixed by the handwritten responses on the form.

"Yeah, but I think that's *another* instance of misdirection. I have no concrete evidence that he ever actually lived in Missoula. But if law enforcement were to go looking for him—say, hypothetically, because of a suspicious house fire in which two people died—they might conclude that he slipped into Canada to avoid police." Dara looked at Jack. "I assume he's wanted for questioning in that case, which is why you hired me?"

"That's part of it," Jack said.

Dara lifted an eyebrow, obviously intrigued by Jack's answer, and Rowan knew that at some point Dara was going to hit her up for the rest of the story about Anderson.

But Rowan wasn't going to be able to tell her anything. She wasn't at liberty to disclose details of the investigation.

"Here's the thing," Dara said, turning back to her computer. "This guy's good. I've done a lot of skip tracing— Ponzi scammers, insurance cheats, deadbeat dads. This guy is way more sophisticated than the people I normally deal with, and he's clever, too. But *still* he's human, which means he's prone to the top mistake that I see over and over."

"Which is?" Jack asked.

"People are creatures of habit," Dara said. "I mean, from a psychological standpoint, it's really hard to sever *all* ties in your life. Even when people want to wipe the slate clean and start over, it's really difficult to pull off. Old habits die hard."

Rowan looked at Jack, and she could see what he was thinking. *Habits like stalking. Rape. Murder.*

Dara tapped the mouse on her notebook computer, bringing yet another screen to life. The screen showed a criminal background check website and what looked like someone's driver's license photo.

"This is Gordon Reilly," Dara said. "Will Anderson's freshman roommate."

"I thought he dropped out his freshman year," Rowan said.

"He did," Dara replied. "But he was there five months, which was enough time for these two to get to know each other. So, I tracked this guy down—"

"How?" Jack asked.

"I can't disclose my methods, sorry," Dara said, not looking sorry at all. Rowan happened to know that some of her "methods" weren't strictly legal.

Dara used the mouse to enlarge the picture. "Anyway, this guy *also* said he hasn't seen Will in years. But he was a great source of info. He told me all about Will's hobbies, which include gaming. And his favorite food—tacos. And his favorite hangout his freshman year, which was a bar on Sixth Street where they accepted crappy fake IDs. And *that* was particularly interesting." Dara folded her arms over her chest. "Most college kids get fakes off the Internet. Not Will, though. This ex-roommate launched into a story about how Will swiped his off some guy who looked like him."

"He stole it?" Rowan asked.

"Yeah, and it was bold as hell, too." Dara looked at Jack. "My take is, this goes back to that whole thing with him working for the call center where people reported their stolen credit cards. According to this friend, Will went to a gym and waited in the parking lot until he saw a guy who resembled him and then *followed him home.* He snuck into the man's house while he was in the shower and stole his wallet."

Rowan looked at Jack.

"Pretty brazen, right? That's why Gordon Reilly remembers it," Dara said. "He said Will was always doing stuff like that, just walking into places, bold as hell."

"We think he has a history of burglary," Jack said.

He sounded composed, but Rowan could tell this info

about Will letting himself into houses had absolutely grabbed his interest.

"If you want to know my theory?" Dara said. "I think he did it again."

"Did what?" Rowan asked.

"Found someone who resembles him and stole an ID. He could be living under that stolen identity now, flying below the radar as much as possible, just using the driver's license as a backup whenever he has to present it for some reason, like buying booze or whatever. But I can tell you this—he's absolutely taking pains to keep his digital tracks covered. It's no wonder you've had trouble finding him."

Jack didn't comment.

"I've seen this sort of thing before, and often it entails a guy using a woman," Dara added. "He takes up with some-one, gains her trust, then starts using *her* identity to dodge the kind of digital footprint we leave when we have to do pretty much anything, from signing a lease to buying some-thing online. Any reason to believe he has a girlfriend?"

"Nothing concrete," Jack said. "But I see how it would help him."

"Anyway." Dara turned back to the screen. "That wasn't the most important thing I learned from this ex-roommate. I also learned that—as expected—Will Anderson is a crea-ture of habit. In this case, gaming. He couldn't stay away. Gordon told me he hasn't seen Will in years, but he crossed paths with him on Reddit."

Jack tensed beside her. "When?"

"Couple months ago. They were on a thread about *As-sassin's Creed*, which apparently Will has been playing for years. Gordon recognized his username and they ended up exchanging emails." She smiled again. "And when I heard that, it was—*boom!*—game over."

"Boom? Why?" Rowan asked.

"Because I got Gordon to forward me the actual email he received from him."

"What did it tell you?" Jack asked.

"A lot." Dara said, and her excitement was palpable. "I used the full email header to track down his IP. And using the IP, I was able to track down the server. And using the server, I was able to come up with a location."

Jack leaned closer. "You got a location?"

"The server traces back to the San Marcos Public Library."

"San Marcos, Texas? That's thirty minutes from here," Jack said.

Rowan shot him a look. "*And* thirty minutes from San Antonio."

"What's in San Antonio?" Dara asked.

"Nothing," Jack said. "When, exactly, was this email dated?"

"October ninth," Dara said. "That's when we know he was last at the library there using the computer. And I believe in all likelihood, he's living somewhere near there now under an alias. I realize what you really want is a *name*, but until I manage to get one, this is the next best thing."

BRYAN STUDIED THE map, enlarging the area around the restaurant.

Evie was right. Mario's Deep Dish Pizza was nowhere close to her new apartment near Zilker Park. So, why had someone put this flyer on her car?

WELCOME TO THE NEIGHBORHOOD.

Bryan opened up his phone and studied the screenshot he'd taken of the pizza flyer before sending it to the lab.

"Don't you have something better to do on a Sunday afternoon?"

He looked up to see Liz cutting through the bullpen.

"Thought you left already," Bryan said.

"Nope." She leaned on the wall of his cube and nodded at the map on his computer. "What're you looking at?"

"You ever been to Mario's Deep Dish?"

"The pizza place up on Burnet Road?"

"Yeah."

"I was there on a date once. Why?"

"Were they crowded?" he asked.

"Packed."

That jived with all the positive reviews he'd found on the restaurant's website.

"I'm trying to figure out why Mario's would be passing out coupons all the way across town near Zilker Park," Bryan said.

"Why do you care?"

He handed her his phone. "Evelyn Wood got that on her car."

Liz frowned down at the photo. "She gave this to you?"

"Yep. Along with the jewelry catalog showing the necklace that was stolen from her house the week before her attack."

"Who wrote this welcome message on here?" Liz asked.

"No idea. But it gave her the creeps, so she collected the flyer with a tissue and put it in a bag for me."

"Well, did you send it in for prints?"

"Yeah."

"And?"

"And nothing," Bryan said. "No prints whatsoever."

Liz's eyebrows arched. "You're kidding."

"Nope."

"The house where she was attacked is less than a mile from this pizza place," Liz said.

"I know."

Bryan held her gaze, and he could see her coming to the same conclusion he had. If—for some strange reason—a Mario's employee had been going around passing out flyers at a random apartment complex nowhere near the restaurant—wouldn't he have left fingerprints?

"Damn." Liz looked at the screen. "She moved, didn't she? Do you know where she's living now?"

"A low-rise over by Zilker Park."

"Doorman?"

"No. But there's keycard entry and security cams."

"Hmm."

They didn't say anything as they stared at the computer screen. If someone wanted to know Evelyn's new address, all he would have had to do was follow her from the house she'd just put up for sale over to her new place.

Would Will Anderson do that? Was he fixated enough on one of his past victims to start stalking her yet *again*? And why would he be focused on Evelyn if his new hunting ground was in San Antonio?

"This asshole is sick," Liz said. "After everything she's been through, now he's taunting her."

"That's my take, too."

"Never in my life have I wanted a collar this bad."

Bryan stared at the computer screen, thinking of Evie swinging her daughter in the air at that park Friday.

Jack walked into the bullpen, and the look on his face put Bryan on instant alert.

"Where's the L-T?" Jack asked.

"I don't know," Liz said. "Why? What happened?"

"We got a location."

EIGHTEEN

ROWAN WOULD HAVE liked to have been in Joy's cozy library again, but instead Joy had set them up at her kitchen table, where they'd spent the evening surrounded by legal pads, laptop computers, and cartons of food from Hunan House.

"Want the last spring roll?" Joy stood up and held out the carton.

"I'm stuffed."

Joy padded barefoot into the kitchen with her dogs trailing after her, probably hoping to get another handout.

Rowan and Joy had developed a surprisingly comfortable rapport over the last few hours. In her home with her husband out of town on a business trip, Joy seemed relaxed compared to the way she'd been that first day. If Rowan had met Joy in any other context, she highly doubted they would have hit it off. It wasn't like Rowan had much in common with a wealthy tech exec who lived in Pemberton Heights. And yet here she was.

"More LaCroix?" Joy called from the kitchen.

"Sure."

She came back with an open soda can and set it beside Rowan.

"Terrible article," Joy said, looking over Rowan's shoulder at the printout of the news story from the *Austin American-Statesman*. Rowan had found the printout in Joy's file. When she'd arrived this evening, she'd been surprised to discover Joy had been compiling research on Will Anderson and his adoptive family.

"Every time I look at that burned-out house, it makes me want to puke." Joy sank into the chair at the end of the table, and Rowan noticed she'd refilled her drink again—vodka cranberry, getting lighter and lighter on the cranberry. "Of all the crazy shit I've learned over the last few days, I think that's what's most disturbing."

"You know, they investigated the fire and ruled it an accident."

Joy lifted an eyebrow. "You believe that?"

Rowan slid the article back into the file folder, along with all the other chilling news stories. "Not really."

Joy looked at her for a long moment. This evening she wore a designer off-the-shoulder workout top and leggings. Even lounging around her house on a Sunday evening, she managed to look fashionable.

"How long have you lived in Austin?" Joy watched her over the rim of her glass as she took a sip.

"I was born here."

"A native. Well *that's* rare. Most of our population flocked here for the tech boom."

"I went to UT," Rowan added.

"Then you know all about WCR."

She nodded.

Joy pivoted her laptop toward Rowan and tapped the mouse. A news article appeared on the screen. WEST CAMPUS RAPIST ATTACKS AGAIN, read the headline. She must have had the story bookmarked.

"You know, back when all this was happening, I had insomnia," Joy said, staring at the screen.

"A lot of people did." Rowan didn't mention that those "people" included herself.

"I was living in a bungalow in Rosedale at the time. This is before I met Michael. I upgraded my security system, had new locks put in." Her ice cubes rattled as she sipped her drink. "I couldn't sleep. I was anxious at night, jumping at shadows all the time." She plunked her glass down. "Kind of like now, ironically. Just the other day, someone left the gate open, and my dog got out. I practically had a panic attack."

Rowan glanced down at the dogs. "Was he okay?"

"He was fine. Someone just left the gate open—probably our pool guy." She pinched the bridge of her nose. "But the point is, I'm a nervous wreck. This whole situation is bringing it all back, only worse now because I'm directly connected to it."

Rowan wasn't used to playing the therapist role, but she felt compelled to at least try. "You're having trouble sleeping again?"

"Nothing a little Ambien can't fix, but yeah." She opened the file folder Rowan had just closed and stared down at the photograph of the blackened shell that had once been the Andersons' home.

"I never met them in person but . . . I always imagined them to be the perfect young couple. So eager for a family that they adopted my son." The wistfulness in her voice made Rowan uneasy. Did she actually feel guilty over what happened?

"How long have you been doing this?" Joy asked. The wistfulness was gone now, replaced with her usual matter-of-fact tone.

"DNA work? Ever since I graduated," Rowan said. "I got my start working in a lab. The genealogy part is more recent."

Joy sat back in her chair, watching Rowan closely. "I want your professional opinion on something."

"All right."

"Do you believe evil is inherited?"

The question surprised her. They'd been focused on genetics and science, and this topic seemed much more philosophical.

"You're talking about the nature-versus-nurture debate," Rowan said, not quite sure how to answer.

"Sort of. I guess I'm wondering if there's a gene for it. Do you think it can be passed down from generation to generation like, say, red hair? Or male-pattern baldness? Can someone be *born* a predator?"

"I don't know, really," Rowan said. "There have been studies showing that particular genes affect impulse control and aggression. And although there is no 'psychopath gene,' certain genetic factors can make a person more prone to antisocial behavior. But upbringing matters, too. Abuse and neglect in childhood have been shown to play a role in violent behavior."

Joy tipped her head to the side, looking unsatisfied with this answer.

Was Joy thinking about her father?

She spoke somewhat neutrally about her mother, who lived in a nursing home in Sage Springs, where Joy grew up. But whenever Arnold Kendall's name came up, Joy's voice turned bitter. Rowan imagined Joy's father had been fairly authoritarian, the sort of man who would pull his teenage daughter out of high school after learning she was pregnant and banish her to live with her aunt.

Joy clearly had no fondness for her late father, which made Rowan wonder why she cared so much about his family tree. They'd spent the last few hours researching Joy's dad's side of the family and looking for online groups dedicated to the Kendall surname. It was a common name, and there were numerous surname projects. But Rowan still didn't really get Joy's fascination.

Joy's interest in her father's history was one of many things Rowan found curious, along with the fact that Joy only ever seemed to focus on this project when her husband was at work or out of town.

"Can I ask *you* something?"

Joy shrugged. "Sure."

Despite the shrug, Joy seemed to brace herself for the question.

"Have you told Michael about any of this?"

She didn't answer right away, and Rowan got the feeling she was about to be lied to.

"I did. After the third night of tossing and turning, he knew something was up with me, so I went ahead and told him."

"And how did he react?" Rowan asked.

"He was surprisingly sympathetic."

"Oh?"

"It was quite a relief, really." She sighed. "He has two teen daughters, and them getting pregnant in high school is his worst nightmare, so I guess that's why he was kind of sympathetic about it. But he doesn't know I'm pursuing all this." She gestured to the files and legal pads spread out across the table. "Michael's not close to his extended family, so he wouldn't understand why I'm suddenly so obsessed with mine."

"Are you?" Rowan asked. "Obsessed?"

"I hired you, didn't I?" She pushed her chair back. "Anything else to drink?"

"No, thanks."

"Why are you obsessed, if you don't mind my asking? You don't seem very close to your father's side."

"Curiosity, for the most part." She seemed to be choosing her words carefully. "And it's important to understand where you came from, don't you think?"

The words put a knot in Rowan's stomach.

"You know . . . you mentioned insomnia. And feeling

anxious," Rowan said. "Are you worried about him finding you?"

"*Him*, meaning my son?" Her voice had an edge to it, and Rowan knew she needed to tread carefully here. Joy was very sensitive when it came to William Anderson.

She topped off her drink again and returned to her chair.

"You know, the media made the link between WCR and the recent homicide in San Antonio," Rowan said. "They've reported that the investigation is active again, but they *haven't* reported what generated the new lead for police." She watched Joy's reaction. "The press isn't aware that investigators are using genetic genealogy, and I happen to know that that information is very closely guarded."

Joy's face remained blank, and Rowan couldn't tell whether Joy believed her.

"That fact may *never* come out," Rowan continued, hoping to reassure her. "Even after they apprehend him, it may never become public where the break in the case came from. Especially if investigators have loads of other evidence pointing to his guilt by that time."

"*If* they apprehend him."

Rowan's stomach knotted tighter. "You don't think they will?"

"One thing I've discovered about my adult son is that he's very clever. Very manipulative. It's a trait he gets from both sides." She crossed her arms. "And it's apparent he's been doing what he does for years now with total impunity, so he must be skilled at avoiding detection."

"So, you *don't* believe they'll find him," Rowan stated.

"Let's just say I'm not holding my breath."

JACK TEXTED HIS location to the team and then settled back to wait. This parking lot was probably another long shot, but Jack was going on seven hours here, so he figured, what the hell? He'd already made three separate loops past every apartment complex in town.

His phone buzzed in the cup holder, and his pulse picked up when he saw Rowan's number.

"Hey, there."

"How's the search going?" she asked, and just the sound of her voice improved his crappy mood.

"It's going."

She waited, probably hoping he'd elaborate, but he didn't.

"Where are you?" he asked.

"Just leaving Joy's house."

"Oh yeah?" He checked his watch. It was after nine. "This late?"

"We were making progress on her family tree. Time kind of got away from us."

Jack pictured Rowan in her little car, driving home in the freezing rain. He wished he could invite her over to his place to warm up by the fire. He'd never really used his fireplace, but Rowan would be a good reason to start.

"Where are *you*?" she asked.

"San Marcos."

"Still?"

"Yeah, things are dragging. I booked a room at the Lone Star Motor Lodge."

"Wow, sounds fancy."

"Free Wi-Fi and breakfast."

"So, are you there indefinitely?"

"Our team is, yeah. For the foreseeable future." He leaned back in his seat and propped his feet on the Igloo cooler he'd brought. It felt good to talk to her, even if it wasn't face-to-face. "We're doing shifts in the surveillance van."

"You must really believe he lives there." She paused. "All based on *one* email? Couldn't he have been traveling through town, just using the library?"

"We've had some corroboration," Jack said vaguely. He didn't want to get into how he'd shown Will Anderson's picture to several librarians, and one had recognized him. She said he'd been in numerous times to use the computers, although she hadn't seen him there lately.

"Corroboration? As in an actual sighting?"

"Something like that," he said. "So, tell me about Joy Kendall. Is she a nightmare to work for?"

"Why would you think that?"

"I don't know. She seems a little high-maintenance."

"That's man-code for you think she's a bitch."

"I didn't say that. She just strikes me as demanding."

"She's successful. What do you expect? I bet the successful detectives you know are demanding, too."

"Point taken."

"Anyway, she's feeling very conflicted at the moment," Rowan said. "She's got a lot of guilt."

"Why?"

"I think she feels partially responsible for what's happening."

Jack gritted his teeth. "There's only one person responsible for what's happening."

"Still, she feels guilty."

Jack could relate, sort of. Logically, he knew he wasn't responsible for William Anderson's latest crime spree. But the knowledge that with better, faster detective work, he might have prevented it continued to eat away at him like battery acid.

"Jack?"

"Yeah?"

"You seem tense."

"Yeah, well. Seven hours in a van will do that."

"Sounds miserable."

It was, but it would be more than worth it if this lead panned out.

"So, you and Joy are getting to be friends, I take it?" he asked her.

"Weirdly, yes, I guess you could say that. We don't have much in common, but I like her. She's got a strong personality."

"You think she knows more than she's telling us?"

"Like what?"

"I don't know," he said. "My radar's up with her. Every time I talk to her, I get the feeling she's being evasive."

"Well, maybe she doesn't want to bare her soul to a police detective. Especially the one who showed up at her door and turned her life upside down."

Quiet settled over them as Jack stared at the fast-food restaurant across the street. The drive-through line was busy with dinged-up economy cars, mostly belonging to college students, judging from the bumper stickers. He watched the people in the vehicles, looking for anyone who even vaguely resembled Will Anderson.

"I'm sorry you're stuck there," Rowan said. "But I guess I'm not, if you think you're making progress."

"We are. It's just tedious. I'm pretty drained, to be honest." He paused. "It's good to hear your voice, though."

No response. The silence stretched out.

"You there?"

"Yeah." She cleared her throat. "So . . . I've been thinking. When all this is over—"

Someone rapped on the door of the van, and Jack leaned forward. "Hang on." He glanced in the side mirror and saw Bryan standing in the street. Jack unlocked and slid open the door, letting in a waft of cold air.

"Holy *shit*, it's cold." Bryan climbed inside and sank into the empty bucket seat. He handed Jack a cardboard coffee cup.

"One sec," Jack told Rowan as he stuffed the drink into the cup holder and slid the door shut. "Bryan just got here."

"I'll let you go."

Jack shot a look at his partner. "I can call you back in a minute."

"No need. Just . . . let me know when you're back in town."

"I will."

"Night."

He hung up and stuffed his phone in his jacket pocket. *When all this is over . . .* What had she been about to say?

"It's fucking *freezing.*" Bryan peeled off the lid to his coffee and tore open a sugar packet. "Aren't you cold?"

"What's with the T-shirt? You know you can't run the heater in here."

Bryan watched him over the brim of his cup as he took a sip. "Hey, you're welcome for the coffee."

Jack sat back in his chair.

"Who was that?" Bryan asked.

"No one."

Bryan shook his head. Then he settled his cup in the holder and ducked his head to peer through the windshield at the Taco Bell across the street.

"Why this place?" Bryan asked.

Jack combed his hand through his hair and tried to shake off his frustration. "I heard he likes tacos."

"Any sightings?"

"No."

"You try grocery stores?"

"I've been by all of them and talked to the management. And I've been by all the big apartment complexes. There's sixty-five thousand people in this town. It's like a needle in a haystack." Jack checked his watch. "You're an hour early."

A sly smile spread across his partner's face, and Jack's pulse picked up.

"What is it?"

"I've got something." Bryan pulled out his cell phone. "You know I told you about the flyer that someone randomly stuck on Evie Wood's car?"

"*Evie* Wood's car?"

"Evelyn. Whatever. Check this out." Bryan swiped at his phone and handed it over to Jack.

"What's this?" Jack asked, staring down at a grainy black-and-white image of a row of cars parked along a street.

"Press play."

Jack pressed play on the video and watched as a figure walked into the frame and slid into a vehicle. A moment later, the taillights glowed, and the car pulled away from the curb. Jack's stomach clenched. He played the video again.

"It's him," Bryan said. "Look at the build."

Jack didn't comment, just hit replay. The guy resembled Will Anderson, it was true. They had the same body type and hair color.

"See?" Bryan asked.

"Hard to tell with the baseball cap."

"Come on. The height, the build, the hunched shoulders, like he's hiding his face. Who passes out flyers looking like that? I'm telling you, it's him."

Jack looked up. "Where'd you get this?"

"The convenience store on the corner. They have three security cams, one trained on the side street between them and Evelyn Wood's apartment building. *This* is the random guy who put that flyer on her vehicle. Here." He reached for the phone and pulled up a second video. Only this one was from a greater distance. But the same figure in a baseball cap and dark-colored jacket could be seen walking down the row of cars and tucking a flyer under the wiper blade of Evelyn Wood's white Toyota.

"See? Her car is the only one that gets a flyer. He's targeting *her*."

Jack glanced up, understanding now why Bryan was so excited.

"What's the date on this?"

"Six days ago." Bryan nodded at the phone. "I got lucky, too. The store manager said they only keep the footage one week back. If Evelyn hadn't given us that tip, this would be long gone."

"Go back to the car video. Is it possible to enlarge it and get a plate?"

"I tried. No dice. But you can see the make and model. We're looking for a black Honda Civic."

"This is good."

"I know." He smiled. "Our haystack just got smaller."

NINETEEN

Rowan was greeted again by the electronic bell as she
entered the office. This time it was one of Dara's office
mates who leaned her head out.

"May I help you?"

"Hi. Is Dara in?"

Dara stepped into the hallway. "Hey, what's up? Did I
forget a meeting?"

"Nope. Just stopping by. You have time for a break?"
Rowan held up a white paper bag and two coffee cups. "I
was at the vital records office, so I had to swing by the
Pastry Place."

Dara gasped as she walked over. "You didn't. Are those
cinnamon rolls?"

"Yep." She smiled at the accountant, who was watching
from her doorway. Jennifer? Jessica? Rowan could never
remember the woman's name. "I brought several. Would
you like one?"

"No, thanks. I'm doing no-carb January." She sighed
wistfully. "Y'all enjoy."

Dara led Rowan down the hall. Once again, she was in her typical jeans-hoodie-boots combo.

Dara glanced at Rowan over her shoulder. "You know what? Let's sit outside. It finally stopped raining."

They passed through the house's small kitchen, which had been converted to a break room, and stepped onto the covered back porch, where there was a patio table and a pair of mismatched chairs.

"I love this outdoor space you guys have," Rowan said, setting the pastry bag and the coffee cups on the table.

"Yeah, I sneak out here sometimes with my laptop when I need a break from my cave."

"Who smokes?" Rowan asked, gesturing at the flower-pot filled with sand and cigarette butts near the back steps.

"Jessica. Drives me crazy. But at least she does it out here."

They settled into chairs, and Rowan took a sip of her coffee as Dara unpacked two enormous cinnamon rolls.

"Oh my God. These are *so* sinful," Dara said, pinching off a corner and popping it into her mouth. "So, what's the occasion?"

"I hadn't talked to you in a while, and I wanted to hear about Nick."

A smile spread across Dara's face. "He's really great."

"So I hear. Skyler said you spent another weekend at his place?"

Dara grinned.

"I'm getting a nonstop-hot-sex vibe," Rowan said, smiling.

"Pretty much." She pinched off another bit of roll. "I mean, we talk a lot, too, but . . . the rest is amazing."

Rowan ignored the twinge of envy. Dara had been through a major low after her last breakup, and she deserved to be happy.

"So, when do I get to meet him?" Rowan asked.

"I'll bring him around sometime. He wants to meet you, too. I told him you guys are like my surrogate family."

Rowan watched Dara's giddy expression. "Are you being careful?"

"Careful?

"Like, did you check him out and everything?"

"Skyler told you to ask that, didn't she?"

"Maybe."

She rolled her eyes. "What the hell is with her? She's so paranoid!"

"We're just worried about you."

"Don't. Nick is *nothing* like Trevor."

Rowan watched her expression as she sipped her coffee.

"And anyway, yes, I checked him out. I'm not stupid. He has a computer science degree from UT. He's never been married. Never been arrested. He's smart and has a really good job." A sly smile spread across her face. "And when we're not working, it's nonstop sex, like you said."

Rowan smiled.

"But enough about me. How's *your* man?"

"He's not my *man*. We're just working together."

"Oh, BS. I saw the way he was with you."

Rowan took another sip. "What do you mean?"

"The way he looked at you when you two were here together."

Rowan didn't comment.

"Are you going to try and tell me you haven't even kissed him?" She studied Rowan's face. "See? I knew it. So, what's going on with you two?"

"I don't know, really. It's kind of up in the air."

Dara watched her closely, obviously hoping for more details.

"I like him but . . . he's a cop, so he basically lives and breathes his job."

"Well, then you have something in common. And speaking

of, tell Jack I'm still working on the alias for him. I spent some time on it this morning but didn't get anywhere. But I haven't given up yet."

Rowan felt relieved for the change of subject. She popped a chunk of cinnamon roll in her mouth. It was warm and spongy, and the brown sugar melted on her tongue.

"How's the investigation coming?" Dara asked.

"I don't know." She dusted the sugar off her fingers. "All I know is that they've shifted focus to San Marcos. Jack and his team have been there since Sunday."

"Doing what?"

"I'm not sure. I guess subtly flashing Anderson's picture around? Or staking out the library? I don't really know. Jack doesn't exactly share all the details with me."

Dara's expression turned serious. "I figured out what this is, you know."

"What do you mean?"

"I saw it on the news how they've linked the West Campus Rapist to that murder in San Antonio. That's what this is about, right? William Anderson is their suspect?"

"No comment."

"I can't believe *this* is the case you wanted my help with. It's all over the news! I assume you told Jack about Olivia?"

"No."

Dara looked surprised. "You didn't tell him your *friend* was one of WCR's first victims?"

"What does that have to do with anything?"

"Well, isn't that why you agreed to help him after telling everyone you were done with police work?"

"I don't know. Probably. But I might have done it anyway. He was pretty determined about getting my help." Rowan sipped her coffee. "He's very persuasive when he wants to be."

"I can imagine. So, are you thinking of going back now?"

"Back?"

"Police investigations. The stuff you were doing before."

"I'm really busy with my adoption work. My referrals are getting off the ground."

"Well, do you *want* to go back to it? Do you miss it?"

"No."

Dara's eyebrows arched.

"Well, maybe a little. I miss the helping-detectives part. I *don't* miss the stress and pressure of being immersed in violent cases. It's a lot—especially now."

"Why especially now?"

"Because things have really taken off, and now every police department in the country is dusting off their cold cases and looking for genealogists to get them new leads."

"That's great for you, right? You could do it like what you're doing now—as a consulting business—and be inundated with work."

"Yeah, that's what I'm afraid of. Being inundated. It was a nightmare—literally. I couldn't sleep, and when I did, I would dream about rapists and murderers. I was having anxiety attacks in parking garages."

Dara frowned. "I didn't know that."

"That's because I didn't talk about it. But I was a mess. Part of it was me not setting boundaries and never having the guts to say no to anything they heaped on my plate. But part of it was the work itself. I felt like I was drowning."

"How come you never said anything?"

"Because what's the point? Everyone's job is stressful."

"You should have told me. I at least could have commiserated."

"Forget it. It's in the past."

Dara looked worried, and Rowan checked her watch.

"Listen, I wish I could stay longer, but I need to run." Rowan stood up and grabbed her purse, and Dara stood, too. "Let me know when you're bringing Nick around. I'm dying to meet him."

"Thanks for the coffee break," Dara said.

"Thank *you*. I appreciate you spending part of your weekend doing that favor for Jack."

Dara leaned in and gave her a hug. "I didn't do it for *Jack*, dummy. I did it for you."

B RYAN GLANCED UP and down the quiet street as he approached the utility van. It was parked beside an easement, which helped, but it had been here all day, and at some point, someone in the neighborhood was bound to get suspicious. He tapped his knuckles on the ice-cold door, and a moment later, it slid open.

"Hey," Bryan said, climbing inside. Once again, it felt like a freezer on wheels. But he'd come prepared this time in a thick sweatshirt.

"Anything new?" Jack asked.

"Nope."

"What's the word from Heidi?"

Bryan settled into the empty bucket seat and looked Jack over. Today his partner wore a black short-sleeved T-shirt, despite the cold, and his hair was mussed, as though he'd run his hand through it a couple hundred times. He had a pair of military-grade binoculars looped around his neck.

"Aren't you cold, man?" Bryan asked.

"I'm trying to stay awake."

Bryan flipped open the cooler and grabbed a Red Bull. "Heidi didn't have any updates."

Jack cursed.

The excitement over Bryan's black Honda Civic lead had mostly fizzled as research revealed twenty-nine black Civics registered within the county. And that didn't include the ones belonging to university students, whose cars were probably registered elsewhere. The task force had divided into two separate teams to stake out the most promising prospects. One was a vehicle registered to a thirty-six-year-old male on the west side of town. The logic there was that it might be Anderson living under an assumed name.

But Jack believed this location was the better lead.

Bryan popped open the drink and took a swig.

"How are things going here?" he asked.

"Slow. No sightings."

He caught the tension in Jack's voice and guessed that he was rethinking his insistence on prioritizing this address. The Honda owner at this location was a woman. But she was thirty-eight—close enough to Anderson's age to be a potential girlfriend.

The real kicker, though, was that her car had previously been registered in Bozeman, Montana.

Coincidence?

Jack didn't think so. He'd been so pumped about the link to one of Anderson's last known locations that he'd insisted on staking this address out himself.

"Here," Jack said, unlooping the binoculars from his neck. "Take a look."

Bryan adjusted the lenses and peered through the windshield at the small duplex two doors down. Sheryl Mason's black sedan was parked in the driveway. It did, in fact, look like the car Bryan had seen near Evie's apartment in the grainy surveillance video.

But that wasn't exactly conclusive without the plate to compare them.

"What do we have on her so far?" Bryan asked, knowing Jack had spent part of his long shift here in the van digging up background on this woman.

"She's thirty-eight, divorced, no kids." Jack consulted a spiral notebook perched on another cooler that served as a table for his notebook computer. "Grew up in Montana. Moved here fourteen months ago."

"Fourteen months?"

"Yep."

Bryan studied the duplex through the binoculars. The place was a dump. The neighboring driveway had an ancient Pontiac up on blocks, and both yards were surrounded by a chain-link fence.

"If we assumed they moved down from Montana together, then he was here a full year before starting up again." Bryan lowered the binoculars. "What do you think that's about?"

"Hell if I know. Maybe something triggered him, like Skinner said. He could have gotten fired. Rejected by a woman. Maybe he's having trouble getting it up."

Bryan lifted the binoculars and studied the house again. "What's she do for a living?"

"No idea. No one's left the house since I've been watching."

"And we're sure there's someone in there with her?"

"No. But there are two TVs on."

Bryan looked at Jack.

"I did a walk-by two hours ago," Jack said.

"If he sees you, we're screwed."

"No one saw me. What I'd really like to do is get a look in the windows."

Bryan lifted the binoculars again. "They have a dog?"

"A Rottweiler."

"You're kidding."

"Nope."

Bryan sighed, lowering the binoculars. Approaching the windows was out. A dog like that would go apeshit.

"We have to wait for someone to leave," Bryan said.

"I know."

"Forget collecting a DNA sample, if we don't even have a *sighting* of someone who fits Anderson's description, this is a giant waste of time."

"No shit," Jack said, and the bitterness in his voice told Bryan just how tense he was after an eight-hour shift that had produced no new leads. For *either* team. It was possible neither of their teams was focused on the right black Honda.

Bottom line, surveillance work was miserable. And that was *knowing* you were watching the right target. If you didn't even know that, then it was an absolute suckfest. After getting this great new lead, Bryan was starting to feel deflated again.

He thought of Evie in the park with her daughter, and he got a sour ball in the pit of his stomach. It had been two and a half months since her attack, and more than two weeks since Amber Novak's murder, and still they hadn't even managed to locate their prime suspect, much less collect a DNA sample and secure an arrest warrant.

"I fucking hate this," Jack said, rubbing the back of his neck.

"I know."

"I'm tempted to go pound on the front door and see who answers."

Bryan's phone vibrated, and he dug it out of his pocket.

"Heidi," he told Jack as he connected the call. "Hey, what's up?"

"We've got a development."

"Are you still at the apartment on Orchard?" Bryan asked.

"Yeah, but the development isn't here. It's the Honda registered to the sixty-eight-year-old male on Carpenter Street."

"Here, I'm putting you on speaker. I'm in the van with Jack. His shift's almost over." Bryan put the phone on speaker and set it on top of the cooler.

"Heidi, what's up?" Jack asked.

"New info on the Honda registered over on Carpenter Street," Heidi repeated.

"The owner is sixty-eight," Jack said, and Bryan wasn't surprised that he'd memorized the details of every damn lead they had going.

"Actually, he's dead."

Jack looked at Bryan. "Dead?"

"Yeah, Liz discovered that when she ran his background. And get this, he's got a son who is forty-two, but his driver's license is showing a Houston address. So, I'm thinking a couple of possibilities. One, the son moved here from Houston, has possession of his dad's car, and hasn't updated his driver's license with his new address yet. Or maybe the son *sold* his dad's vehicle, and whoever he sold it to hadn't transferred the registration for whatever reason."

Jack looked at Bryan. "The Carpenter address, that's a house near the campus, right?"

"Yeah. I left Liz at the other place, and I just did a drive-by. It's a one-story brick with an attached garage. The car's parked in the driveway. I just saw it. The house is owned by someone in Florida, and I think it's a rental property."

"Any sign of a dog on the premises?" Jack asked.

"No."

"Any lights on inside?"

"Yeah. Someone's definitely home." She paused. "What are you thinking?"

Bryan knew exactly what Jack was thinking. He wanted to scope out this rental house with the Honda and try and see if he could get eyes on Anderson.

"Where'd you park the unmarked unit?" Jack asked Bryan.

"Two streets over, right beside the dog park."

"Jack?" Heidi said. "I thought your shift was ending?"

"Not yet," he said. "I'm heading your way."

ROWAN PULLED INTO the parking lot and eyed the neon VACANCY sign. Besides having a pint-size swimming pool, the Lone Star Motor Lodge on I-35 offered free parking and an on-site laundromat. Rowan couldn't imagine why they weren't booked solid.

The sight of the black Jeep Wrangler made her nerves

flutter. Jack was here. Or at least, his car was. It was parked in front of room 116.

Where a light glowed behind the curtain.

Rowan pulled into an empty space in the middle of the lot and cut the engine. She'd come here on impulse, much like the day she had walked into the police station. One minute she'd been skimming news on her computer, and the next minute she was in her car. It wasn't until she was twenty minutes down the highway that she started to question the wisdom of showing up here and interrupting his work.

She grabbed the printout off her passenger seat. It was still raining lightly, so she folded the paper in half and tucked it into her purse before getting out. She glanced around the parking lot, then jogged across the wet asphalt and strode up the sidewalk to room 116.

She took a deep breath and knocked.

Her shoulders tensed as she waited. The muffled sounds of a basketball game could be heard from the TV in the neighboring room. But 116 was silent. On the interstate behind her, an eighteen-wheeler blew its horn as it sped by.

Shivering, she pulled the sides of her coat together and glanced back at the Jeep. Then she knocked again, louder.

TWENTY

"So, now we're down to one?" Bryan asked over the phone.

"I'll go through the list again." Jack ran the towel over his wet hair and then tossed it beside the sink. "Maybe there's something we missed."

"How? We ran down every black Civic in town."

Jack held the phone against his shoulder with his chin as he zipped his jeans. "I'll try the university. They issue parking permits, so presumably they have a list of vehicles."

A knock sounded at the door.

"What good will that do?" Bryan asked. "Unless he's got a girlfriend who happens to be a university student from out of town and he's using her vehicle."

"Hang on. Someone's banging on my door."

"That seems like a long shot," Bryan continued.

"Can't hurt to try."

"Well, you want me to do it? You're on at six in the morning."

Jack opened the door, and Rowan was standing there in

her puffy blue jacket. A jolt of fear went through him. What the hell was she doing here?

"Jack? Hello?"

"Let me call you later." He disconnected the phone.

"Hi." Rowan gave him a nervous smile. "Bad time? I wanted to catch you before your shift starts."

"I just got back." He paused, waiting for her to drop some bomb on him. "Everything okay?"

"Yeah."

She gazed up at him, looking uneasy.

"I was about to go get some food before they close," he said. "You want to come?"

Her eyes dropped to his bare chest, and she hesitated.

"Sure, okay."

He turned and glanced around the messy room. His clothes were everywhere, and he had case files scattered across the nearest bed. He'd told housekeeping to stay away, and the second bed was still unmade from last night.

"Come on in," he said, scooping crime scene photos and reports into a pile and sliding everything into a folder. He grabbed a black T-shirt off the chair and pulled it over his head. Then he shoved his feet into his wet hiking boots and bent down to tie the laces.

"What happened to your arm?" she asked, eyeing his bandage as she stood in the doorway.

He buckled on his holster, then grabbed his leather jacket and shrugged it on.

"I got a few stitches." Ushering her outside, he put the **PRIVACY** sign on the door and pulled it shut with a firm *click*.

"Why did you need stitches?"

He glanced across the rain-slicked parking lot and was relieved to see the **OPEN** sign in the window of the diner next door.

Rowan watched him with a worried look as they started across the parking lot.

"Anderson nicked me."

She stopped in her tracks. "*Anderson?* As in William?"

He touched her arm to get her moving again. "We had an altercation at a crime scene. Or the woods behind a crime scene, I should say."

"He *attacked* you?"

Her voice was pure outrage, and he took her hand. "I'm fine."

"When did this happen? Was this the scrape on your face, too? Why didn't you tell me?"

They approached the diner, and he dropped her hand to open the door. His server from the previous night was behind the register ringing up a customer, and he could tell she wasn't thrilled to see him fifteen minutes before closing. He held up two fingers and pointed at the circular booth he'd occupied yesterday. She handed him a pair of menus and went back to making change.

Jack led Rowan to the curved booth, and she scooted in first. He slid in behind her.

He combed his hand through his hair as he surveyed the nearly empty restaurant. He was tired, famished, and his back was in knots. And he could have used a stiff drink, but they didn't serve alcohol here.

"Jack?"

Rowan stared at him, her deep blue eyes filled with concern.

"I'm fine." He slid a menu in front of her. "Let's order before they shut the kitchen down."

The server came over and set two plastic cups of water in front of them. Strands of gray hair had come loose from her bun, and she looked like she'd had a long night.

"What would you like?" Jack asked Rowan.

"Nothing. I had dinner already."

"Come on. You can't just watch me eat."

She sighed and flipped her menu over. "I'll have a chocolate milkshake, please."

The server looked at Jack. "And for you?"

"A chocolate shake for me, too," he said. "And a club sandwich. Chips, not fries."

She jotted it down and walked off.

Rowan was still watching him, clearly expecting an explanation now that they were alone in the privacy of the booth.

"I can't discuss details of an ongoing investigation," he said. "You know that."

She thrust her chin forward, clearly not happy.

"Can I ask you *one* question, at least? Just say yes or no."

He nodded.

"Have you located him?"

"We're working on it."

Heidi's new lead had been a dead end. Jack had gone to the house on Carpenter and managed to sneak up to the window, and the guy in the living room watching TV was definitely not Will Anderson. So they were back to the female Honda owner Jack had been surveilling all day.

Unless they could come up with another black Civic here in town that they didn't yet know about.

Rowan stripped off her coat and set it on the seat beside her. She wore a snug-fitting gray sweater underneath, and Jack turned his attention to the restaurant so he wouldn't stare at her.

His phone buzzed as a text landed, and he took a few moments to read a message from Bryan. He was going to take the lead on checking with the university for any black Civics belonging to students who had campus parking passes. Jack knew it was a long shot, but they were running out of leads. He texted him a response and put his phone away.

Jack looked up, and Rowan was watching him.

"You seem uptight. I take it that means it's not going well," she said, still determined to elicit some kernel of information from him.

"It's okay. I'm just pretty whipped. What's up with you? I'm glad you came."

"Why?"

"It's good to see you," he said, and she had no idea what an understatement that was. Seeing her, talking to her, just sitting *near* her was the best he'd felt in days.

What the hell was he doing here? He was in a damn diner with her when just minutes ago he'd had her alone in his motel room.

"Jack?" She looked up at him expectantly. She'd asked him something, and he hadn't been listening.

"Yeah?"

"I said, did you see the thing in the *Statesman*?"

"The thing?"

Her gaze narrowed. "You really are whipped, aren't you? When was the last time you slept?"

"I got a few hours last night."

She looked worried again.

"So, you were saying? About the *Statesman*?"

"They ran an article you need to read. It was in this morning's edition, but I didn't see it until tonight when I was surfing around."

The server was back in record time with Jack's sandwich and a pair of red plastic glasses filled to the brim.

"Thank you," he said.

"Anything else?" she asked pointedly.

"We're all set."

She walked away, and Jack turned to watch Rowan dip into her milkshake with a long teaspoon. He loved that she'd ordered a chocolate shake.

"What?" she asked.

He leaned over and kissed the top of her head.

She looked startled, and her cheeks turned adorably pink.

"You were saying?" He picked up his sandwich. "There was an article?"

He chomped into his food as she turned and dug a folded printout out of her purse. She put it on the table and smoothed it flat.

"I hate to be the bearer of bad news, but I came across this article. Or it's a brief, really. Round Rock is reopening the investigation of the house fire five years ago. It says 'new evidence has come to light,' but it doesn't specify what."

She slid the paper toward him, and he leaned over to skim the two-paragraph brief as he chewed his food.

"Is this a problem for you?" she asked.

"It's not good."

"I'm worried *he* might see it. What if he hears about this and then decides to leave? He'll be in the wind again, and all Dara's work will be for nothing."

Jack continued eating as he reread the brief. It didn't have a byline, but he knew someone over at the paper he could call to find out more. Or he could call the retired Round Rock fire chief and see what he knew about it.

"Have you heard from her? Dara?" Rowan slipped a bite of ice cream off her spoon.

"No."

"She told me she's still trying to get an alias for you."

"Let's not talk about the case." He popped a chip into his mouth. "Have you given any thought to that other thing?"

She paused. "Your cold case, you mean? Ramon Huerta?"

"Yeah."

She went quiet for a moment, poking at her shake. "I'm considering it."

"Good."

She gave him a wary look. "What, no hard sell?"

"You said you're considering it. I don't want you to feel pressured."

"Well, I do." She stirred her shake, not looking at him. "Police work, investigations—it's the whole path I'd pur-posely gotten off of."

"I understand. If you can't do it, you can't do it."

Hostility flared in her eyes. "It's not that I *can't*."

The server was back, setting the check in the middle of the table with all the subtlety of a bullhorn.

"Obviously, I can. I'm trying to decide whether I want to get back into this work now."

"If you decide no, it's okay," he said. "You're not the only one who can help me. I just wanted to try you first because you're the best."

She rolled her eyes at the compliment. She was obviously well aware he was using flattery to help his chances. Well, so what? He'd be an idiot not to, and anyway, it was true. He'd never seen anyone with her talent for both the science side and the genealogy side of this work. It was a unique combination that made her extremely good at it.

The conversation dwindled as he finished off his sandwich. He pushed the plate aside and pulled the shake toward him. As he took a big gulp, she snickered.

"What?"

"You put that whole sandwich away in what?" She checked her watch. "Ten minutes?"

"These people want to go home."

She dipped her teaspoon back into her cup, and he smiled as he watched her.

"You're very ladylike with that," he said. "My mom would approve."

"Ladylike. There's a term I haven't heard in a while."

"It's one of my mom's favorites. She was always after my sister to be 'ladylike,' but she was a committed tomboy." He watched her as she scooped another delicate bite. "Do you have any siblings?"

"Two sisters."

"Oh yeah? Are you guys close?"

"Not really. My family's not very close-knit. My parents divorced when I was fourteen."

There was something in her tone, and he studied her expression, curious about the family she rarely talked about. He sensed there was a story there, but she kept her guard up. Still. He wanted her to trust him, but he was going to have to be patient.

She set her spoon down and looked at him.

"What?" She dabbed her mouth with the napkin. "Do I have chocolate on me?"

"No."

The moment stretched out, and he resisted the urge to kiss her again. He didn't know what was up with him tonight. He wasn't one for public displays, and definitely not in a greasy spoon diner.

Jack glanced around. The place had emptied. They'd even turned off the elevator music, and he could hear dishes clattering in the kitchen.

"Come on." He left a tip on the table and grabbed the check. "Let's let these people get home."

He stopped at the register to pay and then joined Rowan at the door.

"Thanks for the milkshake," she said.

He looked out the window. "Damn, it's raining again."

"It's *pouring*," she said, zipping her jacket and peering outside.

He opened the door, and she stepped into the downpour. He followed her out, then grabbed her hand and pulled her beneath the overhang.

"Stay with me," he said.

Her eyebrows tipped up.

"Stay with me and wait this out."

She stared up at him, and the spark in her eyes told him she was tempted.

He leaned down and kissed her. Her mouth was soft, like before, and also cool and chocolaty. He slid his arms around her and pulled her against him. Her body felt stiff at first, but he eased his hands into her hair and kept kissing her, trying to convince her, doing everything he could to keep her from overthinking it.

She pulled back and blinked up at him, her eyes dark and luminous, and he held his breath as he waited for an answer.

He took her hand and squeezed it. She nodded.

Jack smiled and pulled her into the rain.

TWENTY-ONE

H E GRIPPED HER hand as they dashed across the parking lot, getting soaked to the skin in a matter of seconds. She jumped over a puddle onto the sidewalk and then crashed into him as he stopped in front of the door.

"*Shit*," he said as the keycard dropped to the ground.

"Sorry." She bent down to scoop it up and bumped heads with him. "*Sorry!*"

He stood up, cursing and fumbling with the key as they both tried to duck under the overhang, but the water was sluicing off it in sheets, falling right on their backs. It poured down the neck of Rowan's jacket in an icy rush.

"*Hurry!*" she squeaked.

"I am."

The door whisked open, and she stumbled inside with him right behind her.

"Oh my God." She brushed water off the front of her jacket. "I'm *saturated*. How did—"

He caught her arm and pulled her against him, crushing

his mouth down on hers, and she let out a little yelp as his wet hands snaked up under her sweater.

His fingers were cold, but she pressed herself against him, loving the heat of his mouth and the solid feel of his chest. She squirmed out of his embrace long enough to slide her hands under his shirt, too, and he jumped back.

"You're *freezing*," he said, and then kissed her again as she slid her hands around his waist.

She was trembling all over—only partly from the cold—and his body felt warm and solid.

"Rowan."

"Hmm?" She kept kissing him, afraid if she stopped, she'd think this through and come to the conclusion that it wasn't a good idea. It wasn't. She knew that. But her hands on his skin *felt* good, and the same for his fingers dipping into the back of her jeans.

She kissed him harder, pressing as close as she could, trying to fuse their bodies together through their thick, wet clothes.

And then his hands were under her sweater again. The clasp of her bra came loose, and she felt a surge of lust and nerves and anticipation, all rolled into one heady adrenaline rush.

He pulled back. "Let's get this off," he said, setting his hands on her zipper and yanking it down. She wrestled out of her coat, then tossed it aside as he shrugged out of his jacket and flung it on the chair. And then he pulled her against him again, and everything was warmer and drier, and she flattened herself against the firm wall of his chest.

A waft of cool air swept over her as he tugged her sweater up. She lifted her arms, and he had her sweater and bra off in one quick motion. His gaze heated as he looked at her bare breasts and she instinctively brought her arms up, but he pushed them down smoothly as he pulled her back for a kiss.

"Don't. I want to see you," he said, and his breath was hot against her skin as he made his way down her neck and over her collarbone. He backed her against the wall, and she felt the cool smoothness behind her shoulders as his hot mouth settled on her nipple.

She stroked her fingers into his hair and watched as he kissed one breast and cupped the other with his big hand. He felt so good, everything he was doing, and she couldn't believe she was here with him. Eyes half closed, she glanced around the room, vaguely registering the clutter everywhere— files and papers and fast-food cups. This room where he'd spent the last two days immersed in his work was a stark reminder that he was a detective, and that fact permeated everything he did. The thought needled her, along with the nagging possibility that she might be rushing into this, and maybe she should put the brakes on.

He pulled away, breathing hard, and looked at her. "What is it?"

"Huh?"

He cupped his hand against the side of her face. "You all right?"

"Yeah."

He feathered her hair away from her eyes. "You sure?" He kissed her forehead, then her temple, and the sweetness of it made her heart ache. "You got really still there for a second."

His skin smelled wonderful, all warm and masculine, and she leaned her cheek against his biceps as he kissed the side of her neck.

"I'm good." Enough with her stupid thoughts and her stupid caution. She wanted him to touch her. She wanted his hands and his mouth on her, and she was sick of being cautious about every damn thing in her life.

She pulled his head down and kissed him, taking charge of it now and showing him exactly how determined she was to do this now, no distractions. She gripped the waistband of his jeans and felt for his belt buckle. His hand clamped around her wrist.

"Hold on." He kissed her forehead and then stepped back, leaving her standing there half undressed as he turned to unfasten his holster and put it on the dresser. Next came his wallet and keys. As he crouched down to deal with his boots, she reached for the light switch and plunged the room into darkness, leaving only a narrow wedge of white coming from the bathroom.

Then he was kissing her again, and the heat of his bare skin directly against her breasts was electrifying. She slid her fingers into his hair, kissing him deeply as his hands dipped into her jeans again. And then she felt her button loosen and heard the soft rasp of her zipper. He knelt in front of her, unzipping her ankle boots. One by one, he took them off and set them aside, then peeled off her socks, and the whole time she stared down at his dark head as butterflies swarmed inside of her. Then his hands were on her waist, and she felt her damp jeans easing down her legs. She was dizzy, off balance, like she'd been drinking, but she hadn't had a drop of anything, so maybe it was nerves. She rested her hands on his shoulders as she stepped out of her jeans, and the only thing left was a thin bit of satin.

She glanced back at the rumpled bed and kneeled on it as he dropped a condom onto the nightstand. Nerves fluttered inside her, and she looked up at him, trying to read his expression. It was too dark, but she could feel the intensity emanating from him as he stepped over to her.

She scooted to the edge of the bed and traced her fingertips over his chest and his arms, pausing as she reached the white bandage on his forearm. He eased her back and rested his palm behind her, making the mattress squeak as he shifted his weight to his knee and leaned over her.

She touched his bandage lightly. "Are you ever going to tell me about this?"

"No."

He kissed her, settling his weight beside her as he slid her panties off with one smooth motion—a distraction that definitely worked. Then he flattened his hand on her stomach.

"You're shaking," he whispered, kissing her neck.

"I'm cold."

That was a lie, and he knew it, but she didn't want to talk about the nerves that had invaded her body like aliens for some reason. She'd thought about this for weeks, day-dreamed about it, fantasized. But the reality was much more intense than she'd ever imagined, and she knew she was in over her head here. To him, this was a break from his work, a distraction from the tedium. To her, this was . . . something else. Everything was happening too fast to figure it out.

He leaned closer and kissed her as his palm glided, feather-soft, over her skin. Every place he touched tingled, and he stroked his hand lower, grazing her pelvis on the way to her thighs, then her knees, then back up again. It was tickling and arousing and maddening all at once. She arched against him, telling him what she wanted, and then his fingers slid between her legs and the whole world became a bright blur of pleasure.

"You feel good," he said against her temple, and she would have responded, but her ability to form words was gone. There was nothing except his hands and his mouth and the hot, perfect fire he was stoking inside her. She couldn't form a thought about anything besides him, and she gripped his arm, torn between wanting to lose herself and wanting to wait.

"Jack."

"Just go with it."

How did he read her mind like that?

His breath tickled her ear. "It's okay."

"Not yet."

She reached for his jeans and fumbled with the snap and the zipper. He pulled away, laughing quietly as he got up and made quick work of the rest of his clothes.

He planted his knee on the bed and eased her back, hovering over her as he tore open the condom and got it on. He slid her legs apart, and she braced herself as he positioned himself and entered her with a sharp push that made her gasp.

He started to pull back, but she gripped his hips, keeping him anchored.

"No, it's good," she said.

She wrapped her legs around him, and he surged into her, deeper this time, and then she leaned her head back, letting him set the rhythm between them as sensations washed over her. She slid her hands down his back, his hips, pulling him closer as the tension built. His skin was slick and hot, and she ran her nails down his back as she tried to hold on and control it. And then it was too strong, too fast, too much. She broke apart, holding on to him as she gasped his name. He kept going, driving into her, and then he climaxed hard, pinning her with his weight.

She stayed wrapped around him, trying to lock the feeling in place for as long as she could. And then she let her arms and her body go lax. She kept her eyes closed as he pushed himself up on his hands. A moment later he rolled onto his back and groaned.

Rowan sighed blissfully. The bed creaked, and a few seconds later, she heard water running. A moment passed and then he was shuffling with something on the dresser. God, was he checking his phone? A little dart landed in her chest, and she kept her eyes clamped shut because she didn't want to know.

A second later the mattress creaked again as he slid into bed.

"Hey."

She opened her eyes as he leaned over her, propping his weight on his elbow.

"Are you asleep already?"

"Asleep? No." She smiled up at him. "Just momentarily paralyzed."

His eyebrows arched.

She turned into him, nuzzling her head against his chest. She loved the way he smelled, and his skin was damp from exertion.

Quiet settled over them. No more talk. There was just the din of someone's television through the thin wall and the faint sound of trucks on the interstate.

She sighed. "Is it still raining?"

"No."

He slid his arm under her shoulder and rolled her closer.

"I need to go," she said.

"Why?"

His thumb stroked down her arm and up again, and she wanted to purr like a cat. The way he touched her was so natural, and she felt her muscles loosening, all that tension she'd been carrying seeping away.

"It stopped raining," she murmured.

"So?"

"So . . . you have to work."

He didn't say anything, and she knew that he did. Rowan inhaled the scent of him—earthy and musky. She nestled closer, and his warm hand settled on her hip.

She turned and glanced at the clock behind her. She sighed again. She scooted closer and closed her eyes, blocking out the clock and the noise and everything else she didn't want to think about.

"Just one more minute," she said, and then she was fast asleep.

TWENTY-TWO

J OY EYED HER computer on the breakfast table as she walked into the kitchen. She'd checked already. But that was an hour ago.

She sank into the chair. She was becoming obsessed, she knew, but Michael would be home tomorrow, and she'd have to be sneaky about everything again. She tapped the mouse and brought the screen to life, then opened her newly created email account and checked the inbox.

Still nothing.

Scritch-scratch.

She got up and went to the back door, peering warily out at the darkness before undoing the lock. Of course the second Sam stepped outside, Frodo wanted to go, too. She closed the door behind them and flipped the bolt.

Casting a glance at her computer screen, she walked to the refrigerator and freshened her drink. She was almost out of cranberry juice. Not that it really mattered, but she needed to remember to swing by the store and get more before Michael came home. He paid attention to details like how fast she went through the mixers.

Joy returned to the table and sat down again. Drumming her fingernails on the wood, she contemplated her empty inbox. She pulled the legal pad closer and reviewed Rowan's instructions about surname projects. She'd taken all the steps Rowan had shown her, and in the same exact order. She had visited relevant websites, and answered the questionnaires, and provided her contact information. That was twenty-four hours ago, and Joy hadn't received a single response. Not one. What was up with that? These genealogy people were supposed to be *engaged*. Rowan had said so. She'd said even the ones who called themselves "hobbyists" were extremely active with these online groups.

Joy clicked onto one of her bookmarked ancestry sites. The home screen showed a smiling white-haired grandmother and a middle-aged woman who was probably meant to be her daughter gathered around a tablet, talking to long-lost relatives on a video chat.

How very *cozy*. And quaint. How heartwarming it must be to gather around a device invented by one of the world's most notoriously shitty fathers and communicate with your newfound family across the pond.

Joy took a gulp of her drink and set the glass down.

The dogs scratched at the door, and she got up to let them in.

"Sammy? Where's your brother?"

A *ping* from the table had her whirling around. She hurried back to her chair and clicked out of the website so she could see her inbox.

Re: Hoping to get in touch!

Joy tapped open the email and skimmed it.

Dear Jill,

Already, she could tell he was a generation older.

How lovely to hear from a future member of the
Leary family. Congratulations on your upcoming
nuptials . . .

She skimmed the pleasantries and scrolled to the end,
where at last he addressed her question.

Yes, my project has become quite involved, as you have
surely deduced from my many threads in the chat room.
I know some might find it tedious, but this study of the
Leary line truly fascinates me. I have managed to locate
and initiate contact with four distant cousins, as well as
locate an entirely NEW branch of the family back in
Kilkenny, Ireland . . .

Joy scrolled back to the top and reread carefully. Then
she consulted the family tree she had created on her legal pad.

"Damn it."

He still hadn't answered her question, but he'd come
close. Should she respond to him right now and get more
specific, or should she wait?

If she replied now, he'd know she was sitting here at her
computer in the middle of the night. This guy was in San
Francisco, so for him, it wasn't that odd to be answering
emails at this hour. But he knew she was in Texas.

On the other hand, if she waited until tomorrow, he
might take several days getting back to her, and she didn't
think she could wait that long. Her nerves were frayed as it
was. If she had to go through another workday with this
question hanging over head—

"Screw it." She hit reply.

Hi Randall,

So great to hear from you. Thanks for the congratulations!
It's such an honor to "meet" another cousin of Matt's via
email. I feel so grateful to be joining such a big,
welcoming family!!

   One question. You mentioned that you have been in
touch with several Leary cousins this year about your
research project. Could you specify which ones,
exactly? And did you succeed in getting them to do a
DNA kit, too? It's such an exciting project, and I know
Matt can't wait to learn more . . .

Blah blah blah, grateful, blah blah blah, blessed, blah
blah Kind regards, Jill (soon-to-be) Leary.

She reread for typos and hit send.

Then Joy tipped her head back and stared at the ceiling.
"Calm down," she muttered.

But her heart was racing. Her chest felt flushed. She
reached for her drink and paused as she realized it was already low again.

She couldn't keep doing this.

Joy slid her chair back and stepped to the back door.
Where was Frodo? She gazed out at the dark yard, chewing
her lip as she thought about her email. Maybe *grateful* was
overdoing it. She shouldn't have sounded so sappy.

Ping.

Joy rushed back to the computer. He'd replied already.
Her stomach tensed as she clicked open the response.

Dear Jill,

In answer to your question, I have been in touch with
four cousins about my genealogy project: the Porter
girls, Samantha and Sarah (who recently did a DNA kit),
as well as Mallory Leary and Brett Leary . . .

Joy's stomach plummeted. She stared down at the message.

She slapped the computer shut and backed away from the table. Bile rose in her throat, and she rushed to the sink and vomited.

R OWAN AWOKE IN a dark room. Muffled voices came from somewhere nearby, and she sat up in bed. The bathroom light was on, illuminating an open door near the closet.

She blinked at the dimness, trying to make sense of it. There was an adjoining room, she realized, and the door to it was open. Jack was in there talking to someone, probably someone on his team, and he was trying to keep his voice down.

She sat there for a moment, piecing together the events of last night, and her face warmed as she remembered him kneeling in front of her and stripping off her jeans.

A faint buzz sounded—someone's phone. And then the adjoining door pulled shut with a *thud*.

Rowan glanced at the clock, and it took her a moment to grasp the meaning of the flashing numbers. Was it really 1:55? Or had they had a power surge?

She tossed back the covers and immediately regretted it as chilly air hit her skin. She got out of bed and grabbed the first article of clothing she spotted on the floor—a black T-shirt. Slipping into it, she glanced around dazedly. Phone. It would be in her purse. Which was where? She turned, looking around the dim room. Her gaze landed on an open laptop computer sitting on the dresser near a tangle of power cords. Her purse sat beside it, even though she distinctly remembered dropping it on the floor when they'd stumbled into the room together. Jack must have put it there.

She rushed to the dresser, unzipped her purse, and pulled out her phone. It was 5:28. She'd slept here *all night*.

She set the phone down on a pile of papers, and the glow of the screen illuminated a picture. Rowan stared down at it, transfixed by the familiar scene. She knew the chairs, the table, the wind chimes. It was Olivia Salter's back porch. Rowan had sat around that exact table, and the porch had looked the same as this picture—except for the yellow crime scene tape stretched across the back.

Rowan picked up the photograph and looked at the one beneath it. Her breath caught. Olivia's living room. She recognized the furry pink beanbag. There was an evidence marker on the beige carpet next to it—marking God only knew what. Dread filled Rowan's stomach as she set the picture aside and looked at the next one in the stack. This one showed the corner of Olivia's tie-dyed bedspread and more beige carpet. Then a close-up of carpet, along with another evidence marker. Rowan squinted at the little white object in the photo. A metal ruler had been placed beside it for scale. It looked like a wad of gum or—

A tooth.

A human *tooth* on the carpet.

Rowan moved the photo aside. Next was a smaller picture—a Polaroid—and it took her a second to recognize Olivia. She sat on a hospital bed, gaze downcast. Rowan recognized her wavy brown hair, but the entire side of her face was purple and swollen like an eggplant.

Rowan dropped the Polaroid. Her stomach flip-flopped.

A voice near the door sent a shot of panic through her. She glanced around frantically and snatched her clothes off the floor, then she dashed into the bathroom. She pulled the door shut just as the door to the adjoining room opened.

Jack was back.

Shit. She turned on the faucet to give herself cover.

Revulsion gripped her. That snapshot was from the night of Olivia's attack. Had Jack taken the picture? Or some ER nurse? A hot lump clogged Rowan's throat as she tried to get her mind around the image of Olivia beaten almost beyond recognition. Rowan had known what had happened. She'd heard about it through friends. But hearing and *seeing* were two totally different things, and she never should have touched those crime scene photos.

Her stomach roiled and she leaned on the vanity. God, she felt sick. Clammy. She had to get out of here.

A tap at the door.

"Rowan?"

"One sec."

She splashed cold water on her face, then turned off the faucet. She glanced in the mirror and was shocked by her reflection. Her hair looked like a tumbleweed. Mascara was smudged beneath her eyes. She grabbed a rumpled towel off the counter, dampened it, and did her best to clean up her face. Then she smoothed her hair and attempted to tame it by twisting it into a bun. She didn't have a hair band, but it would hold long enough for her to make her escape.

She grabbed her jeans and underwear. The denim was still damp, but she pulled everything on and smoothed the front of the T-shirt. It was Jack's, but he'd have to do without it for now.

She took a deep breath and opened the door.

Jack leaned against the wall across from the bathroom. He was fully dressed, right down to the holster on his hip, and she took a step back in disbelief. His hair was damp, and she realized he'd showered at some point while she had remained sound asleep in his bed after their sex binge.

He stepped over and put his hand on her waist. "Morning." He kissed her forehead.

"I can't believe I slept." She ducked around him, searching for the rest of her clothes. He'd turned the lamp on, and she darted a glance at the pile of crime scene photos on the dresser. Would he know she'd gone through them? There was a new stack of folders sitting atop the pile, and she wondered if he'd put them there intentionally to shield his work from view.

"You okay?"

She turned around. "Fine." She grabbed her socks and boots and went to the chair closest to the door to pull everything on.

He came to stand beside her, folding his arms over his chest as he watched her zip her boots.

"My shift starts in a few minutes," he said.

"I know. Sorry."

"Why?"

"I didn't plan to stay here. I know you've got work. Okay if I borrow this?" She motioned to the T-shirt she was wearing.

"Sure."

She spied her sweater on the floor by the nightstand. She scooped it up, snagging her bra, too. She grabbed her purse off the dresser and stuffed everything inside.

"Rowan."

She looked at him.

He stepped over, gazing down at her with a furrowed brow. "What's wrong?"

"Nothing. I'm leaving." She retrieved her phone from the dresser, then tucked it into her back pocket.

"You don't have to race out of here," he said. "Sleep in if you want. They'll have coffee in the lobby at seven."

"As tempting as that sounds, I can't. I've got an early meeting with a client, so—" She spied her down jacket on the back of the chair and grabbed it. "I need to take off."

He eased closer, gazing down at her again with those sharp brown eyes that saw way too much.

"What's the problem?"

"No problem."

He darted an impatient glance at the ceiling. "Why are you lying?"

Her chest tightened. "I'm not lying."

"Yes, you are. I know your tells."

"My *tells*?"

"Something's wrong. Why won't you just talk to me?"

"Nothing is wrong. Like I said, I have a meeting to get to."

He watched her for a moment. "All right. Can I call you later?"

She shoved her coat under her arm. "Aren't you working?"

"Yeah, but I can talk on the phone. And maybe when this operation wraps up—"

"You know what? Focus on your work. You need to concentrate and I"—she reached for the door—"I'm getting behind on my own stuff. I can't really deal with this right now."

"Deal with what?"

"This—whatever. Hookup."

His eyebrows arched. "Hookup? That's what you want to call it?"

"I don't know—thing. Sex. *Whatever*." Panic bubbled up inside her, and to her horror, she felt tears welling in her eyes. "Call it whatever you want, but it's not going to happen again. I shouldn't have even come here!"

He drew back like she'd slapped him. "Okay. You mind telling me—"

"Forget it, all right?" She jerked open the door. The latch caught it, and she let out a frustrated huff.

Jack stepped over, calmly pressed the door shut, and undid the latch.

She opened the door again and glanced up at him, and he was staring down at her like she was crazy.

"Good luck with your case."

She ducked under his arm and walked out.

TWENTY-THREE

JACK CLIMBED INTO the van.

"Did you talk to Heidi? We had a sighting." Bryan's voice sounded like he was jacked up on caffeine or adrenaline or both. "Just fifty-five minutes ago."

Jack sank into the seat beside him. "She told me."

"Telephoto lens, man. This is freaking *huge*."

"Who took the pictures?" Jack grabbed the binoculars off the floor and peered through the lenses at the house.

"Some guy on Heidi's team. He dressed up as a utility worker and climbed up a telephone poll with a camera and got the shots."

Jack adjusted the focus and stared at the duplex.

"Jack, what's wrong?"

"Nothing."

"I thought you'd be psyched."

"I am."

"Yeah, I can tell."

All the windows in the front of the house were dark, with

the exception of a faint glow in the small, high window at the end of the house—likely the bathroom.

"Here, look at the pictures." Bryan picked up the laptop computer sitting on the cooler and handed it to Jack. Jack stared down at the surveillance photograph on the screen showing a woman standing at the kitchen sink—the kitchen across the street, presumably. The woman looked to be filling a coffee pitcher with water.

"Scroll through. *Look*." Bryan reached across him and tapped the arrow.

Jack's blood ran cold at the next image. A man stood at the sink.

William John Anderson.

In the bright overhead light, there was no mistaking him. Jack knew it was him.

"Here. See?" Bryan handed Jack his cell phone, and on the screen was Anderson's old driver's license photo. The photo was a decade old, but it didn't even matter. The two pictures were clearly the same guy.

"It's him," Bryan said. "Fucking *finally*. We found him."

Jack glanced up at Bryan. His hair was sticking out in different directions, and he badly needed a shave. He looked a little unhinged, actually—a direct result of spending the night in a surveillance van.

"Jack. Dude, you're killing me. What's with the non-reaction?"

Jack looked at the photograph again.

It was definitely Anderson.

He tapped the back arrow to review the previous shot on the computer screen. The woman at the sink was Sheryl Mason of Bozeman, Montana. And the car in the driveway was a black Honda Civic. All of those facts piled on top of each other meant Bryan was right.

They had located him at last.

"It's him." Jack looked up.

"No shit, man. That's what I'm *saying*."

The radio crackled to life and Bryan grabbed it from the cup holder.

"We have movement at the back door," a voice said, and Jack recognized Heidi on the other end. She was supposed to be in an unmarked police unit one block over.

"Looks like . . . a male and a female in the utility room. He's putting on a coat."

"Who's she talking to?" Jack asked Bryan.

"They've got someone on the roof of a vacant house two doors down. He's been watching with binoculars and relaying info."

"Someone's stepping outside now," Heidi said. "The male subject is exiting through the back door. One sec." She paused. "Okay, I'm hearing he's alone."

A dark figure stepped into the driveway, and Jack's pulse picked up. The car's taillights flashed as the man popped the locks. Jack lifted the binoculars. No luggage, and his hands appeared empty except for the keys as he slid into the car.

"That's him." Jack handed Bryan the binoculars. "Heidi, what's your twenty?"

"I'm one block east in a blue Kia. I'll tail him."

Jack looked at Bryan.

"We should go, too. We need to stay on him," Jack said.

"What about the van?"

"Someone can come get it. We need to be on him like a tick."

Jack watched through the windshield as the car backed out of the driveaway. Despite the lack of luggage, Jack couldn't stop thinking about the news brief Rowan had shown him. And he knew she was right—that story or any of the other recent media coverage might be enough to spook this guy into skipping town.

Jack grabbed the radio. "Heidi, he just pulled out. He's headed your way."

"I see his headlights."

"Don't let him make you."

"I got it."

"We're going to grab a car and catch up with you."

"Roger that."

Jack gave Bryan the radio and touched the door handle. "You ready?"

"Let's go."

They climbed out of the van and were hit with a blast of cold air. At least it wasn't raining still.

"Where'd you park?" Bryan asked.

"One block over, by the dog park."

Keeping to the shadows, they made themselves as inconspicuous as possible as they walked briskly down the street. The sky was lightening over the treetops, and soon people would be out walking dogs and getting into cars and heading to work and school.

Jack's breath formed a cloud in front of his mouth. He pictured Rowan rushing out of his motel room with her coat stuffed under her arm.

How had everything gone sideways so fast? He didn't get what had happened between when he'd left her sound asleep in bed and when she'd raced out the door almost in tears.

They rounded the corner, and Jack spotted the car he'd just parked. It was an old beater with door dings—much more useful for undercover work than an unmarked police unit, which any half-alert suspect could spot a mile away.

Jack started jogging, eager to catch up with Heidi.

"Where do you think he's going this early?" Bryan asked as they got into the car.

"No idea." They had no indication of where Anderson worked or if he even had a job. Or he could be getting the hell out of town this morning.

"Check in with Heidi," Jack said.

As if on cue, her voice came over the radio.

"All right, he's moving east, toward the interstate."

Jack cursed.

"Okay, we've got a turn signal," she added. "He's turning south on the frontage road. I repeat, *south* on the frontage road."

Bryan looked at him. "Step on it."

Jack hit the gas.

B RYAN SPOTTED HEIDI's car at the edge of the truck stop parking lot. She looked inconspicuous—just a shadowy silhouette behind the wheel. Bryan tugged down the brim of his baseball hat and walked between two big rigs fueling up on diesel. The restaurant was crowded, and Bryan hoped he was going to be able to get a table with a view of the subject.

He and Jack had almost come to blows just now. Jack had wanted this job for himself, but Bryan had insisted that Jack couldn't follow Anderson into a restaurant when he'd already been in a physical confrontation with the man. Yes, it had been dark at the time, but if Anderson had gotten a glimpse of him at some point, then Jack's presence here now could blow everything.

Bryan pulled open the glass door and stepped into the warm alcove. He opened the inner door and held it for a pair of long-haul truckers.

As Bryan stepped into the restaurant, the smell of bacon hit him. His stomach grumbled, but he ignored it as he scanned the morning breakfast crowd. Anderson was seated midway down the counter facing the kitchen.

"Just one?"

A young server with curly dark hair grabbed a menu from a bin beside the register.

"Yeah, could I have that two-top table by the window?"

"Sure." She ushered him through the dining room and sat him at a narrow table with a view of Anderson's back.

"Coffee to start?" she asked.

"Sure. Thanks."

She hurried off, and Bryan put his phone on the table beside a pair of syrup dispensers. He tapped a quick message to Jack and Heidi.

He's on a stool at the counter.

Bryan surveyed the row of customers. Anderson had a mug in front of him, and he was hunched over something he was reading.

Alone? Jack asked.

Looks like, Bryan responded.

Bryan was still rattled by their argument, even though he'd won. Jack had demanded to be in here, even knowing it put the operation at risk, and Heidi had intervened over the radio to side with Bryan, which had pissed Jack off more. Jack was normally so even-keeled, and Bryan didn't know what the hell his problem was—beyond the obvious fact that this drawn-out stakeout was shredding everyone's patience.

The server returned with an empty mug and a coffee carafe. "What else can I get you?" she asked, filling the mug.

"Just this for now."

She looked annoyed and started to walk away.

"Wait." Bryan gave her a flirty smile even though he was pretty sure he looked like hell from his overnight in the van. "Would you mind doing me a favor?"

Her face instantly turned suspicious. "What?"

Bryan nudged his jacket open and pulled his badge from the inner pocket. She looked intrigued.

"There's a guy at the counter there," he said. "Dark green jacket."

"Yeah?"

"Would you mind walking by and taking a look at what he's reading?"

She hesitated, but only for a second. "Sure, I can do that."

"Thanks."

She walked away, and Bryan watched from the corner of his eye as she stopped to fill a few more cups before going back behind the counter. She clipped an order to the line by the pickup window and then made her way down the row of counter stools, topping off coffees.

He still alone?

This message was from Heidi, and Bryan pictured her sitting in her car in the parking lot, watching customers file in, probably trying to memorize people and their vehicles in case she needed to run the license plate of someone who was here to meet Anderson.

Still solo, Bryan typed back.

A few minutes later, the server was back with a plate of toast he hadn't ordered.

"The guy in the Dodgers hat, right?" she asked.

"Yeah."

"He's looking at a map."

Bryan's pulse picked up. "A map?"

"It's one of those laminated foldout ones, like we sell in the gift shop."

"Did you happen to see what it was?"

"I didn't get that close." She dug a few packets of strawberry jam from her apron pocket and set them on the table. "But there's a picture of the Alamo at the top."

A map of San Antonio.

"Thanks," Bryan said. "I appreciate your help."

She tipped her head to the side. "Anything else I can get you?"

"I'm good. Thanks again."

"Sure thing." She smiled and set his check on the edge of the table.

As she walked away, Bryan texted out an update. He wasn't surprised when Heidi responded immediately.

San Antonio?!! he's planning again

Bryan chomped into his dry toast and cast a subtle look at Anderson. Was he camped out here at this truck stop so his girlfriend wouldn't see what he was up to? Was that why he hung out at the library, too, using their computers? Or was he stopping here for breakfast on his way somewhere?

We need that sample ASAP

This from Jack, as though Bryan wasn't already acutely aware of how badly they needed to get their hands on a DNA sample.

Bryan watched Anderson and tried to catch the eye of the server again, but she had her hands full delivering food. And then she stopped to take an order.

Finally, Bryan managed to snag her attention, and she swung by his table with an empty tray tucked under her arm.

"One more thing." He smiled again. "He's drinking coffee, right?"

"Yeah."

"Could you offer him a to-go cup?"

"We don't do to-go cups."

"Could you make an exception? It would really help me out."

She glanced at the counter, then looked at Bryan. "Sure, okay."

"Thanks."

She walked off, and Bryan ate the rest of the toast, washing it down with a slug of coffee. Then he pulled a clear latex glove from his pocket and tugged it onto his right hand as subtly as possible. From the corner of his eye, he watched the server go back behind the counter and stop to talk to Anderson. Bryan held his breath and waited.

Anderson shook his head. Then he got up from his stool, and Bryan felt a rush of panic.

He's leaving, he texted.

Bryan pretended to be reading his phone while in his peripheral vision, he watched Anderson cross the restaurant and stop at the register.

No to-go cup in his hand. No toothpick. No chewing gum. They were going to have to tail him around and wait for another chance to collect something, and that was assuming he didn't go straight home now. Or hell, maybe jump on I-35 and leave town.

The server caught Bryan's eye from behind the counter. She gave him a shrug, and Bryan responded with a slight nod. He grabbed his check off the table and headed for the register, trying to time it so he didn't bump right into Anderson as he was paying.

On his way, he passed Anderson's stool and used his gloved hand to snatch the napkin off the top of the breakfast plate. The napkin wasn't even unfolded, but maybe the lab could get something off it. He slipped it into his pocket and headed for the register.

A skinny guy in an apron was ringing up Anderson's tab, and Bryan hung back.

Six feet.

Six feet between him and the sick son of a bitch who had eluded investigators for years. Bryan looked him up and down, battling the urge to tackle him to the ground and slap the cuffs on. The guy was big—probably 210 or 220—and Bryan's chest tightened as he pictured his meaty hands closing around Evelyn Wood's neck.

Bryan looked away and tried to put a neutral expression on his face.

"Have a good one," the cashier said.

Anderson stepped away and grabbed a peppermint from

a bowl. He twisted the wrapper open with his teeth and then reached for the door.

"Everything okay today?"

Bryan looked at the cashier. "Yeah." He handed over a twenty, then glanced back, desperate not to lose sight of that candy wrapper.

Anderson was stepping through the outer door.

"Keep the change," Bryan said, and rushed out just in time to see Anderson drop the wrapper onto a trash bin by the door. It was one of those trash bins with an ashtray on the top, and Bryan saw the glint of cellophane beside a cigarette butt.

It was going to blow away.

Bryan pushed open the outer door. Anderson stood on the sidewalk now zipping up his jacket. Bryan darted a look at the candy wrapper just as a latex-gloved hand reached down and snagged it. Bryan's heart lurched.

Heidi.

She walked right past him, no eye contact as she tucked the evidence inside her coat and entered the restaurant.

Bryan stepped away from the door, averting his gaze from Anderson, who was now crossing the parking lot to the black Honda.

Turning his back, Bryan pulled his phone from his pocket and texted the team.

Candy wrapper. Heidi made the grab. U record it?

They needed a video, or some defense lawyer someday was going to be screaming about chain of custody. Bryan stared down at his phone, clenching his teeth as he waited for an answer from Jack.

Affirmative. Got it on vid.

TWENTY-FOUR

A DULL THUMPING NOISE roused Rowan from sleep. *Thump thump.* She tried to lift her head but then dropped it back on the bath mat.

Thump thump thump.

Where was Oscar?

Was he pawing at his cabinet again, trying to get to his food?

Rowan squeezed her eyes shut. God, how long since she'd fed him? She couldn't remember. She didn't know how long she'd been in here, drifting in and out. Her stomach clenched, and she pulled her knees closer.

"Rowan?"

She hunched her shoulders at the voice.

"Rowan? Are you—shit." Boots appeared in front of her eyes. Then Jack crouched down in front of her.

She covered her face with her hand and curled into a ball.

"What the hell happened?"

"Go away," she croaked.

She squeezed her eyes shut, wishing she could melt through the floor. She heard cabinets opening and closing and then the faucet running.

"Here." A cool, wet towel pressed against her forehead. "Can you sit up?"

"Please go away."

Miraculously, he did.

But a minute later, he was back again. His hand slid beneath her and lifted her shoulders off the floor.

"Can you sit? You need to drink something."

The instant he said it, her mouth felt dry as dust, and she squinted her eyes open.

Jack knelt in front of her. He wore his leather jacket and a black baseball hat she'd never seen before.

She closed her eyes to keep from crying. She looked disgusting. She had vomit in her hair. It was spattered on the floor around the toilet, too.

"Can you drink something?"

She nodded a little, and he held a glass to her mouth as she took a sip.

The water felt cool on her parched throat.

She waited a moment and then took another sip.

"When did you get sick?" he asked.

"This morning."

"Was it something you ate?"

She shook her head. "Stomach flu. Skyler had it yesterday." She looked at him blearily. "How did you get in here?"

But he wasn't paying attention. He was opening the linen cabinet, rooting through the shoebox where she kept her medicines and Band-Aids.

"You have a thermometer?"

"By the bed."

"Okay, hold on to me."

Before she could grasp what that meant, he scooped her up in his arms. She gripped his jacket, hoping she wasn't going to throw up on him.

He carried her into the bedroom and gently set her down on the unmade bed. Then he disappeared again.

Rowan squinted her eyes and looked at her dim room. Dirty clothes covered the floor. Her blinds were shut, but strips of fading daylight seeped through. It was evening. Wasn't it?

She closed her eyes and tried to think. Today was Wednesday. She hadn't seen him since yesterday morning.

He came back, and she heard a *thunk* as he set something on the rug beside the bed.

"Here's a bucket if you need to throw up again."

She winced and turned onto her side.

Then the mattress sank as he sat down. "Rowan, look at me."

She squinted her eyes open.

"Do you need to go to the ER?"

"No." She closed her eyes. "It's just a bug."

"Are you dehydrated?"

She took a deep breath. "I'm thirsty."

"There's water by your bed here. Can you drink some more?"

She nodded.

He helped her sit up, and she took another sip. Then another. It tasted good. The last time she'd tried to drink, it had come back up, along with everything in her stomach.

She lay back on the pillow and tried not to envision how repulsive she looked. And smelled. She hadn't showered in two days.

Her eyes flew open as she remembered the stakeout. "Did you find him?"

Jack just looked at her. He nodded.

"Did you arrest him?"

"Not yet."

"Why not?"

He grabbed the thermometer off the nightstand, and it made a beep. "Here." He put it into her mouth, and she watched him, trying to absorb what he'd just told her as he stared at her with those bottomless brown eyes.

Why had he come here?

Her stomach clenched, and she sank back against the pillow. She wanted to die. Every bone in her body hurt.

The thermometer beeped, and he pulled it out.

"One hundred."

She sighed and turned onto her side. "It's down."

"Are you sure you don't need to go to the doctor?"

"Yes."

"Want me to call your mom or your sister?"

"No."

She closed her eyes as a wave of nausea washed over her. *Please please please don't let me puke on him.*

The mattress shifted, and she felt a rush of relief. He was leaving. She heard his boots on the floorboards in the hallway and then the kitchen.

What time was it? She groped around the rumpled bedding beside her and found her phone. She tapped in the passcode and stared at the screen.

It was 5:40 P.M. She had a bunch of text messages, including several from him, but just looking at them made her head throb, and she tossed the phone aside.

Jack was back. "There's some ginger ale here by the bed."

"Thank you."

"And some Ritz crackers, if you're up for it. I couldn't find any saltines."

"Thank you."

"Rowan."

She opened her eyes.

"I can't stay here," he said. "I have to get back."

"I know."

"Are you going to be okay?"

"Yes."

She opened her eyes fully and looked him over, taking in his clothes, his boots. There was a brisk tension about him, and she knew he was on his way to work. More surveillance? Just the thought exhausted her.

He reached over and picked up her phone. "You've got half a battery left. I'm going to put this here." He set it on the nightstand beside the ginger ale.

"Thanks."

He gazed down at her, and guilt swamped her. She'd been such a bitch to him back at the motel. She should probably apologize, but all she could focus on right now was how desperately she wanted him to leave.

He leaned down and kissed her forehead.

She groaned. "Don't, you'll get sick."

The sheet settled over her, and she winced from the pain.

"I'll put the hide-a-key back in your flowerpot."

"Thank you."

"We need to talk about your security setup, by the way. It's crap."

She sighed.

"If you need anything, call me."

"Thanks."

His footsteps faded. She lay there, every cell in her body aching. She heard the front door open.

It closed with a soft *click*.

JACK STARED THROUGH the binoculars at the front of the house. If he had to spend another entire night here, he was going to lose his mind.

He lowered the binoculars and stretched out his leg that was falling asleep. They'd switched from a van disguised as a utility truck to a less conspicuous minivan in front of a house where the owners were out of town, and the new vehicle didn't have nearly the same space to spread out. Jack grabbed his phone from the cup holder and checked his messages. Still nothing.

He called Liz.

"Lasco."

"Hey, it's me."

"Any movement?" she asked, and he caught the excitement in her voice.

"No. What's the status with the lab?"

Her weary sigh on the other end made Jack's gut clench.

"I talked to Hood," she said.

"Well, were you going to tell me?"

"I just got off the phone with him. Calm down."

"What's the story?"

"Still waiting."

Jack gritted his teeth.

"There's an issue with the sample. They're having to rerun everything, and he thinks it will be tomorrow."

"*Tomorrow?* What the fuck?"

"I know you're frustrated."

Frustrated didn't begin to cover it. Jack was livid. He'd spent four days swigging coffee and Red Bull and freezing his ass off in a parked car. He was pissed off at Hood, pissed off at Heidi, pissed off at Heidi's team, and he and Bryan were barely on speaking terms.

"Sorry," Liz said. "I know it sucks."

No, she didn't know. She hadn't been stuck in a van for four days.

"I thought this was expedited?" he said. "The lab was supposed to turn this around in less than twenty-four hours."

"That's what I thought, too, but they ran into a glitch with the sample. I don't know what to tell you."

"Tell me when the fuck we're going to get our DNA back so we can get a fucking arrest warrant and get this fucker in handcuffs."

"Hey. I get you're frustrated, but don't take it out on *me*. I'm as impatient as you are."

Jack rubbed the crick in his neck.

"And, anyway, *right* is more important than *fast*, at this point," she said.

"What's that mean?"

"It means just what it says. We need to make sure we're right about this."

Irritation burned in his chest. "How the hell would we be wrong about it?"

"I don't know. I'm just saying, let's run the DNA test and be sure."

Jack tossed the binoculars into the seat beside him. "I already *am* sure. It's William John Anderson in that house right now. I've been tailing him to restaurants and gas stations and the goddamn grocery store. I've seen him with my own eyes."

"Yes, but do we really know it's *him*? WCR? Do we really know *Will Anderson* is the guy who raped eight women in Austin and murdered another in San Antonio? I mean, what if the genealogist is wrong, and we've got the wrong guy here?"

"She's not wrong."

"How do you *know*, Jack, unless we test the DNA evidence?"

Jack clenched his teeth.

"Look, I understand this woman is good. And I also know you like her personally—"

"What's that mean?"

"Jack. Give me a break, here. Everyone knows you're sleeping with her. That doesn't mean we all get to throw our procedures out the window and rely on her boundless talent. People screw up! Even pretty genealogists who you happen to have a hard-on for! So we have to get confirmation before we go in there guns blazing and arrest this guy."

Jack leaned back in his seat, fuming. Liz was right. He knew that. But he wasn't happy to learn she and everyone else had picked up on his personal relationship with Rowan.

And he was even less happy with the reminder that

Rowan could have made a mistake. If she had, it would screw up everything. From an investigation standpoint, it would be a logistical nightmare.

"Hood told me he'd call the minute the lab gets back to him," Liz was saying. "I'm guessing that will be mid-morning."

"Call me when you hear."

Jack hung up.

Was it possible he was jumping the gun here? Maybe. He could admit—to himself, at least—that Liz had a point. This entire investigation had become focused on a suspect based on Rowan's work product. And she'd been out of the police investigation game for several years. What if she'd overlooked something?

What if Joy Kendall had another male relative who might be responsible for the DNA profile recovered from the second victim's fingernails? Rowan was good at her job, yes, but still she was human, and she could have missed something.

And that something could torpedo the whole case. Jack didn't think she'd screwed up. But he was beginning to wonder if his attraction to her was affecting his judgment.

He couldn't stop thinking about her. He'd burned through two hours of his last break—hours when he should have been sleeping—to drive to her house and see her after she'd ignored his messages. What the hell was wrong with him? He wasn't one to hover. Or smother. Usually, *he* was the one backing away from relationships—as Heidi knew better than anyone. The minute he realized Heidi was auditioning him for the role of husband and father, he was out.

But something with Rowan was different. The thought of a commitment with her didn't spook him like it usually did. The opposite, in fact. Maybe because she was so clearly pulling away from *him*, he was more inclined to chase her.

Typical male bullshit, he knew—the sort of stuff he'd

heard his sister complain about for years. But it was just what he felt. He liked Rowan. A *lot*. The sex had been great, too, and he had the scratch marks on his back to prove it. So, why was she dodging him? Even before she'd come down with the flu, she'd been ghosting him, and if he hadn't gone over there and scraped her up off the floor, she'd probably still be shutting him out. He'd done something to upset her, but he had no clue what it was, and now he was trapped in a damn surveillance van waiting on backlogged lab work and bureaucratic red tape—the two things he hated most about his job.

Jack scrubbed his hands over his face. He needed to snap out of this shit mood. Spending hours cooped up in a cold, dark van was making him loopy. Not to mention short-tempered. He'd gotten into it with Bryan, even though Jack knew Bryan was right—after wrestling with Anderson in the woods, Jack couldn't then tail the guy closely without risking blowing his cover. Which meant Jack was relegated to staking out the house while Bryan and Heidi followed him into restaurants and stores and wherever he happened to go. They still didn't know what he or his girlfriend did for a living, only that they didn't leave the house much except to run errands or walk their dog. Back in Montana, the woman had had a cosmetology license, but Jack had found no evidence that she had renewed her license here or worked for any of the salons in town.

And it had been years since Anderson had made an ATM withdrawal or deposited money, as far as Jack knew. What the hell were they living off of? Jack was beginning to think that Anderson's sister had lied and that she'd been aiding and abetting her brother all along.

Jack's phone buzzed, and he checked the screen.

Rowan.

He connected. "Hey."

"Hi. How's it going?"

"Slow. How's it going with *you*?"

"Better," she said. "I had some soup."

"That's good."

It was great to hear her voice, but this time, he kept that reaction to himself.

"The ginger ale helped, too. Thank you for coming by."

"Sure."

She got quiet.

A light went on in one of the front windows, and Jack grabbed the binoculars.

"Jack?"

"Yeah?"

"I'm sorry about the other morning when I blew up at you. I was kind of out of sorts."

He adjusted the lenses and waited.

"Hello?"

"Are you going to tell me what was wrong?"

She went quiet again, and he waited for her to lie to him and say it was nothing. Frustration gnawed at him. She was so guarded about her feelings. He wanted her to open up, but he couldn't force her. He wasn't the best at relationships, but he knew that much.

He was going to have to be patient, even though his patience was in extremely short supply right now.

Another light switched on inside the house. Then the radio crackled, and Jack's heart lurched.

"Rowan, I need to call you back."

"Is everything okay?"

"Yeah, but I have to go."

"Be careful."

He clicked off as Bryan's voice came over the radio.

"We've got movement at the back door," his partner informed him. "Looks like . . . male subject exiting. He's going out to the driveway. You seeing this?"

"Got it," Jack said as a shadowy figure stepped onto the driveway.

"Can you confirm it's him and not her?"

"Affirmative. I've got eyes on him now."

The car was unlocked, evidently, and Anderson got in without the lights flashing on. A moment later, the taillights glowed.

"He's backing out of the driveway," Jack said. "Can you follow?"

Nothing.

"Bryan? You copy?"

"Copy that. I'll take the lead."

TWENTY-FIVE

First it was the truck stop on I-35, where he bought a lotto ticket and a sixteen-ounce Icee, according to Bryan.

Then it was the YMCA, where he made a loop through the parking lot but didn't stop.

And now it was a dog park, where he'd spent the last twenty minutes sitting in his car in the dark in the parking lot near the public restroom.

Jack stared at the back of the Honda from the dark shadow beneath a giant oak tree down the block.

Static came over the radio.

"Still there?" Bryan asked.

"I don't like this."

"What about it?"

"The park, the neighborhood."

"What the hell's he doing there?" Bryan asked.

"Nothing. That's my point."

"Think he's waiting for a dealer?"

Jack had been wondering the same thing. But they had no indication that Anderson was into drugs.

"Maybe a hooker?" Bryan suggested.

"I don't know."

Jack caught movement in his side mirror and turned around to look. Just a cat running across the street.

"I'm going to do a drive-by," Bryan said.

Bryan was parked one block over, which was close enough to move into position to tail Anderson again, but not close enough to be noticed.

"Don't let him see you," Jack said.

"I won't."

Jack checked his watch. It was after eleven now. He checked his mirrors again, looking at the lawn where the cat had come from.

This location bothered him.

He didn't like the park, the trees, the one-story houses. He didn't like the utility easement two blocks away that he'd passed on his way here.

"Fuck."

Jack grabbed the radio. "What?"

"He's not there."

"What do you mean? I'm looking right at him."

"No, *he's* not there. The car is there, but he's not in it."

Jack's pulse jumped. "I didn't see him get out."

"Well, he did unless he crawled into the back seat and went to sleep. I'm going to get out and do a walk-by."

Jack stared at the car parked in the shadows. It was near a streetlamp. How could he have missed Anderson getting out of it?

A dark figure moved near the playscape. Bryan. Jack recognized the way he moved, even in the dimness. A moment later, the figure disappeared into the shadows.

Jack glanced around, pulse racing now as he looked at his surroundings just as Bryan's voice came over the radio.

"He's gone."

"Fuck."

Jack shoved open his door. He glanced around. He took

out his phone, set it to silent mode, and sent a message to Bryan.

I'm out of the car. Switch to texts.

If Anderson was lurking nearby, Jack didn't want him overhearing the radio comms.

Jack looked around, bracing himself against the cold as he surveyed the area.

He visualized the utility easement in his mind. It cut a narrow swath through the east side of the neighborhood, and Jack set out for it.

Where r u going? Bryan texted him.

Utility easement, he replied. The wooded area behind the houses.

I'll cover the street side in case he comes this way, Bryan responded.

Jack spotted the gap between houses at the end of the street. That was it. He broke into a jog, unzipping his jacket for easy access to his weapon. He looked at the houses as he passed them—some dark, some with porch lights on or windows glowing. The homes were one story, probably three- and four-bedrooms, some no doubt with sliding doors in the back.

Was this reconnaissance? Was he looking for a victim here? But this wasn't his hunting ground.

Jack's chest tightened as he surveyed the area. Maybe it was. For all Jack knew, he could have already scoped out this area long ago. They'd been so focused on San Antonio they hadn't expected him to be working close to his home base. But they'd been watching the man for only *four days*, and he'd been living here for months. Maybe he'd previously canvassed this whole neighborhood and had a selection of targets all picked out. Everything about this place felt horribly familiar.

Jack's phone vibrated, and he saw Heidi's number. Bryan had probably called her.

"What the heck's happening?" she demanded. "I thought you guys were staking out the house?"

"He's on the move," Jack whispered.

"You were supposed to call for backup if that happened. I'm at the motel."

"Get a car over to the subdivision northeast of the campus."

"What subdivision? Give me a street."

Jack halted and glanced around him. The sign on the corner was too far away to read, so he tapped into the map on his phone.

"I'm on . . . Apple Tree Lane. Sending you a screenshot." He captured the image and hit send. "I'll update you when I get eyes on him again."

"You *don't have eyes on him*?"

"No."

Jack hung up and broke into a jog, keeping to the shadows along the street as he neared the dark gap between the houses. It was partly cloudy tonight, but in the light of the half-moon, he could make out the tall silhouettes of power lines.

Jack jogged into the brushy area beneath the towers, quickly finding a trail through the grass, probably used by dog walkers and runners. Some of the trees looked spindly and skeletal with their bare branches. But there were enough bushy junipers to provide adequate cover.

He ducked under the shadow of a huge oak tree and stopped to get his bearings.

Jack's heart thundered.

He was here. Somewhere nearby—Jack could *feel* it.

Jack slid his phone into his pocket and closed his eyes. He took a deep breath and slowly let it out, relaxing his shoulders. He tried to tune into the sounds all around him.

First it seemed quiet. But then he registered the distant whir of traffic on the interstate. And the rush of wind through the trees. And a dog barking, probably several blocks away.

The dog was as good a clue as any, and Jack set off toward it. He kept to the shadows, wishing his eyes would adjust faster so he could see in the darkness.

The dog started up again, closer now. Or maybe it was a different dog. Something was setting them off.

A faint creaking noise caught his attention. Jack pivoted toward it. Where the hell had it come from? He went totally still, straining to hear more.

Should he move toward the barking dogs or the creaking sound?

Jack changed course, easing through the brush toward the direction of the creaking. Maybe it was a gate or a garage door.

A wind gusted up, rustling the branches all around him, and Jack took advantage of the noise to quicken his pace. When the wind died down again, he stopped.

He was in a densely wooded area behind a row of houses. The walking trail through here was behind him, maybe thirty feet, and he was now positioned much closer to the back fences. Above the fence line, he could see roof after roof and the tops of windows.

Where the hell was he?

As soundlessly as possible, Jack eased branches out of his way and moved toward the nearest fence. In the dimness, he could see the fence was totally smooth—no gate back here. Another gust of wind, and he used the noise cover to plow through the brush to the next house over. This fence was a different story. Jack found a back gate.

Silently, he tried the latch. But it was locked from the other side.

He moved on to the next house. A cloud passed in front of the moon, and everything went pitch-black. Jack stopped, waiting for more light so he didn't run smack into a tree.

His phone vibrated, and he read the message from Bryan.

I'm on Apple Tree. No movement here. Where r u?

Jack texted back, Woods behind houses.

A dog barked nearby, and Jack froze. The sound was muffled, like it came from indoors, but something—or someone—had caught the dog's attention. Was it someone outside?

Jack waited, straining to hear. Then he moved through the brush, trying to be as quiet as possible as he swiped through branches. He reached a gap in the woods and spotted a gate.

It stood open.

Only a few inches, but the gate was definitely ajar. Had this been the creaking noise he'd heard earlier?

Jack eased his gun from the holster. He crept toward the gate and slowly pressed his fingertips against the weathered wood.

Creeeeak . . .

He cursed inwardly and stopped.

Anderson had gone through this gate. Jack was certain of it. So, was he in this yard now?

The wind gusted, and Jack took advantage of the noise to muffle the sound as he pushed the gate open a few more inches. Sucking in his breath, he squeezed through the opening.

He was in someone's backyard now. No porch lights, but light streamed through a kitchen window, spilling onto a back patio surrounded by empty planters. The home was a brick one-story with an attached garage, and Jack eyed the overgrown hedge that lined the back of the house.

Was Anderson back here?

Jack crept around the garage, taking care not to bump the trash cans as he emerged in a side yard near the driveway. Another gate there stood wide open.

Jack's pulse jumped as he stared at it.

Wide open. He was setting up exits for himself.

Jack walked through the gate, checking the bushes along the driveway. The garage was closed, and a white Mazda was parked in the drive. Based on the pink NAMASTE bumper sticker, Jack guessed the car belonged to a woman.

A flagstone path connected the driveway to the front door. Jack stood on the driveway, looking around. He spied Bryan's car parked down the street.

Jack tucked his gun back into his holster and approached the front door. The bluish light of a television flickered behind the blinds in the front room.

He rang the doorbell. And waited.

The porch light went on, and Jack pulled out his badge and held it up to the peephole.

The door swung open, and a woman stood there, wide-eyed with alarm. She wore reindeer pajamas and had her hair up in a towel.

He held up his badge again. "Evening, ma'am. I'm Detective Jack Bruner."

A little dog came scurrying around the corner, yapping.

"Pumpkin, *no*." She reached down and scooped the poodle into her arms.

"Sorry to bother you." He tucked his badge away. "We had a report of a prowler in the area and wanted to check to see if you heard any disturbances?"

"A . . . what now?"

"Have you heard any noises, possibly in your backyard?"

"No."

"Has your dog there been barking at all, maybe alarmed about anything in the last half hour or so?"

"No." She hugged the dog closer to her chest. "Who reported the prowler?"

"Ma'am, are you alone here in the house?"

"Yes. My husband is in Houston tonight."

Jack's pulse picked up.

"Would you mind if I took a look around the backyard, ma'am?"

"Not at all. You want to go through the house or—"

"I'll go through the gate. Please check your door locks and make sure they're secure."

He left her staring after him with her dog clutched in her arms.

Jack strode back around the house, cataloging everything he knew. This woman's gates were open. She was home by herself. Her husband was out of town.

But she had a dog.

WCR never picked houses with dogs, but everything else fit.

Jack went back through the gate, retracing his steps around the back of the garage. Anderson was *here*. Call it a hunch or gut instinct or whatever, Jack could practically *feel* him lurking nearby.

His phone vibrated with a text from Bryan.

Fence jumper!! Two houses over.

Jack shoved his phone in his pocket and raced through the yard and out the back gate.

He stopped by the fence, looking for movement in the trees. Two houses over *which way*?

A large dog barked, and Jack took off toward the sound, plowing through branches. Thorns stabbed at him as he pushed through the bushes.

Rustling in the trees to his left. A shadowy figure darted through the brush.

Jack took off after it. "Police! Stop!"

The person ducked into the thicket, and Jack sprinted after him. No creek bed this time, no uneven rocks to turn an ankle. Jack plunged through the scrub brush, batting at leaves and branches as he tore after the figure.

Jack's heart thundered. The guy was fast, elusive, moving in and out of the shadows as Jack struggled to stay in pursuit.

Jack's toe caught on a rock, and he crashed to his knee, cursing, but immediately scrambled back up.

He couldn't miss this time. Not again.

Jack charged through the thicket, using his left arm to shield his face from the sharp points as he pulled out his gun. Once again, he was so close, *so close*, and yet he knew that he was losing ground, missing his chance.

Branches rustled ahead. Then the tree cover disappeared, and the dark figure dashed into the clearing.

Jack poured on the speed, pushing himself to the limit. Anderson was thirty yards away, then twenty yards . . . ten . . . five.

"Police! Stop!"

On a surge of adrenaline, Jack tackled him, and they crashed to the ground. Jack caught an elbow in his ribs as he tried to wrestle Anderson's arms behind him. He cursed and kicked, trying to heave Jack off. A fist connected with Jack's jaw, snapping his head back, and he saw red suddenly. He jammed a knee into Anderson's spine and shifted his weight onto him.

Suddenly Bryan was there, pinning his ankles, and Jack managed to get the cuffs on his wrists.

"It's him?" Bryan asked as Jack roughly patted him down for weapons.

"Yeah."

Jack felt something hard tucked into the back of Anderson's waistband. He reached in and pulled out a long leather sheath.

His hunting knife.

Jack glanced at Bryan as he flung the knife away, and Anderson's struggling intensified.

Sirens sounded in the distance.

"I called for backup," Bryan said, handing Jack a second set of cuffs, and he clamped them on, just to be sure, as the wailing sirens got closer. Jack sat back on his knees, catching his breath as Anderson scowled up at him.

"Hey, fuck you," Anderson snarled, and Jack battled the urge to punch him in the mouth.

Instead, he took a deep breath and said the words he'd been saving for years.

"You're under arrest."

TWENTY-SIX

"STILL NOTHING."

Bryan glanced up as Heidi strode into the conference room.

"Let me call you back," Bryan told his lieutenant. "Detective Rollins is here with an update."

Bryan got off the phone, and the fiery look in Heidi's eyes told him something was very wrong.

"What happened?" he asked.

"*Nothing*, I just told you. He's not saying a word."

After his initial outburst, the suspect tentatively ID'd as Will Anderson had clammed up, not uttering a word to Jack or anyone as he was Mirandized and loaded into a police car. The FBI profiler had said Anderson might be more apt to let his guard down around female cops, so Heidi and her partner had been the ones to bring him in.

Jack stepped into the room. He still had leaves in his hair, and the knees of his jeans were black with mud.

"Where is he?" Jack demanded.

"In an interview room," Heidi said. "He's just sitting

there, cooling his heels. He didn't say a single *word* on his way in here."

Jack muttered a curse. "Did you ask him about the knife?"

Another recommendation from Skinner—bring up the weapon they had found on him and see what he had to say about it.

"He didn't take the bait, just stared out the window the whole time."

Jack's mouth tightened. He was still clearly hyped up from the foot chase. Not to mention getting punched in the jaw.

"What do you think we should do?" Heidi asked Jack. Her lieutenant was supposed to be in charge here, but everyone knew Jack was the expert on this guy. "I know the profiler, in his infinite wisdom, said we should let him stew awhile, but I don't know. I think we should take a crack at him *now* before he gets dug in."

"Sounds like he's already dug in."

"Did you offer him something to drink?" Bryan asked.

"Yeah, but he just stared at me." She rolled her eyes. "I think he's been watching a few too many *CSI* shows. If we want his DNA, we're probably going to need a judge to sign off."

"Speaking of DNA, what's going on with our sample?" Bryan asked.

"Hood is checking."

Jack's brow furrowed, and Bryan was beginning to think this was the primary source of Jack's off-the-charts stress level right now. They were *still* waiting for confirmation on the DNA sample they had collected at the truck stop yesterday morning. Until they had it, there was the possibility that Rowan's research was flawed, and they'd zeroed in on the wrong guy.

Yeah, skulking around people's yards at night wearing all black and carrying a hunting knife made him look guilty as hell, but still. Anderson hadn't had gloves on him.

Or a ski mask. So maybe tonight was merely a dry run. Or a reconnaissance mission.

Or maybe—and Bryan hoped to hell this wasn't the case—they had arrested the wrong man, and WCR was still at large.

Heidi sighed. "So, if he isn't talking at all, at least there's one bright side—he hasn't lawyered up yet."

"He will," Jack said.

"How do you know?"

"Because he's smart." Jack checked his watch and looked at Bryan. "We should get going on that search warrant for his house. I want to be ready to move as soon as we get that DNA match."

"Assuming we get it," Heidi said.

"We'll get it."

She shot a look at Bryan, probably wondering if he shared Jack's certainty. She turned to Jack with a raised eyebrow. "Has it occurred to you that *maybe* the reason for the holdup is that something is wrong, and the sample's not a match?"

Jack's expression darkened, but he didn't answer.

"I'll help you with the warrant," Bryan said. He didn't mind writing them and he needed something to do. "Can we use your workstation?" he asked Heidi.

"Have at it. I hate paperwork." She gestured to the bull-pen. "I'm the corner cube by the break room. My computer passcode is C-O-R-A."

They started out the door, and Heidi's phone chimed.

"Hold up," she said, yanking the phone from her pocket. "Rollins."

Bryan looked at Jack. He had gone rigid as his attention was fixed on Heidi's face.

"Yeah. Okay." She turned to look directly at Jack. "Got it. Thanks." She clicked off. "That was Hood. The DNA from the candy wrapper came back."

"And?"

"It's a match with the rape kit. We got him."

* * *

ROWAN PLUCKED HER earbuds out and listened. Was someone at her door? She checked her watch. It was just past noon, and she wasn't expecting anyone today.

She heard the sound again and hurried across the house, stepping over the pair of laundry baskets parked in the middle of her living room. She smoothed her hair, then checked the peephole and felt a jab of disappointment when she saw that it wasn't Jack.

She opened the door. "Hi," she said, ushering Lila inside. "What's all this?"

Lila held up a grocery bag. "Soup for the sickies."

"That's so nice," Rowan said, feeling guilty now. "You didn't need to do that."

"I just dropped some off at Skyler's." Lila glanced around the living room. "Are you actually *cleaning* today? You must be feeling better."

"I am. Come on in."

Rowan took the bag, and Lila followed her into the kitchen, sidestepping the vacuum parked by the sofa.

"Sky said you were a day behind her, so I figured you'd be curled up in bed still," Lila said.

"How's she doing?"

"A little better."

"Good. She sounded wiped out when I talked to her this morning." Rowan set the bag on the counter and peeked inside. "Oh my gosh. Is this homemade?" She pulled out the plastic Tupperware container.

"My grandma's recipe. Good for the soul."

Tears sprang into Rowan's eyes. "Lila, that's so thoughtful. You didn't need to go to all this trouble."

"It's no trouble. Geez. Don't get all weepy on me."

"Sorry." Rowan grabbed a dish towel and blotted her face. "I'm emotional today. I don't know what's wrong with me."

"It's the flu. It knocks everything out of whack." Lila leaned back against the counter. She wore an oversize sweatshirt and jeans, and Rowan remembered it was her day off.

Lila crossed her arms and looked her over. "So. How's Jack?"

"I slept with him."

Lila's face brightened. "Ooh! Good for you. How was it?"

Rowan turned and put the soup in the fridge, stalling for time as she tried to figure out how to describe it. Intense. Amazing.

Terrifying.

She thought of the warmth of his body as they'd slept spooned together with his arm draped over her waist.

"Uh-oh." Lila watched her with a wary look. "Someone's falling hard."

"I'm not falling." Rowan rolled her eyes. "I just like him, I think."

"Good."

"How can you say it's good when you don't even know him? God, *I* barely even know him. This is stupid."

Lila shrugged. "Well, I know he's a cop, so at least you don't have to worry about him running off with your credit card."

"Speaking of, how is Dara?" Rowan said, eager to change the subject. She wasn't ready to analyze things with Jack yet.

Lila sighed, and Rowan went on alert.

"What happened?"

"Trouble in paradise," Lila said.

"Oh no. What is it?"

"Apparently, she went over to see him, and his ex-girlfriend was there."

"*There* there? Like they were together?" Rowan asked.

"I don't know the details, just that Dara's upset. Nick

told her she was just stopping by and there was nothing to it, but it was late at night, apparently, and Dara's not buying it."

"That sucks." Rowan fisted her hand on her hip. "She seemed so excited about how everything was going."

"I know. And so soon after Trevor the Douche." Lila shook her head. "She really didn't need this right now."

"Well, maybe it's really nothing and they'll work it out," Rowan said.

"Yeah, but you know Dara. She has trust issues."

"Don't we all."

"Yeah, but hers are man-specific," Lila said. "But you're right. Who knows? If he's really all that great, he'll find a way to make it right with her. And if he's not, good riddance. If he's a cheater, better to find out early."

Lila was right, but the thought was still depressing. Dara had seemed so happy just the other day.

Lila glanced at the clock on the wall. "Well, I need to run. I've still got a bunch of errands."

Rowan walked her to the door. "Thanks for the soup. That was really sweet."

Lila put her hand on the doorknob and looked at the laundry baskets on the floor. "Rest up today. Don't get carried away cleaning and have a relapse." She opened the door, and cold air wafted inside.

"Lila . . . about Jack. Please don't tell Dara and Skyler anything."

She smiled. "I won't. But what are you so worried about?"

"I don't know. Just that it may have been a onetime thing. I don't really want to talk about it with everyone when it's in limbo."

She raised an eyebrow. "Skyler said he came by here to see you when you were sick. Doesn't seem like limbo to me. But, hey, my lips are sealed."

"Thanks. And thanks for the soup."

"No problem." Lila squeezed her hand as she stepped through the door. "Love you, babe. Get some rest."

"I will."

Rowan stood in the doorway shivering as she watched her leave. Then she locked the door and padded across the house in her sock feet, glancing at the laundry everywhere. She'd started on a big cleaning binge to try to find an outlet for all her nervous energy. Now she still had chores to finish, but she'd lost her motivation suddenly.

She grabbed a bottle of water from her fridge and went into the sunroom, where Oscar lay curled up on a pile of papers by her computer.

Rowan sank into the desk chair and stroked his fur. He was sulking because she'd ejected him from the bed so she could wash the sheets. She scratched his favorite spot under his chin, and he responded with a low purr.

Sighing, she dug her phone from her pocket and checked the screen. Nothing new from Jack. She hadn't heard from him since seven this morning when he'd sent her a text.

We arrested him.

Those three simple words had jarred her awake. She'd been shocked and then relieved and then panicked, for some reason. Her emotions were all over the map. She'd been expecting Jack to call with more details, but she figured he must be buried in work. She'd been watching local news, but she hadn't seen any announcements yet, so they must have somehow managed to keep it under wraps for now, maybe while they questioned Anderson or notified his victims.

The quiet wouldn't last forever, though. It was a high-profile story, and the press was sure to sniff out any new developments.

Oscar yawned and stretched his paws, and Rowan scratched his tummy.

She glanced at her sleeping computer and tapped the mouse to bring the screen to life. Just before she got sick, she'd been doing some research into Jack's cold case project. She still hadn't decided whether to take it or not.

But really, she *had* decided. Deep down, she knew what she was going to do. She was going to help him. She couldn't *not*. The case bothered Jack deeply, and after some preliminary research, she understood why. Ramon Huerta was a throwaway kid, someone who—through no fault of his own—never had a chance. Every adult in his life had failed him, and she knew Jack couldn't stand to add his name to the list. Whether anyone else cared or even noticed, Jack was committed to solving the case and holding someone accountable.

Jack's unrelenting determination kept coming back to her again and again. He was a good man. He was strong and committed and, above all, tenacious. And she admired those qualities, but they worried her, too, because she could feel herself getting pulled in.

Someone's falling hard.

Lila had figured it out in a minute. She was like a sister, and it was pointless for Rowan to lie to her.

Rowan closed out of the news article she'd been reading on her computer. She had several other tabs open, various genealogy websites she'd been using to create Will Anderson's family tree. One of the open pages showed a new message in her inbox. It was a contact from one of the surname projects Rowan had queried weeks ago when she originally started her research. Will Anderson's DNA analysis had resulted in two matches, and she had focused her effort on the closer match that ultimately led her to Joy Kendall. This email was someone she had contacted about the weaker match, a distant cousin from a different branch of Will Anderson's family.

Dear Ms. Healy,

Thank you for your interest in the Leary Surname
Project. I have been researching our family line for
months now, and it has certainly been a labor of love!
But with the help of some newly digitized records, I have
at last been able to fill in some branches on our family
tree. Several relatives recently took a DNA test, and I
am hopeful that even more information will be
forthcoming . . .

Rowan skimmed through the long paragraphs. Like so
many other genealogy buffs she'd met, this man had plenty
of time to focus on his pet project and tended to be verbose.
But he was also thorough and detail-oriented, so that was
good. She scrolled to the end of his message, hoping for a
link to the family tree he was so proud of. He didn't disap-
point.

"Thank you, Randall," she murmured, clicking it open.

The Leary family tree appeared on the screen, and
Rowan scanned the diagram, alert for any names that she
didn't already have on her whiteboard. Quite a few were
new, but she zeroed in on one person immediately.

Brett James Leary.

According to her research, he was Anderson's biological
father.

She stared at the name, thinking of Joy and how agoniz-
ing this whole process had been for her, how much guilt
she'd been grappling with since Rowan and Jack had shown
up at her door. Did Brett Leary even know he had a son out
there? Even if he was aware, he likely had no clue that his
son had grown up to be a rapist and murderer.

Rowan clicked on Leary's name to learn more, but the
biographical information available was scant—just a birth
year and county where the birth was recorded.

Rowan stared at the screen as a ball of dread filled her

stomach. She clicked open a browser and ran a search on the name. A cold, queasy feeling came over her as she scrolled through the search results. One of the results included a photograph. Rowan clicked it open and clutched her hand to her chest.

"Oh, Joy," she whispered. "Oh no."

TWENTY-SEVEN

SAGE SPRINGS LOOKED eerily familiar.

Joy cruised through downtown, scanning the store-fronts as she passed the Cotton Gin, Hal's Hardware, the Dreamy Creamery. The High Noon Saloon occupied the corner, a pair of six-shooters painted above the door. They were still going with the western theme here, apparently, which attracted tourists. But the county had fallen on hard times in recent years, and whatever tourist dollars they were getting weren't enough to counter the effects of de-pleted gas wells and thirsty cattle.

Joy rolled to a stop at an intersection and eyed the Dairy Queen, where a group of teenagers gathered around picnic tables. Despite the temperature, the girls wore crop tops and razor-torn jeans, and they tossed their hair and flirted with a Jeep full of boys in the drive-through line.

Joy checked the time. It was only one o'clock, and they should have been in school still. Was off-campus lunch a thing now? Back when Joy was in school, the football coach would have been out here in his pickup yelling at his players to get their asses back to class or they'd be running laps.

The light turned green. Joy drove several blocks farther and hooked a left at the library. Tucked behind it was a brick church surround by towering pecan trees. Joy turned into the parking lot. It was practically empty, but she pulled into a space right beside the long white van used for work camps and field trips.

Joy glanced around. The air was crisp, the sky blue. The weather was cooperating today, and if she could stand the chill, she wasn't going to need to put the top on her convertible anytime soon. Joy smoothed her ponytail, which had kept her hair from turning into a giant tangle on the way here. She adjusted the rearview mirror and took her time putting on lipstick before collecting her Louis Vuitton bag off the seat.

She got out and looked around, taking in the quiet neighborhood as she zipped her suede jacket. Then she strode up the sidewalk and entered the office.

The smell hit her immediately. Musty hymnals and stale coffee. Joy squared her shoulders and stepped up to the counter.

"Good morning." She smiled down at the owl-eyed receptionist, whose window looked out at the parking lot and Joy's shiny black Mercedes.

"May I help you?"

"I'm Joy Kendall, and I have an appointment with the reverend."

The woman blinked up at her. Then her gaze dropped to the datebook in front of her. She flipped it open, and Joy tried to read the handwritten notes.

"Uh . . . an appointment this afternoon? I don't see anything here."

"We spoke on the phone." Joy lifted an eyebrow. "Perhaps he forgot to mention it?"

"Well . . . he's out of the office just now." She cleared her throat and looked up with a nervous smile. "Is it possible you're mistaken about the time?"

"Nope. One o'clock." She checked her Rolex. "He told me he was available. And what is your name?"

She tore her eyes away from the diamond bezel on Joy's watch. "Uh . . . I'm Leanne. I keep all of his appointments, so—"

"Well, sounds like there's been a mix-up. Do you have some paper?" Joy nodded at the spiral message pad beside the old-fashioned desk phone. "I'll leave a message for him, and maybe we can reschedule."

"Uh, certainly. That's fine." She handed up the notepad.

"Thank you." Joy dug a pen from her purse and wrote her name in flowing cursive, followed by her cell number. "Tell you what, my battery is low. I'll also leave the phone number of where I'm staying, too, just in case." She smiled at Leanne, who was still transfixed by the watch. "He can give me a call when he gets in. Do you expect him soon?"

"I don't know."

"No? Well, that's fine." Joy finished writing the message and handed back the pad. "Thank you for your help, Leanne."

"Of course."

Joy left the office and braced herself against the chill as she strode back to her car. She slid behind the wheel and spent a few moments lingering and scrolling through her phone before backing out and exiting the lot.

One stop down, two to go.

Cold wind whipped around her head as she picked up Main Street again and retraced her route. She passed the cemetery on the outskirts of town and hung a left onto Wood Hollow Trace. If memory served, it was a twenty-minute drive along a windy two-lane road that hugged the river and then intersected a highway.

When she reached the juncture, she checked the map on

her phone just to make sure. She'd never actually driven this herself. Or paid much attention.

She hung a left onto the highway and drove another ten minutes until she reached the turnoff.

ANGELHEART RANCH 2 MILES.

Joy took the turn. She scanned the barbed wire fence on either side, taking in the familiar pastures and trees. Eight summers she'd come here, but the grass had been green, not yellow, under the bright July sun.

The fence went from wire to wooden, and she tapped the brakes as she spotted the private drive up ahead. Joy checked her mirror for traffic and pulled over. She bumped along the shoulder and rolled to a halt.

ANGELHEART RANCH read the wrought iron sign above the gate. No more Camp Angelheart, and changing the name was a smart move. A ranch was more versatile, not to mention profitable. It could be used during the non-summer months for corporate off-sites, weekend retreats, weddings. The venue had been written up in articles—no doubt the result of someone's PR efforts.

Joy got out. Her suede Uggs sank into the sodden ground as she trekked to the gate. It was locked, of course. She stepped onto the wooden fence slat and slung her leg over, then hopped down.

A chill darted down her spine as she looked around.

The road through the trees was familiar. She remembered the giant boulder on the left, then the gray windmill on the right as the road curved around. She walked briskly, keeping her cold hands buried inside her jacket pockets as she neared the main campus, which consisted of half a dozen buildings around an athletic field. The grass was yellow here, too, and the archery targets at the end of the field were shrouded with canvas covers.

Joy's pulse picked up as she recognized the low limestone buildings. There was the dining hall, the craft hut, the main office with the flagpole out front. On the hill behind the office was a row of wooden cabins. Even though she hadn't been here in years, she could still name all the cabins on the girls' side, from Guppy Gulch all the way to Robins' Ridge, where the sixteen-year-olds stayed.

Joy trekked past the craft hut and stopped at a wooden sign pointing to Campfire Hill. She gazed up the slope, interested to see that the steep, rocky path she remembered had been replaced by concrete steps—probably so kids like her wouldn't sprain an ankle and end up in the infirmary.

Joy walked past the dining hall and then the outdoor chapel, which consisted of cedar-plank benches arranged in a half circle under a canopy of trees. Joy paused to look as the cypress limbs swayed gently in the breeze. Once upon a time, Joy had sat there under the dappled sunlight and felt close to God. She hadn't felt that way in a very long time.

She kept walking and came to the office, where the camp director spent his time when he wasn't teaching archery or giving campfire talks. Reverend Brett didn't work here anymore. He was Reverend Leary now, and he'd moved up in the world. She stopped in front of the steps for a moment and then circled around to the back, passing the post office window where kids would line up for mail. At the back of the building, she found the screened-in porch that served as the infirmary. There was still a wooden sign above the door showing a little red cross.

Joy's chest tightened. It looked different now. The mesh screens had been replaced by glass. Heart thudding, she approached the door. She tried the handle, but it was locked securely, and she felt a jab of bitter irony. She cupped her hand against the window and peered inside.

The screened-in porch was a sitting room now, furnished with sofas and rocking chairs. Joy remembered a row of gray cots covered in soft blue blankets. She remembered the rotating fan in the corner, the counter filled with glass jars containing cotton balls and tongue depressors. She remembered the smell of rubbing alcohol and the mini-fridge where Nurse Amy kept cans of ginger ale for home-sick campers with queasy stomachs.

Joy remembered the cot on the end, where she'd spent the night—or most of it—beside Becca Foster, who had gotten sick after the Saturday picnic.

A silent, useless rage welled inside her as she thought about it now. A sprained *ankle*. What the hell? Joy should have been back at her cabin with an ice pack, not stuck in here for two full days. It was all a setup, a manipulation, and she'd been too naive to see it. She remembered Brett coming in, smiling as he paid Joy and Becca what he called a "house call." He'd brought a deck of blue Bicycle cards, and he'd sat on the end of Joy's cot and teed up a game of gin rummy.

You're good, Joy.

She remembered the dark room that night and listening to the chirp of crickets over the rotating fan. She remem-bered the low squeak of the screen door and a whispered voice.

Joy, are you sleeping?
Joy, wake up.
Joy, come walk with me.
Joy, Joy, Joy . . .

"Hey."

She jumped, startled, and glanced up. She was seated on the ground, staring up into a leathery brown face. The man wore green coveralls and work gloves and held a rake in his hand.

"That your Mercedes?"

She cleared her throat. "I'm sorry?"

"The car at the gate." He looked her over with a combi-nation of interest and disapproval.

"Oh." She stood up and swayed slightly as the blood

rushed to her feet. When had she sat down? And her cheeks were wet. She wiped them dry. "Yes, that's me."

"This is private property," he said gruffly. "No visitors allowed."

"Oh. Well, I was just leaving."

She gave a brisk nod and walked past him, folding her arms in front of her as she started down the path.

"You a camper?"

She turned around.

"What?"

"A camper." He smiled. "We get them sometimes. People come back to show their kids."

She stared at him for a moment.

Then she shrugged. "No kids," she told him, and walked away.

TWENTY-EIGHT

"Hey, where the hell are you?" Bryan asked, and Jack could barely hear him with all the noise in the background.

"Something came up."

"What?"

"Something *came up*. I'm not going to make it."

"Man, you're killing me. This is *your* collar. Get your ass over here. Everyone in here wants to buy you a beer."

Jack highly doubted that. And anyway, his mission tonight didn't include getting hammered and waking up with a hangover when Heidi's lieutenant had scheduled another press conference bright and early in the morning. As Jack had suspected, the guy was a publicity hound and had had no qualms about jumping in front of reporters to take credit for leading the task force that finally apprehended the notorious WCR.

"You guys have fun," Jack said. "I'll catch up with you tomorrow."

"You're serious?"

"Yeah, I've got something I need to do."

Bryan laughed. "Yeah, I got it. Tell her hi for me."

Jack tossed his phone in the passenger seat and turned on his brights as he scanned the roadside for landmarks. The iron cactus came into view, and he slowed.

He was going to catch a ton of crap for skipping out on the Icehouse tonight. But he didn't care. Rowan was dodging him, and he needed to find out what was going on. She'd been sick, but there was more to it than that, and he wanted to talk to her in person. She'd lied to him multiple times now, and although he suspected she had her reasons, he was ready for a real conversation.

He passed the limestone wall, and his headlights swept over the red barn. No lights on there, but Rowan's porch light glowed, and her Corolla was parked under a tree, meaning she was home.

The door to Rowan's car stood open, and Jack felt a prickle of unease as he pulled up beside it. The interior light was on, too, but the car looked empty.

Jack got out of his Jeep and glanced around. Was she heading out somewhere and she'd gone back inside to get something?

He mounted the porch steps and tried the door. Locked.

He knocked and waited. No answer.

Glancing over his shoulder at the car, he went down the steps and started for the barn. Maybe she was with Skyler.

A screen door slammed in the distance. Turning in the direction of the noise, he saw a shadowy figure running across the yard near the ranch house.

"Rowan?"

No answer.

He rested his hand on the butt of his gun as he walked toward the shadow. The person was moving quickly in the direction of Rowan's house.

"Hey."

The figure halted. "Oh my God! You scared me."

Relief washed over him as Rowan stepped into the glow of the porch light.

"What are you doing here?" she asked breathlessly.

"Looking for you." He stepped closer. "What's wrong?"

"I'm on my way out."

"You left your car door open."

"Crap, I forgot." She combed her hand through her hair. It was damp, as though she'd just jumped out of the shower. She wore jeans and a sweatshirt and had flip-flops on her otherwise bare feet. "My car's low on gas and I need to take Skyler's."

"Rowan, what's wrong?"

She looked at him, eyes wide. "What?"

"It's thirty degrees out and you're practically barefoot."

"Oh." She glanced down. "I'm in a hurry."

He rested a hand on her shoulder. "Stop and take a breath."

She sucked in a breath and blew it out.

"Tell me what's the matter."

She bit her lip, and he saw some kind of war going on in her mind. To tell him or not? Whatever it was, he wanted her to trust him.

"Where are you going?" he asked, trying an easier question.

"Can you drive? I'll explain on the way."

"Fine."

She jogged to her car and closed the door, then went around to the passenger side of his Jeep and jumped in.

He got behind the wheel. "You want to lock your car?"

She glanced up from her phone and waved him off. "No need."

Jack bumped over the grass and looped around to the driveway. "So, is Skyler home or—"

"I don't know where she is. Probably at the Duck."

He glanced at her in the seat beside him as he made his way down the rutted driveway back to the road. Her cheeks were flushed, and her sweatshirt was on inside out.

"You still have a fever?"

She looked up from her phone. "What? No. I'm all better."

He trained his gaze on the road, waiting for her to finish scrolling. She muttered a curse and dropped her phone into the cup holder.

He rolled to a stop at the highway. "Which way?"

"Left."

He turned left on the highway and gave her until he had it in fourth gear to collect herself.

"Tell me what's going on."

She took a deep breath. "It's Joy. I'm worried about her."

"Why?"

"I think she's in danger."

"Danger? From what?"

She clutched her hands in her lap. "I don't *know* exactly. I just know she's in some kind of trouble."

Rowan took a deep breath and blew it out, and Jack waited for her to explain.

"So . . . Joy's been very upset. Paranoid. She's been having trouble sleeping," Rowan told him. "I mean, I get it. The WCR thing—*everyone* is jumpy. I've had insomnia, too. I feel like I'm in college again."

Jack darted a look at her.

"This has been traumatic for her," Rowan went on. "I thought it was the whole adoption thing—us dredging up her past and all that—but then we had this conversation when I was at her house working with her, and I realized it was more than that. She's not just anxious, she's really *afraid*. To the point where she's having panic attacks."

Jack glanced at her, not liking where this conversation was heading at all. "You're saying she's afraid for her safety?"

"Right. I mean, I thought maybe she was being irrational, and I tried to talk her out of it. I tried to tell her that he won't *know* it was her—"

"'He' as in Anderson?"

"Yeah, I tried to reassure her that the police won't reveal who tipped them off to his identity, in case she was worried about him coming after her."

They reached a juncture of two highways, and Jack stopped. "Tell me where we're going."

"Sage Springs." She picked up her phone and tapped open a map. "Take a left."

"The *town* of Sage Springs? That's forty-five minutes away."

"I know."

Jack hung a left.

"So, I told her right, didn't I?" Rowan looked at him. In the greenish glow of the dashboard, he could see the stress on her face. "You guys keep that information under wraps, don't you? The names of family members who give you identities and DNA samples?"

"We try. But sometimes it comes out, especially when a case goes to trial," he said, knowing it wasn't the answer she wanted to hear.

Rowan shook her head. "Well, I suspected that, but I tried to reassure her anyway. And I thought I understood what her anxiety was about. But today I realized I didn't understand anything at all."

He looked at her. "What happened today?"

TWENTY-NINE

ROWAN STARED AHEAD at the two-lane highway. Just saying everything out loud put a cramp in her stomach.

"This afternoon I was clearing up loose ends," she said.

"Loose ends?"

"With the Will Anderson case." She glanced at him. "Back when you gave me this, you made it clear everything was urgent, that you were on a *ticking clock*, that you needed answers ASAP. So, as soon as I had something, I pulled up and handed it over. But it wasn't comprehensive yet."

"How do you mean?"

Rowan looked at him. Even in the darkness, she could see the tension in his face, as though maybe he sensed what she was going to tell him.

"You wanted a lead, and I gave you a lead," she said. "I gave you his birth mother. That was what I had, based on my strongest match. But there was another match—a weaker one—on another branch of his family tree, and I had already started down that path, making inquiries, when everything started falling into place around Joy Kendall and the Kendall family. Well, I finally heard back from someone on the paternal side of the family. It's the Learys, by the way."

"Who?"

Rowan grabbed her phone from the cup holder and opened the page she'd found. It was a brief news story in the *Sage Springs Ledger.*

She glanced in the side mirror. "You need to pull over to look at this."

Jack checked the rearview and then veered onto the shoulder. He parked and put the hazards on.

"This is Will Anderson's birth father." She handed him the phone. "Brett James Leary."

Jack took the phone, and his expression hardened. He looked up at her.

"He's fifty-nine," Rowan said. "He was thirty at the time his son was born. Joy was *sixteen*. Her high school boyfriend isn't the father—this fucker is."

Jack looked down at the image. He scrolled past the photo to the article beneath it.

"He was the youth pastor at a church at the time," Rowan said. "I looked him up. That was twenty-eight years ago, and now he's the head pastor there. A fucking rapist."

"Does Joy know you know all this?"

"No." Rowan sighed. "Although, I'm sure she knows I'll figure it out. She probably assumes everyone will eventually, that her whole life will be put under a spotlight." Rowan took a deep breath. "So, I called her today to talk through all this, and I couldn't reach her, so I went by her house, and *that's* when I started to get alarmed. Something's wrong, Jack."

"Why do you say that?"

"Her maid answered the door, and she was worried, too. She said yesterday Joy told her she would be working from home today, but Joy hasn't been there at all, and she missed an appointment with her landscape architect. And also—this is weird—she left two days' worth of food for her dogs."

Jack just looked at her. "Where's her husband?"

"Out of town on business, according to the maid. So, I left another message at the house for Joy to call me and went home. I ate dinner and took a shower, and when I got out, I realized I had a voicemail from Joy. I almost deleted it, too, because I didn't recognize the number. It sounds like she's having an emotional meltdown. She's weepy and slurring her words."

"You think she's drunk?"

"Probably." Rowan picked up her phone and clicked into the voicemail. "And she takes prescription sleeping pills, too. Not a good combination." She hit play and handed the phone to Jack.

"Rowan . . ." Joy's voice filled the car. "I got your message. *Messages.* I got all *three.*" Ice cubes clinked against a glass. "I can't come to the phone right now, unfortunately. It's old-home week. I'm in my hometown taking a trip down memory lane. This whole thing has been . . . a tough journey. And the guilt . . ." Her voice trailed off, and Jack looked at Rowan. "The cycle . . . that I've *allowed* to happen is ending. Finally." Her voice quieted. "We don't want to become our parents, but it's inevitable, isn't it? I spent my whole *life* trying to be different from my mother. And I ended up the same in so many ways. Weak and cowering . . ."

Jack looked at Rowan, his face grim.

"But I need to *thank you*, Rowan, for doing what you did," she continued. "Someone had to stop it—"

"Stop what?" Jack asked.

"I don't know. Her son?"

"—I'm sorry I wasn't strong enough when I needed to be. That's on *me*." More ice cubes rattling. "So . . . if I don't see you again . . . thank you, Rowan."

Silence filled the car. Jack looked at her.

"See?"

"I don't like the 'if I don't see you again' part," he said.

"I know!"

He handed her the phone. "She sounds volatile."

"Volatile? More like suicidal."

JOY TUCKED THE paper bag into her purse as she left the gas station. Hunching her shoulders against the cold, she jogged to the other side of the street and crossed the parking lot of the Blue Iguana Inn. The light was on in the lobby, and she yanked open the glass door.

The purple-haired guy behind the counter glanced up.

"Any messages?" she asked.

He just stared at her.

"Joy Kendall. In casita seven."

"Uh. No." He glanced behind him at the wall of wooden cubbies. "No messages."

Joy let the door whisk shut, and he returned to whatever he'd been doing on his phone.

She trekked across the parking lot, glancing around for any new cars. No black Cadillac sedan, although she hadn't really expected one, had she? She glanced at her watch. It was almost ten.

She dug through her purse for her key. It was attached to a carved wooden iguana, probably so guests wouldn't forget to return it to the lobby when they checked out. Joy unlocked the door and stepped into the little cottage. The place had Saltillo tile floors and Mexican blankets on the ends of the two queen beds. She set her purse on the chair and stripped off her jacket. It was cold and drafty, but she didn't want to turn on the heater.

Joy went into the mini-kitchen and took her bottle of Grey Goose from the fridge. She poured some over ice and added a splash of cranberry from the bottle in her purse. She took a sip and then went to check the back porch.

She'd left the light off, but she could still see the two

matching rocking chairs in the moonlight. Beyond them was a lawn that sloped down to the creek. She unlocked the door and pushed it open. The creek was full from the recent rain, and her casita was close enough to hear water rushing over the rocks.

Joy left the door ajar. Then she switched on the lamp, casting the little seating area in a soft yellow light. Retrieving her purse, she went into the bathroom and closed the door. The vanity was covered in colorful tiles, and she set her purse beside the sink, then reached into the shower and turned the water to hot.

Slowly, Joy peeled off her clothes, dropping several hundred dollars' worth of designer activewear onto the cold tile floor. Standing naked before the mirror, she took a swig of her drink.

She looked good for forty-five. Better than most women her age, and certainly better than the men. At work, she was surrounded by guys, most of them with paunches and man-boobs. But they got away with it, of course. Put a man in a Porsche, and no one gave a shit about his appearance.

Joy turned to the side and gazed at her stomach. She had scars from plastic surgery, but they were nearly invisible. No one ever noticed them, including Michael, who knew her better than anyone.

Tears stung her eyes as she studied the body she'd worked so hard for. What a waste. She'd spent her whole life hiding and lying and trying to forget. But some part of her had known it wasn't possible.

She twisted her hair into a knot and stepped into the shower. The hot water sluiced over her shoulders and down her back. She gave herself three full minutes—just enough to warm her blood and loosen her muscles—and then she stepped out.

It was time.

She dumped the rest of her drink down the sink. Then she dried off with the white towel and draped it over the rack. She had hung her robe on the hook when she checked in, and now she wrapped herself in the cool white silk before grabbing her purse and emerging from the bathroom in a cloud of steam.

Joy glanced at the back door before crossing the suite and dropping her purse onto the floor beside the bed. The air was even colder now, but the shower had warmed her up. She stripped back the covers and sat down. Pulling her phone from her purse, she saw two more messages from Michael and one from Rowan. She flipped the phone face down on the nightstand.

Her gaze fell on the shiny pearl grip sticking out of her purse. Joy reached for the pistol. It felt cool and heavy in her hand, and she traced her fingertip over the short silver barrel. She'd never liked guns. But she liked this one. Of everything in the big display case, this one had caught her eye. Petite yet powerful. Everything about it suited her, and she'd known it was hers the instant she saw it.

Joy reached over and switched off the lamp. The room was cold and quiet and dim—the sole light coming from the lamp in the living area. She lay back on the bed, nestling her head against the pillow and her pistol beside her. She gazed up at the ceiling and waited for her eyes to adjust. She took a deep breath and tried to relax, but her heart was racing.

Forgive me, Michael. You didn't sign up for this, I know. But neither did I.

A hot tear slid down her cheek. Then another. And another. She rested the pistol on the bed and wiped the tears away.

"TURN HERE," ROWAN said as they neared the juncture.

"Are you sure?"

She studied the map on her phone. "It's faster, according to this."

"Okay, but I've never been on this highway." Jack hung

a right. "What about when we get there? How are we going
to know where she is?"

"I don't know. Look for her car? I mean, it's a tiny little
town. There can't be many places to stay."

"You want to try texting her?"

"I did."

"What about her husband?"

"I don't have his info. But I might be able to get it."
Rowan scrolled through her phone and found her latest call
from Dara.

She picked up on the first ring.

"Hey, it's me," Rowan told her. "I need your help."

JOY'S HEART LURCHED at the knock. She held her breath
and waited. Thirty seconds later it came again, louder.

She didn't move. She lay stone still, not even breathing
as she strained to hear.

Nothing.

No more knocks or footsteps, only the distant rushing of
water behind the cabin. Then . . . something. A faint rustling in the bushes. Or was she imagining it?

A soft thud on the back steps. Joy held her breath, heart
pounding wildly as she heard the soft rasp of footsteps on
the porch. Then the faint but unmistakable *creak* as the
back door opened and he stepped inside.

"Joy?"

The low voice in the darkness was dizzyingly familiar.

"Are you asleep?"

She sat up in bed. "No."

He crossed the living room to the sleeping area, and she
took in his appearance. He wore a flannel shirt with the
sleeves rolled up. His hair had thinned, and he looked older
now, thicker through the middle. But he had the same tall,
broad-shouldered build that could command an audience.

He stepped closer. "What are you playing at?" he growled.

"Playing at?"

"Who do you think you are showing up here and making a scene?"

His words sank in, and icy rage filled her. "Who do I think *I am*? I'm the girl whose life you ripped apart. Do you even remember?"

His scowl answered her question.

He stepped closer to the bed, and her heart rate kicked up. "Who did you talk to?"

"No one," she said. "Yet."

He slapped the switch on the wall, and the room lit up. Joy blinked at the brightness, and he glared down at her.

"What do you want?" he demanded. "Why are you here?"

"I came to tell you your secret is out, and there's nothing you can do about it."

His face became red and mottled with useless fury. She recognized the look—she'd felt that way a thousand times herself, and she almost felt sympathy for him but—

"You *bitch*." He lunged toward her. She screamed, but the sound was lost as his hands clamped around her throat.

She tried to pry off his fingers as his angry red face loomed over her and she fought for breath. The pain was intense as his hands squeezed out all air, all sound. She bucked, trying to get his weight off her as the hands clenched tighter and panic took over. She clawed at his hands, his eyes, his cheeks. She slapped at the bed as her vision tunneled and dimmed.

No, no, no!

But there was no sound, only his monstrous face, and the realization that she'd made a terrible mistake.

Her hand fell on something hard, and she closed her fingers around the grip. She smashed the pistol against the side of his head, and he jerked back, dragging her with him by the neck.

Pop!

THIRTY

Jack whipped into the parking lot.

"Oh my God. Was that a *gunshot*?" Rowan looked horrified as he screeched to a halt beside Joy's black Mercedes. "Jack?"

He jerked his gun from the holster. "Stay here. Do *not* get out!"

He jumped out of the Jeep and raced up to the door of casita seven.

The weight was crushing her, suffocating her, compressing her lungs. Joy shoved at his shoulder, but it didn't budge. She heaved with all her might, and his massive body fell to the floor with a *thud*.

Pounding at the door. Joy kicked the covers away and glanced around, frantic.

Boom.

The door burst open, sending splinters flying. Jack Bruner rushed into the room, gun drawn, and Joy's heart skittered. He looked from her to the groaning body on the floor beside her feet.

Joy flung the pistol onto the bed and held up her hands. "He attacked me," she croaked, but her voice was barely audible.

Jack rolled Brett Leary onto his back, and the wound in his side gushed blood all over the tile. Jack patted him down and then glanced up. He reached across the bed and grabbed her pistol, then tucked it into the back of his jeans.

"He attacked me, and I shot him." Joy rubbed her neck, transfixed by the growing puddle of blood.

"I called 911."

Joy glanced up to see Rowan standing in the doorway, looking like a deer in the headlights.

"Get *back in the car*!" Jack bellowed.

Rowan didn't move. "I called 911," she repeated, looking at the splintered doorframe. Then she looked at Joy. "Are you all right?"

Joy stepped backward, bumping into the bed. She sat down, clutching her neck. Her throat felt like it was on fire, and she stared down at the expanding pool of red.

Jack grabbed the pillow off the bed and yanked the case off it. He wadded the fabric and pressed it against the wound. Seconds later, it was saturated.

Joy blinked down in shock. *I killed him.*

I killed him killed him killed him. He's gone.

"Joy."

She glanced up, and Rowan was standing there, holding her arm. "You're bleeding, Joy."

She looked down, startled by the streaks of scarlet on her white robe.

"Here, sit down," Rowan tried to steer her to a chair. "Are you injured?"

"No, I'm—" She watched as Jack reached over and dragged a sheet off the bed to stanch the bleeding. "It's his."

Shaking off Rowan's grip, Joy stepped back. She stared

down at the face that had haunted her for twenty-eight years and watched the color drain out of it.

Joy sank to the floor and pulled her knees to her chest. A siren sounded in the distance. It drew closer and closer and was joined by another. She felt numb. Cold. Detached.

She pressed her forehead to her knees and waited.

THIRTY-ONE

THE NORMALLY SLEEPY Sage County Sheriff's Office was a hive of activity. Jack sat in front of a borrowed computer and watched the deputies rushing back and forth as they pieced together the circumstances surrounding the shooting death of Brett Leary.

Joy had given a brief statement at the scene, but when deputies attempted to interview her again at the hospital, she'd wisely declined and called a lawyer.

"Do you think they believe her?"

Jack glanced up at Bryan, who leaned on the wall of Jack's borrowed cubicle. Bryan had shown up here after Jack called him with the news of what had happened. It wasn't their jurisdiction, but his partner had come anyway.

"Who?" Jack asked.

"Joy Kendall. Do you think they question her self-defense story?"

"What's to question? She's got a ring of bruises around her neck. He attacked her in her bed."

"No, I know that," Bryan said. "I'm just having a hard

time picturing it, and I bet they are, too. I mean, the guy's a *pastor*."

"Yeah, well. Not all predators show up in a ski mask."

Jack scanned his report one last time and then saved it. He logged out and pushed back his chair.

"I'm out." He stood and grabbed his keys.

"You don't want to talk to the sheriff after he wraps up in there?"

Jack glanced at the closed office door. The sheriff had been meeting with the county prosecutor for the last half hour, probably trying to figure out how to message this.

"No." Jack checked his watch. "I need to get home."

"I think I'll hang around," Bryan said, "see what details I can scoop up."

"Keep me posted."

"I will."

Jack nodded and walked out, aware of people watching him as he stepped from the bullpen into the empty lobby.

Almost empty.

Rowan sat alone in a chair near the door, and Jack felt a rush of alarm as she glanced up from her phone.

"What are you doing here?" he asked.

She dropped her phone in her purse and stood up. "Waiting for you."

"I thought you got a ride with Lila?"

"Turns out, she's working tonight." Rowan shrugged. "So, I decided just to wait."

Jack stepped closer, filled with both worry and relief. She looked almost as shell-shocked as she had back at the inn when the parking lot had been packed with emergency vehicles. After coming to the sheriff's office and giving a statement, she had told Jack she was getting a ride home. He'd been racing to wrap up his paperwork so he could go see her, and now she was standing right in front of him.

He took her hand. "Come on."

He ushered her out of the office into the cold night air. It was almost one A.M., and he couldn't remember when he'd felt more drained. It had been a marathon day. A marathon *week*.

He stopped on the sidewalk and took off his jacket, then draped it over her shoulders.

"You don't need to—"

He kissed her and cut her off. Then he wrapped his arms around her.

"Thanks for waiting," he said.

She stared up at him with those deep blue eyes, and he realized he hadn't held her like this in days. It felt good, so good it worried him.

"Are you really done for the night?" she asked.

"I'm done. Let me take you home."

B Y *HOME*, JACK meant his place, and Rowan talked herself out of all her reservations as she took him up on his offer to make herself comfortable. She borrowed his shower, and when she emerged from the bedroom clean and once again wearing a borrowed T-shirt, she discovered he'd made a fire in the fireplace.

Now she stretched out on the sofa under a fleece blanket, staring at the flames as his hand stroked over her hip. Their first time together had been fast and desperate, but tonight was slow and sensual.

He glided his hand down her side and kissed the back of her neck.

"You smell good," he murmured.

She looked at him over her shoulder. "It's your shampoo."

"Not that. You." His mouth moved down her neck as his hand slid between her thighs.

She rolled over and stared up at him. His skin looked gold in the firelight, and she reached up to trace his jaw.

"You never told me about this, either," she said, running her fingertip over the swollen bruise.

Jack gazed down at her, and she braced herself for something evasive.

"He resisted arrest," he said.

"Will Anderson?"

He nodded. "We followed him from his house. He was prowling around someone's backyard, opening gates, unlocking things. I think it was a dry run."

A chill moved through her, and she shuddered. "God. It's so lucky you were there."

"It ended up being a foot pursuit. I tackled him in the woods, and he landed a punch."

"But you got him under control?"

"With Bryan's help, yeah. He's a big guy. It took two of us."

Rowan watched him, picturing the scene. She hadn't expected so much detail. Usually, Jack was very tight-lipped about his work.

He propped his weight on his elbow and looked down at her. "Now can I ask *you* something?"

She tensed. She had a feeling she knew what he was going to ask.

He stroked his finger over her collarbone. "What happened the other morning?"

She didn't respond.

"Don't say 'nothing.'" He gave her a sharp look. "You were almost in tears. I've been trying to figure out what I did—"

"You didn't do anything."

She sat up, pulling the blanket over her. He sat up, too.

She blew out a breath. "I saw the crime scene photos on the dresser. And the Polaroid of Olivia."

His eyebrows tipped up with surprise.

"We're friends."

He frowned. "You and Olivia Salter?"

She nodded.

Jack tipped his head back. "Fuck." He raked his hand

through his hair and looked at her. "Why didn't you tell me, Rowan?"

She could see he wasn't happy about this.

"At first, I didn't know."

He scooted back, pulling the blanket over his lap as he leveled a look at her. "You didn't know what, exactly?"

"What your case was about. All you told me was it was a serial sex offender. It wasn't until later that I figured out it was WCR."

"You should have told me then that you personally knew one of the victims."

"Why? That was the whole reason I took the job. I wanted to help you find him."

The furrow in his brow deepened as he watched her.

Rowan looked at the fire. "But . . . you're right. I know I should have said something. It's one of the reasons this whole thing has been difficult. Back when Olivia was attacked, it turned her entire life upside down. She became depressed and withdrawn from everyone. And it affected her friends, too. All of us were shaken by it."

Jack just looked at her, and she could tell he didn't approve of her keeping this information from him.

"I'm sorry." He took her hand and squeezed it.

"Why are *you* sorry?"

He shook his head. "I feel like shit that we didn't find him sooner. This investigation dragged on for years, and we couldn't catch a break."

She watched his expression, and she knew he felt guilty, as though he were personally responsible for the actions of some sadistic psychopath.

Do you believe evil is inherited?

Rowan thought of Joy and the guilt she'd been dealing with, too, knowing she'd given birth to someone like that.

Jack grabbed his boxer briefs off the floor and pulled them on. He walked into the kitchen. Was he angry with her? It was difficult to tell.

She wrapped the blanket around her shoulders and went into the kitchen. He pulled a bottle of water from the fridge and set it on the counter.

"Are you upset?" she asked.

"I wish you hadn't seen those pictures."

"Me too."

She hadn't meant to stumble onto them—they were just there in his room. And that was part of the issue. Jack was immersed in his work, always, and if she spent time with him, then she was exposed to it, too. This was why she'd told herself she would never again date a cop.

Although "dating" didn't even begin to describe this. They had yet to have a normal evening that wasn't interrupted by work. And Rowan knew that wasn't likely to change. Jack's job was part of who he was.

He leaned against the counter and watched her. "And I'm sorry this has been hard for you."

"Hard for *me*?"

"Yes."

"Will Anderson being locked up is way more important than whether something is hard for me," she said. "I mean, that's the whole thing, right? That's why I can't get away from this work. Whether it's Ric or you or whoever, I always end up getting pulled back in."

"You're good at it," he said. "People want your help."

She stepped closer and looked at his bare chest. Finally, they were having the conversation that had been weighing on her for weeks.

"I'm tired of resisting," she told him. "Maybe you called it from the start."

He frowned. "What's that mean?"

"Maybe I'm going to go back. I don't know." She shook her head. "I'm so confused. I can't seem to decide what's the right thing to do."

He brushed her hair out of her eyes. "You're tired. You've been sick and you haven't slept." He nodded at the clock on the microwave. "And it's three in the morning. Not the best time for making decisions."

She rested her head against his chest, and he wrapped his arms around her. She heaved a sigh.

He sighed, too. "I knew you were lying when you said nothing was wrong."

"Okay, fine. But I don't have *tells*."

"Yeah, you do."

She closed her eyes. Maybe he was right. And if he was, then that meant he knew she was keeping other things from him, too. But intimacy had never been easy for her.

Someone's falling hard.

She pulled back and looked up at him, at those deep brown eyes, at the strong lines of his face, and at the nasty bruise he'd just told her about. She'd become so attached to him in so short a time. What if she was alone here? What if she truly let her guard down and he backed off?

"What?" he asked.

She shook her head.

He lifted an eyebrow, clearly aware she was holding things in again. But she didn't want to dump all of her insecurities on him.

He dropped his hands to her hips and pulled her against him. He was attracted to her. At least she knew *that* for sure.

"I'm taking a comp day tomorrow," he said. "I've spent the last week on stakeout, and I need some time off. Will you spend it with me?"

She looked up at him. "When was the last time you took a comp day?"

"Hmm . . . never?"

"In that case, how can I say no?"

THIRTY-TWO

B RYAN HEARD BOLTS clicking before Evie opened the door.
"You're early," she said, pulling the door back.

"Yeah, hope I'm not catching you at a bad time."

"Not at all."

She ushered him inside, and he wiped his shoes on the welcome mat before stepping into the apartment. The place was only partially unpacked, and cardboard boxes lined the wall. The living area had wood floors and a sliding door that opened out onto a fourth-floor balcony. Bryan recognized some of the furniture from his original visit to her previous place.

"You want coffee?" she asked, leading him past a granite kitchen island. Today she wore a T-shirt and jeans, and her feet were bare.

"I'm fine, thanks."

Beside the breakfast table was a child-size easel with a big drawing pad propped on it. He glanced around.

"Bella's not home," she said, guessing his question. "She's with her dad this weekend, so I've been knocking out chores." She tipped her head to the side. "Do you by chance know Chinese?"

"Chinese?"

She smiled. "Today's project." She stepped into the living room, where a shelving unit lay flat on the rug.

Bryan walked over and surveyed the little pile of screws on the floor next to an unfolded instruction sheet.

"Those are the leftovers."

He glanced up at her.

"But I don't think I'm supposed to have so many extras."

"Yeah, that's probably not good." He crouched down beside the shelving unit and set the file he'd brought with him on the rug.

"Where'd you get this thing?" he asked.

"It was on clearance online." She came to stand beside him. "Guess now I know why."

He spied a plastic bag underneath a piece of foam and tore it open.

"You forgot the feet," he said.

"Oh. How did I miss those?"

He examined the shelf for a moment, then attached the four wooden feet to the bottom with the remaining screws. He set the shelf upright and stood up.

"Nice. Thank you." She sighed. "And this is why I shouldn't start projects at two in the morning."

Bryan rested his hands on his hips and looked at the shelf. Then he turned to her. "Trouble sleeping?"

"Yeah." She pursed her lips, looking at the shelf instead of him. "It's weird. I thought after the arrest, things might go back to normal. Or at least, *more* normal."

Guilt needled him as he noticed how tired her eyes looked. She was already under stress, and his visit wasn't going to help.

"So." She turned to face him and crossed her arms. "What was it you wanted to talk about?" She glanced down at the manila folder he'd set on the floor.

Bryan scooped up the file. "You mind if we sit down?"

She led him to the kitchen island and pulled out a bar-stool. Bryan took the one beside it, feeling nervous now, although he wasn't sure why. She'd asked him to keep her posted on this, and that's what he was doing. But now he wondered if he should have left her alone.

"We executed a search warrant at William Anderson's home."

She gave a stiff nod and stared down at the folder, obviously dreading whatever he'd brought to show her.

"We recovered a stash of items that we believe belonged to some of the victims."

The collection had been found deep inside the garage of the house Anderson shared with his girlfriend, Sheryl Mason, whose name was on the lease. Anderson's souvenirs were discovered in a toolbox buried inside a big plastic bin filled with camping equipment—cookstoves, flashlights, tin dishes. The top tray of the toolbox was filled with nails and screws, but underneath was a treasure trove of evidence, including a set of car keys, a charm bracelet, a gym card.

A silver locket.

Bryan opened the file and slid it in front of Evie. He watched her face as she looked down at the eight-by-ten crime scene photograph showing a silver locket displayed atop a blue tarp. A metal ruler had been positioned beside the locket for scale.

She stared down at it, not moving or even blinking.

"Is it yours?" he asked, although he could see the answer on her face.

She gave a slight nod, still not taking her eyes off the photo.

"I hate that he touched it," she whispered.

"I understand."

"Is there a picture of the inside?"

Bryan slid the photograph behind the second one in the stack. This one was a close-up showing the locket open.

She frowned. "Where's Bella's picture?"

"This is how we found it. It was empty."

Her gaze jumped to his. "He took out her picture?"

"Presumably."

She winced and looked away.

Bryan closed the folder. The missing picture was one reason he'd needed confirmation from Evie that this was her necklace. But now he wished he'd found a better way to go about this.

She opened the folder again and flipped back to the first photograph. She gazed down at it, shaking her head. Then she slid it back.

"Well, that's it." She sighed. "It's really him."

"You thought we had the wrong guy?"

"No." She glanced at him. "I mean, maybe part of me. You can't imagine the crazy stuff that goes through my mind in the middle of the night. But that's conclusive enough for me."

From Bryan's perspective, the DNA match was conclusive enough. Not to mention the size twelve Adidas sneakers they had found in his closet that would no doubt eventually be determined to match the footprints found in Evie's backyard. Combined with all the items in the toolbox, the physical evidence against Will Anderson was overwhelming. Any trial would be a slam dunk, and he would be lucky to get a plea to avoid death row.

Of all the cases Bryan had worked, this one deserved the death penalty. But he knew how the system worked, and he could live with prospect of Will Anderson spending the rest of his life in prison—which was where his biological father should have ended up, too.

Bryan's chest tightened with frustration as he sat there in Evie's kitchen thinking about the many people WCR had hurt or killed. Will Anderson had caused so much damage that would last a lifetime. And meanwhile, the man whose cruel act had set everything in motion had suffered for only a moment.

But at least Brett Leary couldn't add to his list of victims. Joy Kendall had seen to that.

Bryan closed the folder. "Thanks for taking a look. We appreciate the confirmation."

"Thank you." She covered his hand with hers. "Seeing this helps."

Her hand was warm and light on his, but she pulled it away and tucked it in her lap.

Bryan looked at her, not knowing what to make of the gesture. But he knew he needed to go.

He got up from the stool and she did, too. He picked up his file and walked to the door.

"If you need anything, don't hesitate to call me. *Us*." He turned to look at her. "Detective Lasco has some resources she can put you in touch with. Counseling, support groups, things like that."

"Yes, she told me."

"That's good."

He gazed down at her, suddenly uneasy with the thought of not seeing her anymore.

"Thank you again," she said. "I'm glad you came by."

Bryan nodded, even though he had no idea whether she meant it or was just being polite.

She put her hand on the doorknob. "This probably sounds weird but . . ." She cleared her throat. "Call me sometime. If you want to, that is." She smiled up at him, and this time he knew.

She opened the door.

THIRTY-THREE

Rowan stepped outside to get the last of the groceries from the trunk as Jack jogged up the driveway. He'd been gone nearly two hours, and his gray T-shirt was completely soaked through.

He met her at her car and grabbed the two cases of soft drinks.

"How far did you go?" she asked.

"Twelve," he said, shutting the trunk.

"Really? You made good time."

"It's all right."

Jack had started training for a marathon a month ago, and he was working up to long distances. It seemed to be a good stress reliever for him.

He followed her up the steps and into the house.

"Whoa." He stopped short. "What happened here?"

When he'd left this morning, the place had looked normal. Now furniture was moved, the rug was rolled back, and a giant heap of sheets and towels covered the sofa.

"I mopped," she said.

"Why?"

"Just . . . because. I felt like it."

He followed her into the kitchen, and she started putting groceries away.

"You said you were going to relax today. Why the sudden cleaning frenzy?"

"Can't I clean my house if I want to?"

"Sure, but why would you want to?"

She slung a salad kit into the fridge and shut the door. "Because I feel like it, okay? Is that all right with you?"

He looked at her for a long moment. Then he stepped around her and put the soft drinks on the floor of the pantry.

The washer buzzed, and she went into the other room to transfer a load of towels. As she started the dryer, she heard the back door open and close.

Rowan sighed and ran her hand through her hair. She grabbed a warm sweatshirt that had just come out of the dryer and pulled it on. Then she went into the kitchen and filled a Yoda glass with ice water.

She joined Jack by the creek. His shoes and socks were in a pile beside him, and he was soaking his feet.

"Isn't that freezing?" She handed him the water.

"Feels good."

She sat down on the grass beside him and pulled her knees to her chest to keep her shoes out of the creek. It was a chilly March day, and they had woken up with the wind howling against the windows and Oscar curled at their feet.

Jack turned to look at her. His hair was wet from his run, and his skin was flushed.

"Sorry I snapped at you," she said. "I'm in a bad mood."

"What's wrong?"

She sighed. "My mom called."

He leaned back on his palms and waited patiently for her to explain.

"We don't see each other much. But she wants to have dinner next Thursday."

"Your birthday."

She glanced at him. "How did you know that?"

He gave her a *get real* look.

She gazed out at the leaves floating atop the water. She'd been putting off this conversation for weeks. But it was time to have it. Nerves fluttered inside her as she thought of his reaction. His family sounded so normal. Just the other day, his mother had called to tell him his cousin in Dallas had had a baby.

She looked at him. "So . . . I told you how my parents split up when I was fourteen. I'm not real close to either of them anymore."

"Why not?"

She watched a leaf swirl on the surface of the water and then float downstream.

"You know that night we were at the Duck and you asked me if I'd ever researched my ancestry? I didn't tell you the truth about that."

"I know."

She looked at him. "How?"

He shrugged. "The look on your face. And I didn't really believe you would devote your whole life to genealogy and never trace your own family."

Rowan glanced away. She should have known he'd know. From the very beginning, she'd felt like he could read her thoughts.

She took a deep breath. "Five years ago, I tested my DNA and learned that I'm an NPE kid."

"What's that?"

"It stands for 'non-paternity event,' which basically means my father isn't who I thought. My mom had an affair and . . . well, I'm sure you can guess the rest. My dad knew about it, but they decided to stay married, probably for practical reasons. They had two kids already and bills to pay. But it was never a love match, at least in my memory."

Jack watched her, and she wished she could read the look on his face.

"After I found out, I confronted my mom. I could see why they kept this from me when I was little, but *now*?" Bitterness welled inside her. "They should have told me after the divorce. Or if not then, when I turned eighteen. They had *no right* to keep it from me."

Silence settled over them. Rowan plucked a weed from the ground and tossed it into the creek. She watched it swirl and spin.

"And the thing is, even as a child, I always *knew* my dad felt differently about me than my sisters. He was always aloof. That's his basic personality, yes, but with me, there was always this underlying disapproval. I made good grades, I never got in trouble, but still I could never please him." She shook her head. "I had this hang-up about it for *years*, and my mom knew it, and she did nothing. She never would have told me any of it if I hadn't discovered it for myself." She swallowed the hot lump in her throat. "I don't think I'll ever forgive her for that."

She stopped speaking, and there was just the sound of the rushing water and chirping birds.

"Do you know who your biological father is?" Jack asked.

"Yes." She didn't say his name because it still felt alien to her. "He lives in Arizona with his second wife. They have three grown kids—my half siblings. Anyway, I've never reached out to him."

"Do you think you will?"

"Maybe someday. I don't know." She picked at the grass. "I've seen for myself how sometimes these things don't go well. Right now, I don't really feel like setting myself up for more disappointment. I've got enough stuff to work through."

She looked at the creek again. Her heart was thrumming now as she told him this thorny secret that had been poking at her insides for years. She'd wanted to share it with him sooner, but she'd felt awkward and embarrassed. She still did.

"Rowan."

She looked at him.

"Thank you for telling me."

She shrugged. "I wanted to give you a heads-up, you know? My family's a mess."

"A lot of families are. Mine definitely isn't perfect."

"But mine's worse than most. Truly."

He looked at her for a long moment, and she wished she knew what he was thinking.

"It sounds like you're dealing with a lot," he said, "but the whole thing isn't a reflection on you. You know that, right?"

"I know," she said, even though she had a hard time believing that. "Anyway, Skyler and Lila and Dara are like my family now. We're all kind of misfits. I've never really wanted to have kids or to get married. Until you came along, I never thought . . ."

She stopped and looked away. She hadn't meant to go there, and she could feel him watching her.

He picked up her hand. She looked at him.

"I've been thinking about it, too," he said.

Her heart did a little flip-flop. His eyes were dark and serious, and the understanding in them made her throat feel tight.

He lifted her hand and kissed her knuckles. Then he settled their joined hands on his leg.

"So, this birthday you've got coming up," he said. "How about we spend the day together?"

She blinked at him, caught off guard by the sudden shift in topic. "Doing what?"

"Something fun." He smiled at her. "I noticed there's a mountain bike in the back of the barn. Is that Skyler's?"

"It's mine. But I haven't been on it in ages. I'd probably wipe out."

"No, you won't."

"I might."

"If you do, then I'll pick you back up." He squeezed her hand. "Come on. There are some good trails around here. We'll start small, no big hills. It'll be fun. And then I can take you out for lunch someplace nice, and we can toast your birthday."

She smiled and looked at the creek. She couldn't remember the last time she'd done something special for her birthday. She'd gotten into the habit of ignoring it.

She shot a look at him. "Thursday is a workday."

"Yeah?" He leaned back on the grass and tugged her with him.

"Since when do you take time off in the middle of the week?"

"This is the new me." He propped himself up on his elbow and looked down at her. "Less addicted to work. More addicted to other things."

They both knew he meant sex, and she smiled up at him. He leaned down and kissed her. His mouth was warm and seeking, and she could tell he was trying to distract her from her angst about everything. And she let him. She loved kissing him, and she loved that he liked to take his time with her.

When he eased back, his expression was serious.

"Does it freak you out, what I said earlier? That I'm thinking about our relationship long-term?"

She shook her head. "I've been thinking about it a lot."

He traced the neck of her sweatshirt with his finger. "You know, I dated this woman once—"

"What was her name?"

"Heidi." He frowned. "Why?"

"Because I want to know you. And that includes past girlfriends."

She sat up and turned to face him. He sat up, too, and rested his arm on his knee.

"Anyway, she said she wanted to move in together. I kept making excuses why I didn't want to, and finally we broke up. Our last argument, she told me I needed to grow up and start taking life seriously." He looked at Rowan. "The thing is, I've always taken life seriously. That wasn't the problem. I just wasn't ready for that kind of relationship then. Everything is different with you."

Her eyes filled with tears, and she looked down.

"Hey." He tucked a lock of hair behind her ear. "Why are you crying?"

"Because. That's so sweet."

He leaned his forehead against hers. "I love you, Rowan."

She sniffled. "I love you, too."

He wrapped his arms around her and held her against him, and it felt warm and *right*, the way it always did. She pressed her cheek against his shoulder and let the feeling of pure contentment wash over her. She'd never felt it with anyone else. He held her close until she eased away.

"Do you really want to take a day off work to go mountain biking?

He laughed. "*That* was your takeaway from this conversation?"

"It was the most shocking thing you said."

He sighed. "Yes, I really do."

"Good." She smiled. "Then it's a date."

Keep reading for an excerpt from
Laura Griffin's next Texas Murder Files novel,

LIAR'S POINT

THE BEACH WAS deserted again.

On sunny days it was the good sort of deserted, empty and peaceful like a postcard. But today's sky was cold and colorless, and the beach just felt bleak. The wind nipped at Cassandra's cheeks, and she wished she hadn't come.

Focus on the breathing, not the pain.

She set her gaze on the foamy waterline and tried to get into the zone. The tip of her nose felt frozen, and her knuckles were numb as she pumped her arms.

Almost there. Just a little more.

She should be used to this by now. She'd been coming here for months on her evenings off. The route to the lighthouse from her apartment was a perfect two-mile loop that was both scenic and invigorating.

Her mind shifted to the stress that had prompted her to come out here and freeze her butt off when what she really wanted to do was pour a fat glass of wine. Today had been crazy, even for a Saturday. Her classes had been filled to capacity, and then she'd had to pick up two classes for Reese, who was out sick.

Or so she'd claimed. Reese had a new boyfriend, and Cassandra had her doubts about that excuse. But she'd filled in anyway, without complaint, because she owed Reese a favor.

Pounding out her frustration on the sand, Cassandra focused on the lighthouse. Perched upon a grassy hill, it looked gray and lonely in the waning daylight. During the summer, the lighthouse was packed with people climbing to the top for a panoramic view of the island's south side. But the visitors' lot was vacant now—not a tourist in sight.

Up ahead, a little blue car was parked on the beach near the dunes. Cassandra scanned the shoreline for its owner but didn't see any walkers or wade fishermen. She looked out at the waves.

A low buzzing noise pulled her attention back to the beach. She glanced up, searching for the drone. She couldn't see it, but the menacing hum told her it was there. She halted and stared up at the sky.

A red-haired boy darted out from a sand dune, with an excited black dog bounding behind him. The kid looked up, and Cassandra saw that the noise was a remote-control airplane. The plane did a series of rolls and loops. Then a man joined the boy and took over the controls to bring the plane down for a smooth landing.

Cassandra resumed her run. She focused on her breathing again, sucking in big gulps of air, then blowing them out. Like magic, the anxiety faded, and her limbic system began to settle down.

Just a dad and his kid. Don't be so paranoid.

The wind whipped up, making her eyes water as she neared the lighthouse. She sprinted the last twenty yards, then stretched her arms above her head and turned around. The boy and his dog were leaving now. The dad loaded them into a pickup truck and walked around to the driver's side. He drove in a circle on the beach and disappeared behind the dunes.

Cassandra spied the solitary blue car again. Something about it needled her.

She glanced around. Still no shell-seekers or fishermen, and she gazed out at the churning surf. Had someone gone for a *swim*? It was freezing. But maybe that was the point. Cold water could grab you by the chest and squeeze the breath right out of you. It was terrifying but exhilarating, too, and she understood the allure.

Even so, this end of the island had a notorious rip current. You'd have to have a death wish to swim out here alone, especially at sundown.

Cassandra veered toward the car, unable to stay away. Jogging toward it, she studied the tinted windows, the dinged door. She caught sight of something hanging from the rearview mirror, and her heart lurched. A dream catcher. A small white feather dangled from the hoop.

She jogged straight up to the door and looked through the window. Someone was asleep in the front seat. Long brown hair, pale arms.

Cassandra's breath caught, and her stomach did a somersault. Panic gripped her as she noticed the flies.

N ICOLE FELT NAKED.
It wasn't the minidress or the strappy sandals. It wasn't even the weird slit that left the entire side of her thigh on display.

It was the Smith & Wesson .40 caliber pistol—or absence of it—that was making her feel exposed. She was so accustomed to those twenty-nine ounces riding on her hip, and the lack of weight was making her antsy as hell.

She checked her phone, then flipped it over.

Nicole glanced around the restaurant, which was wall-to-wall couples, of course. She'd never been in here before, and the decorations grated on her nerves. They were going for elegant, she knew—this was the Nautilus, after all—and it wasn't like the place was covered in pink balloons. The bloodred rosebuds on every table looked nice, actually. Ditto for the votive candles that emitted a soft glow. Really, it was the glitter that was giving her hives, all those tiny gold hearts sprinkled across her table like pixie dust. Just the sight was making her feel even stupider than she already did in this ridiculous dress.

She checked her phone again.

For the first time ever, she had a date on Valentine's, and not just any date. Tonight was *the* date. She and David had gone out three times already. The last time had ended with intense kissing in his car, which definitely would have continued if he hadn't been called into work. Nothing like being summoned to an autopsy to kill the mood.

He wanted to make it up to her, though. Those were his exact words when he'd invited her to this expensive restaurant. And so Nicole had squeezed herself into a low-cut black dress that gave her the illusion of boobs, borrowed her sister's stilettos, and come here to meet him for dinner.

"Are we still waiting?"

Her server was back again with that pitying look that was almost as annoying as the glitter.

She smiled up at him. "We are."

"And would you like some wine, perhaps? Maybe a cocktail?"

"I'm good." She nodded at her half-finished water. "Thanks."

He walked off, leaving her to her silent phone. No text, no voice message. She'd even checked her email, but zip.

Nicole looked around, sure people were staring at her. God, the white-haired couple behind her was already paying their bill.

Her phone vibrated on the table, and she snatched it up.

"Hello?"

"Where the hell are you?"

Not David. She closed her eyes.

"I'm out. Why?"

"Didn't you get the call?" Emmet asked her, and she pictured him at the police station surrounded by the typical Saturday-night chaos.

"I'm off tonight."

"Not anymore."

Her phone beeped with an incoming call, and she checked the screen.

"Listen, that's Denise. I have to go." She hung up with Emmet and took the call.

"Hey, what's up?"

"The chief asked me to reach you. He needs you at a scene."

Damn it.

Nicole pushed her chair back and grabbed her purse. "Does he know I'm off tonight?"

"Yep."

She unzipped her little black clutch and left a ten on the table. They were going to have to bus it, even though she hadn't ordered anything.

"Well, what's going on?"

"One sec," Denise said and cut over to another call. When things were busy, the Lost Beach PD receptionist doubled as a dispatcher. She was also the chief's right hand, doing everything from managing his calendar to deflecting reporters who called in from time to time.

The front of the restaurant was packed with waiting couples. Nicole scanned the bar and the area around the hostess stand but didn't see any tall, handsome doctors looking around for their date. It was 7:32. She'd officially been stood up.

"Nicole?"

"I'm here." She squeezed past the people and pushed open the door. A cold gust hit her, and she stepped back.

"He needs you at Lighthouse Point right away. And keep it off the radio."

"What's going on?" she asked again.

"I'm not sure."

"Well, what did he say?"

"He said, 'I need Lawson at Lighthouse Point ASAP. Keep it off the radio.' That's all I have."

Nicole hunched her head down, wishing for her jacket as she strode across the parking lot. It had filled in since she'd arrived.

"What's your ETA?" Denise asked.

"I'll be there in three."

"Roger that."

Nicole slid behind the wheel of her pickup and started it. Cold air shot from the vents, and she turned the heat to max. She set her purse on the passenger seat and backed out, still looking for David's black Pathfinder in case he was pulling in late. He wasn't.

She should shake it off. He had a demanding job, like she did. It was unpredictable. Maybe he got tied up at work and forgot to call.

But really, that only made her feel worse. She'd been looking forward to this all week. She'd planned her outfit and put on makeup and spent half an hour straightening her damn hair. This was why she didn't go out. She hated the BS. She was much happier at home binge-watching TV with her cat.

The lighthouse came into view, and Nicole's pulse picked up. Three, four, *five* emergency vehicles—four cruisers, plus a fire truck. No ambulance, which was a worrisome sign. Everyone was parked in the lot, but the action appeared to be centered on the beach where some portable klieg lights had been set up. Nicole whipped into a space beside the fire rig and scanned the crowd as she shifted into park.

She reached into the back and rummaged around. There was a flannel shirt, an LBPD windbreaker, and a rain poncho. No shoes, damn it. She had a pair of waders in the toolbox in back, but the mud boots she normally kept on hand were on her balcony at home, drying after she'd hosed them off.

She grabbed the windbreaker, then unzipped her little black purse and slid out her backup pistol. A tube of lipstick fell out, too, as if to taunt her.

She got out and pulled on the jacket, then tucked the gun into the pocket, along with her badge. Not that she needed her detective's shield. Even at a glance, she could see she knew everyone out here.

She crossed the parking lot, attempting to look confident, which worked fine until she reached the sandy trail leading to the beach. She considered kicking off the heels and going barefoot, but there might be glass on the beach, plus her sister had threatened her within an inch of her life if anything happened to her precious Jimmy Choos.

"*Don't* leave them at his house," Kate had said. "And if he has a dog, put them up high."

"I'm not going to end up at his house."

"Yeah, you will."

"I will not."

"When he sees you in that? You will, trust me."

Nicole strode across the sand to the group of men milling in the shadows near the klieg lights. A perimeter had been cordoned off around a small blue Subaru. The only person inside the yellow scene tape appeared to be their CSI, who wore a white Tyvek suit and a purple face mask. Miranda was just back from maternity leave and no doubt had plenty of things she'd rather be doing on a Saturday night. She crouched beside the car's passenger-side door and snapped a photograph.

Nicole headed for the cluster of first responders. Adam McDeere saw her and did a double take.

"Whoa." He looked her up and down and seemed to get stuck on her cleavage. "Where were you?"

"Out. What's going on?"

He cleared his throat, still distracted. "We got an OD. A jogger called it in 'bout an hour ago."

Nicole looked at the car. "Where's the ME's team?"

"They came and went. It was pretty straightforward. No blood."

"Is it a suicide?"

He raked a hand over his buzz cut. "No note or anything. But who knows?"

"Lawson!"

She glanced up, and Brady was waving her over. She went to talk to him, and his brow furrowed as he looked her over.

"What do we have, Chief?"

"Drug OD," he said. "There's a bottle of pills spilled across the passenger seat."

"All right."

The other guys turned to look at her, and she felt their gazes moving over her bare legs.

"Any note?" she asked.

"Not that we know of. We don't have her electronics yet."

So it was a woman. Nicole turned to check out the car again. Emmet knelt beside Miranda now, shining his flashlight inside the vehicle. Their heads were close together, and they appeared to be examining something.

"I need you to interview the witness."

Nicole turned back to Brady. The chief wore his typical weekend attire of a barn jacket over a flannel shirt and jeans. He'd been off duty, too, but it didn't look like he and his wife of thirty-plus years had been out celebrating.

"We tried to get her statement already, but she was pretty hysterical. Having some kind of panic attack, she said."

"'We'?"

"Owen was the first one here."

She glanced at Owen, who had stepped away from the group to talk on his phone. He stood in the shadows with his back to everyone, as though he wanted privacy.

So, Owen Breda hadn't been able to get a statement from the witness. Not exactly typical. Owen was one of their best detectives, and his easygoing charm put people at ease, particularly women.

"Where is she now?" Nicole asked.

"Over there." Brady nodded toward the water.

Nicole turned and suddenly noticed the figure seated on the sand about thirty yards away. The person was little more than a shadow, really—just a dark silhouette sitting still as a statue.

"What's she doing?" Nicole asked.

"No idea." Brady said. "Woman's a space cadet. We couldn't even get an address out of her."

In Brady's book, a "space cadet" could mean someone who was high or flakey or habitually out of it, for whatever reason.

Nicole looked at the woman again. "Is she local?"

"She works at the Banyan Tree."

Nicole turned to see Emmet walking over. "You interviewed her?"

"As much as I could." He stopped and frowned down at her, hands on hips. "She kept having breathing issues."

"Does she need a paramedic?"

"I tried. She didn't want one. Said she just needed some space."

Nicole looked at the woman again, then back at the chief. "I'll go talk to her," she said, zipping her jacket.

"Find out if she saw anything suspicious," Brady instructed.

"I will."

"It looks like a suicide, but you never know. Ask her if she saw anyone else around before she found the car."

Nicole bit her tongue. Did he think she didn't know how to conduct an interview?

"And pin down her timing," Brady added.

"Got it."

She felt Emmet watching her and turned to look at him. He wore his usual leather jacket and jeans, but the hint of cologne told her he'd been on his way out somewhere when he got the call.

"Want me to go with you?" he asked.

"I'll handle it."

Nicole set off for the water, skirting around the glare of the portable klieg lights. In the distance, people were milling on the sand, no doubt wondering what all the fuss was about. It was the off-season, but the island still had plenty of snowbirds and full-time residents who liked to walk the beach at night, and all the first responders had caused a stir. No media yet, though, which was one bit of luck. But it wouldn't be long. Suicide or not, a death on the beach would at least be worth a news brief in the mainland paper.

The witness sat cross-legged on the sand, her posture ramrod straight. The dark braid down her back went all the way to her waist. Her hands rested on her knees, palms up, and Nicole stopped in her tracks. Was she meditating?

Stepping closer, Nicole picked up a faint hum. She *was* meditating. This was a new one. Nicole didn't know the etiquette here, but it didn't matter. Someone was dead, and the police needed a statement.

"Excuse me?"

The humming stopped. The woman's chest rose and fell. Then her head swiveled to face Nicole while the rest of her body remained stock-still.

"I'm Detective Lawson, Lost Beach PD." She pulled the badge from her pocket and held it up. Even in the dimness, she could see the woman's expression didn't change. "Mind if I ask you a few questions?"

A slight nod.

"I understand you came upon the car and called it in?"

Another nod.

She definitely was *not* hysterical. She seemed unnaturally calm, like maybe she was on something. She wore black leggings, sneakers, and a gray sweatshirt that looked a hell of a lot warmer than Nicole's thin windbreaker. She was sitting on a jacket, too, probably to protect her clothes from the wet sand.

Witness Interrogation 101: eye contact.

Nicole stepped closer and crouched down, tucking her knees under her jacket as her dress rode up.

"Cold out here, huh?" Nicole smiled.

"There's a front coming in."

"Do you jog out here often?"

"Three times a week. On my evenings off."

"And where do you work?"

She took a deep breath and blew it out slowly. "I teach yoga at a studio downtown."

"The Banyan Tree?"

She nodded.

"Sorry. I didn't catch your name."

Another deep breath. The woman's eyes looked almost black in the dimness. She had pale skin, and Nicole wondered how long she had lived here. Most full-time residents had year-round tans unless they constantly slathered on sunscreen.

"Cassandra Miller."

Nicole took the little spiral notebook from the inside pocket of her jacket. "Is that with a C?"

"Yes." She eyed the notepad with a wary look.

"And your home address, Cassandra?"

She rattled off the address of an apartment complex in

town several blocks off the beach. Then she surprised Nicole by volunteering her phone number. With a twinge of satisfaction, Nicole jotted everything down. Already she'd managed to get more than Owen.

"So, you mind telling me about what happened? How you came upon the vehicle?"

The woman turned her face to the water and took another deep breath. Deep breaths seemed to be a big thing with her.

"I was nearing my midpoint."

"'Midpoint'?"

"I always turn around at the lighthouse."

"All right."

"I noticed the car when I first passed it."

"What time was this?"

"I don't know. About ten after six?"

Nicole made a note. "Did you see anyone inside?"

"No. I thought it was empty."

"Did you get a close look at it?"

She shook her head. "I was running. Then I reached the lighthouse and turned around, and that's when I got a weird vibe."

"A vibe about what?"

"Just, you know, a *feeling*. I knew something was off. Something about the car bothered me."

Weird vibe, something off, Nicole scribbled.

"I thought maybe someone was swimming or surfing. The waves are high today. But there's a riptide here, and there are warning signs all over the place. I started to get worried that maybe someone was out there alone."

She took a deep breath and blew it out for an eternity as Nicole waited, her pen poised above her notepad.

"And then?"

"Then I jogged over for a closer look, and that's when I saw the dream catcher." She glanced over her shoulder at all the cops. "I recognized it."

"Recognized what?"

She turned to face her. "The car. The dream catcher. All of it seemed familiar. I looked closer, and sure enough, it was her."

Nicole leaned closer. "You're saying you *know* the person who—"

"Yes. She's one of my students."

Ready to find
your next great read?

Let us help.

Visit prh.com/nextread